Return Journey

Rosemary Kay

HEADLINE
REVIEW

First published in 1996
by HEADLINE BOOK PUBLISHING

First published in paperback in 1996
by HEADLINE BOOK PUBLISHING

A HEADLINE REVIEW paperback

10 9 8 7 6 5 4 3 2 1

ISBN 0 7472 5339 0

Printed and bound in Great Britain by
Cox & Wyman Ltd, Reading, Berks

HEADLINE BOOK PUBLISHING
A division of Hodder Headline PLC
338 Euston Road
London NW1 3BH

Rosemary Kay was born in Glasgow and grew up in Edinburgh. After graduating from Edinburgh University and meeting her husband, she went to Cambridge, where she qualified as a teacher. With her husband and three daughters she has lived in Boston and Scotland and now resides in London. *Return Journey* is Rosemary Kay's first novel.

To Barry

CHAPTER ONE

'Our Father, which art . . .' My mouth slacked to a sulk. A tremor lifted my closed lids. Under a blurred edge, down the slide of my nose, I looked at my hands folded on the hymn book in my Harris Tweed lap.

From lip to lip the murmured prayer ran round. 'Thy will be done on earth, As it is in heaven.'

This used to work. This was the time I gave myself, the only public time in the week: I discounted the hours alone in my room. This overwhelming surge of hopelessness was new. Come on. Come on. I pressed my knees together, felt the knob of my anklebones, my leather insteps squeaky tight. Think of his hands.

Looking up from my place in the choir stalls at the end of the second row I had as good a view of the congregation as the minister. All heads were bowed. Except – and what could Ninian Orr, sitting there beside two parents, possibly know? Or care? I ducked and gave him my dipped lashes and the pert tag of my wool beret.

Toes knocked the pew ends. The Sunday School children were shuffling out. They paused at the bottleneck in the aisle by the south transept and watched in wonder Mr Sturrock's black skirts move up the miniature spiral of staircase to the eyrie of his pulpit. Teachers rotated heads and shepherded the lambkins and their innocence out through the vestry door.

With the other sinners, I remained.

The minister breasted the pulpit and clasped the edge. Coughs stuttered about, giving cover to the checking and shooting of cuffs. My neighbour arched her wrist, took a deep breath and, as she gently expelled it, withdrew from her pocket a box of Imps: confectionery of the Devil. She nudged me. I picked out one crotchet nugget with my fingertip and applied it to my tongue. I raised my head for the reckoning, sat

1

po-faced and waited. The sweet began to smoulder. I resolved,
as usual, to concentrate. Liquorice and eucalyptus. There was
some message here for me, something that might help.
Sentence after sentence must make sense. The Imp burned into
the interstices of my head.

'Come on! Come, come, come!' Dorcas had leaned over the
gate and sung like that, a coloratura call for the cows. Except,
they were not cows . . .

Mr Sturrock was like the vulture at the zoo. He craned forward,
bald-pated, cadaverous. His white-of-egg eyes swelled behind
rimless spectacles. But his was no downy ruff; the dog collar
pulled the flesh of his extending neck into wrinkles taut as
loom threads. Dropping my false attentive gaze, I caught
Ninian Orr drop his from me and felt a blush rush up. I parted
my lips and tried to ventilate the chemical explosion in my
head. My eyes watered. I gave a little shake, a little toss, looked
up again by a route round the side aisles avoiding the Orrs'
pew, and travelled to where the rafters of the roof vault soared,
to the bosses and the square grilles and down again by the
chains of the electric lamps which I wished were lit. This plain
November morning light in this plain Edinburgh parish
church was cold. Oh, for a hailstorm like I remembered once. It
had made the windows dark as Ballachulish slate. Lights had
gleamed. Brass had twinkled. The church had been a refuge
then. Mr Sturrock, human enough, briefly, had referred to the
weather, made a joke – about God's Wrath, of course: he was
an Old Testament man.

Perhaps it was the lighting made my mother prefer the
Sunday evening service. I had gone with her once. Although
lamp-lit then, the church was almost empty. There was a
mellowness at night from all the rows of empty waxed wood
pews. Because there were no young people, I did not like it and
did not go again.

She did not come on Sunday mornings often now. I used to
watch her from the choir, pick out the turned-back brim of her
hat which arched above a brow no longer quite smooth, amid
the sea of faces, the good morning congregation. Surrounded
by others and smiling with her upper lip when she caught my
look, my mother stood, lonely as Lot's wife. It was less painful
not to be reminded. At home we had our little ways but

outside it was different. It must be easier for God too, now: He was spared the simultaneous conflict of the mother's and the daughter's prayer. When one came in the morning, another in the evening, it gave Him more time to . . . well, to do what He could.

> Here's the church,
> Here's the steeple.
> Open the door,
> Here are all the people,
> Beatie Brown et al.

The Orrs' pew was near the front. Mr Orr was a lawyer. Mrs Orr was Captain of the Girl Guides. Ninian was unusual among the older boys in that he still attended church. I liked his looks. He was tall with something of the tubercular poet in the pallor of his skin. Under a dark forelock lurked brooding brown eyes, eyes that looked a lot at me.

The cows were really wee bulls, Dorcas said. 'Come on! Come, come, come!' She sang with the confidence of the country born, her outstretched hand reaching for the muzzles of the black and white beasts ambling towards our corner. 'Look! See that tuft underneath . . .'

In the pew behind the Orrs sat the Moggachs. Brother and sister, one curiously fat, the other thin, neither bonny, flanked their parents. A pair with a pigeon pair – wasn't that what that blessing was called? Wilma was in the Communion class. Her blackheads were not so obvious in the vestry on Wednesday evenings as they would be when we met outside on the street in half an hour.

It was time I joined. The Catholics got you earliest. The Church of England just made it. By the time the Scottish Church asked you the age of reason was awkwardly advanced. I was still going to the classes. I was, however, balking. The deaconess kept trying to coax me up on to the truth path. At the beginning I had looked for clues in her earnest parchment face but I found I bridled at the pained expression which crossed it when I plied her with questions about Faith and the Trinity. The time-honoured phrases, as familiar to me as the lines of the hymns, when examined, made no sense. I had

3

looked at the grey canvas of the tubular chairs stacked round, at the treacle varnish of the tongue-and-groove, the sheepskin mittens on the seat, the handbag set on the green linoleum, and found in the flame of the gas fire purring away the only warm and magical thing.

Wilma had not asked one question yet. They, that little gang, the Wilmas, Jeans and Marjories, good at the pained expression too, would join 'no bother', become members, take Communion, and, I cringed, for it seemed almost an incestuous thought, they would probably marry the pimply boys, the boys from the Scouts, the Youth Fellowship, the Badminton Club, the ones who followed them back from the chip shop, the guffawing shuffling troop. After a game or two of musical chairs, all – I considered Wilma's open-mouthed moon face – most would pair off, breed and spawn.

'Oh, naughty!' Dorcas had squealed.

The wee bulls were crowding towards us to get her bunch of grass. One of them had mounted another. She said they did that, to practise. What for? I nearly said. Then I saw. A long pink rod was growing from that innocent white tuft. It emerged like a weird fifth leg. Where had it come from? How? Where was it to go? The animal rolled one dopey eye as if denying it had anything to do with him.

'Imagine having that shoved up you!'

Oh, Dorcas.

The minister's arms were spread, the sleeves of his cassock stretched like black wings. He launched into the ether. He would find me out. He found us all out. We were not Cains in the land of Sodom and Gomorrah. The remote crags of adultery, caverns of incest, ravines of murder were not his hunting ground. He hovered over the parochial plains of greed, the screes of stinginess, discovered valleys of hypocrisy, lighted above glinting rills of deceit, green seams of jealousy, and each pause in his harangue imprinted an awareness in each heart, sitting with stony face on the hard pew, the specificity of his or her own particular sin. Mr Sturrock's thin lips rucked. The Avenger prepared to swoop. I had lost myself in impure thoughts. I had, as usual, lost the flow. But the general drift was familiar . . . Recognising the breaker as it came, I crouched and braced myself. I squeezed my arms: my breasts

4

touched. To cancel that brief silky confluence I hunched my shoulders into the penitential itchiness of my Shetland sweater.

Whoosh. The rush of air came blasting through.

Breathe on us, breath of God.

From behind the organ console, the toe-cap of the choirmaster's shoe, a resting point for my travelling gaze throughout the sermon, vanished. Pages riffled. Then I heard the embarrassing commotion, the not-mute-enough preparatory tap dance on the pedals. The congregation lifted their eyes again. They brightened. Wrists were read. Brows darkened. The minister was into injury time. Discreet coughs gave intimation. But he knew. He came winging in. We all received humbly enough, and with some relief, the final Blast of the Trumpet.

'Now let us stand together and sing hymn number . . .'

The organ gave the gathering note. First off the mark, the chief soprano stood. Less professional but more modest and more gentle, we others rose around her.

> 'Eternal Father, strong to save,
> Whose arm hath bound the restless wave,'

My singing came from a source deeper inside than I fathomed at any other time. Its resonances filled me, body and soul. It was a cry. My singing was all a cry, a musical shout, the loudest vent I gave to anything.

> 'O hear us when we cry to Thee . . .'

Oh, but this hymn above all hymns – why this hymn today? My despair surged back. It was my hymn.

The faces of the congregation, the Orrs, the Moggachs, the doctor, the deaconess, mothers, elders, became a blur. I sang out to somewhere beyond. The words were the words of a myth: the Father, Christ, Holy Spirit addressed by the hymn meant a trinity of verses, a chance to dive into the cadences of the tune three times. In my Sunday School days, in my easy innocence, I thought this had been written just for me. In the sidelong glances of the grown-ups, the sad sloping smiles, the occasional touch of blessing on my head, I had felt the warmth of sympathy.

5

The final solemn notes of the phrase fell:

'For those in peril on the sea.'

My father had drowned, my story went. 'Daddy's gone away, Beatie. Away across the sea.' The terrors of the deep were real. In the tumult of the waves men in yellow sou'westers fought sheeting rain on slanting decks. My picture of the odds against him came from the advertisements for Lifebuoy soap. 'O hear us when we cry to Thee/For those in peril on the sea' . . . but as a child my jaw did not ache, my lips did not tremble like this. Then my small heart brimmed with pride as for heroes gone. Now, my heart was tight.

Ninian was staring at me. I mouthed the final verse. Could he tell? I managed a faint finish. 'Thus evermore shall rise to Thee/Glad hymns of praise from land and sea. A-men.' We stood with our hymn books up. The last chord of the organ faded. Then we sat.

'Now let us pray.' I would not do this any more. 'Humbly we ask forgiveness of Thee . . .' No. My clasped hands began to slip. What was the use? I had begun to miss the bedtime one, the 'God bless Mummy, and Granny and Grandpa in Heaven, and everyone I love and know. And those I don't. And keep them safe. Look after the poor . . . Feed . . . Help . . .' Nightly I rattled through the childish phrases. Nightly I had paused, then concentrated all my powers upon the final wish. I would lie still afterwards, crouched sideways on my pillow. When I opened my eyes it was always dark. The spotlit hand appeared out of a velvet blackness. It was a strong male hand. Beautiful. Masterful. The long fingers stroked a sculpted limewood block. They pushed in upon the turns. They explored the contours and felt along the grain.

When I got home from church there was a smell of braising meat. My mother was speaking on the telephone in the hall. She turned her back and covered her ear with her hand.

'Parklea,' she spoke in that emphatic tone you use with the deaf, 'is in the lea of the park – near Arthur's Seat.' She rolled her Rs and narrowed her vowels when she addressed Englishmen and other foreigners. 'We're just off the Dalkeith Road. Good bus routes, the 33, 19 and – oh, very quiet. Very quiet, indeed,' she sniffed, 'and private.' I went past her up the stairs.

The boiled cabbage had reached the landing. 'A good Scottish breakfast,' she was saying, 'but not the evening meal. "Private"? That means no alcoholic beverages to be consumed on the premises. That's what "private" means.'

Oh, it meant more than that. I pushed open my bedroom door.

I knew the way these conversations went. Over the years my mother had learned to offer little carrots like bus routes, seclusion, proximity to the Palace of Holyrood, but her telephone manner lacked charm. Its clipped Edinburgh ring betrayed her resentment at having to admit paying guests. She never advertised but was on some Tourist Board list. When advances were made it was as if she defied their approach. In the summer we almost got into the swing of things, but in the off season, as this was, we might as well have shut up shop. But my mother muttered, 'Needs must,' and went to the phone with sucked in cheeks. A Sword of Damocles, the intrusion of strangers upon the house, hung above my head, unlit, like the porch light, but always there.

I opened my wardrobe door, stood before the mirror. Had I looked like that when I passed the Orrs? I should have pulled my beret down to the side a bit and let my hair fall in front of my shoulders. There. I was rather like that French singer, Juliette something. The beret should be white, though. And I needed a black polo neck. Look. Make my eyes round. Not bad eyes, really, the grey irises with the pupils very white. Dorcas once said with my hair and brows and what she called my 'olive' skin, they should have been cinnamon balls, proof of my Italian blood. But they were my mother's eyes . . . He had! Ninian had been going to speak to me. When I was shaking hands with Mr Sturrock, I saw him standing beyond the holly bush on the outside of his family group. Then he moved when I came near – suddenly swung his shoulder out or something – I was so sure he was going to speak to me I looked away. So sure! I had gone past then and he hadn't. And he couldn't because Wilma and Marjorie galumphed up – at least Wilma galumphed (even in her new high heels she moved like a rhino) – 'Beetee! Beetee!' one on either side of me, Bibles in hand. 'Are you coming on Wednesday night?' I raised an eyebrow. I could do that. Did he, Ninian, see me do that, I wonder? Quite arch. I've never seen my mother do it. Perhaps I inherited the trait from my father. Trick not trait. Just trick.

7

I grasped a hanger from the rail. I closed my coat and my image of myself away.

My mother was still on the phone when I went down. This was persistence indeed on the part of the caller.

'We do weekly rates,' she was saying, 'but never the evening meal. I am not a *student* landlady.' This was a lower breed. 'You say now you are not a student.' She looked up at me with the corner of her mouth tucked. 'What are you then, if I may ask?' Her eyes went wide: 'A doctor! Oh.' The tone changed. I was at the turn of the stair. 'Mrs Jamieson told you about me – Mrs Jamieson of Number 50? You're her cousin . . . That was nice. Yes. Well . . . Goodbye now.'

'Who's that?'

'Some English doctor.'

'Is he coming?'

'Phoning back.'

'Must we?' Though we had several spare bedrooms upstairs I had to share the main bathroom with the guests. My mother had a small one of her own which opened off her room. When there were lots of visitors it did not somehow matter so much but when there was just the one, and that one a man, I disliked having to do this.

'Mrs Jamieson's a nice enough wee woman.'

On Sundays we ate lunch at the oak table in the dining room, a large high-ceilinged room with a bay window to the front. The table had bulbous giant acorn legs and leaves that folded in upon themselves and were extended only at Festival time.

The bisected grapefruits with their cherries were already out. Mother always ate the cherry first, popped it in her mouth, over and done, as if she did not want anyone to notice.

'Sermon long?' she asked.

'He overran a bit.'

'What was it about?'

'Sin.'

'Tt.'

'I can't stand sin. I don't feel guilty. I try to. But I don't. What's this doctor?'

'A doctor's a doctor, Beatie.'

'There's other kinds. Doctors of Philosophy – even Agri-culture.'

'In Edinburgh, a doctor's a doctor.'

The silver plate was coming off our spoons. This gave a metallic tinge to the taste of the citrus and made me eat it quickly. My mother, though, nursed each segment to her palate as if she savoured the taint, and swallowed with deliberation.

'Were there many at church?'

'Mm.'

'What about the teaching then?'

I had promised to think about it. Mother kept discussions about my future for this particular time. She was not subtle. 'I can't decide,' I hedged. Our school turned out more teachers than any other in the city. I did not like the maidenly image of those who stood before me in their black gowns repeating the same lessons day after day. 'I wish . . .' I ate my cherry and paused with my spoon in the air.

'You know what I think, Beatie. Atholl Crescent is a good solution. Not academic. But sensible.'

'Mother!' It was appalling. She thought if I got a Diploma in Home Economics we could make the house into a hotel, still private, but posh, unlike a guesthouse. My training would be short and I would never have to leave home. 'What would my father have said?'

'What indeed?' She stretched for my dish and with a clenched mouth stacked the grapefruit skins. The main course was served in silence from the sideboard.

'Can I have a black polo-neck jumper for my birthday?'

'But I've cut out a skirt.'

'I need a jumper.'

'This meat's not good.'

'Gravy's nice.'

'Silverside.' She chewed her sibilants. 'In my home we always had a big roast. Sirloin on the bone with the eye of the fillet in it. Gigot of lamb – a whole one. No cheap cuts.' Her knife sawed the grey slice. 'Succulent. Sweet.' Her expression was tragic. 'Not tough as an old leather boot.'

'This *is* your home, Mother.' I looked down to avoid her face. 'It's *fine*.' But across the table the rhythm of her eating faltered. The fork fell to the plate. 'Are you not hungry, Mummy?'

The large eyelids drooped.

'If you're tired, you'd better go up for a nap. You can have pudding later. Baked apples, is it?' It was always baked apples. My grandmother had made apple pie.

9

'I wanted,' her tone was utterly weary, 'to sew.'

'That doesn't matter, Mum. Just get up to bed. I'll fill a hot-water bottle for you.'

Sundays were so long.

I cleared through, put on the kettle and started washing the dishes. Ninian's brown eyes swam up through the steam. I kept the idea of him before me.

Mother was already in bed when I took the bottle up. Her legs stuck out like rods under the clover candlewick. 'Thank you, dear. Please pull up the quilt. I don't know what I'd do without you.' She had taken to saying this in recent months.

'Have you got your book?' She was always on at me about my dreaming but she could not be without her library book. The inevitable plastic-coated historical romance lay on the bedside table.

I went downstairs noisily to give the illusion of life in the house. I wiped the table mats: the Forth Rail Bridge, the Jamaica Bridge, the Auld Brig at Alloway, banged the bundle square. I was sure Ninian had been about to speak. Positive. Curse Wilma and Marjorie for being such limpets. 'Damn!' The sound of my voice dropped into the silent house like a penny down a well. I fetched the cutlery through to the dining room. I set up a chant, one from our primary school sol-fa song books: 'Scots, wae hae . . . wi' Wallace bled . . . Scots, wham Bruce . . . has aften le . . .' With each breath I shot a knife or fork into the drawer. 'Welcome to . . . your gory bed . . . Or to victorie!' The question was: if my mother was the way she was and I felt I was different, was I like my father?

I ate my baked apple from the bowl on my lap as I sat in the kitchen corner beside the Rayburn. Then I drew up my legs and hugged my knees. Was there any good in looking back? My future, in the immediate term, meant a history essay on 'The Causes of the Scottish Reformation'. My only way out of this house was by passing exams and going to university. I returned to the dining room and spread my books on the table. I chose the seat facing the window so that I could watch whatever life, if any, passed by along the crescent. It was still light outside but I brought the standard lamp over and set it ready by my elbow. I switched on the radiator. From charcoal to reluctant red the bar grew orange and the smell of toasting dust began to rise, a smell that usually helped me settle for solitary studious hours. But I kept staring out the window. In the street not a child called or a car passed – a typical Scottish Sabbath. I kept my eye on it all the same.

A male figure was approaching on a bicycle. His body was bent over the dropped handlebars, yet his jacket was suddenly familiar, as was his dark forelock. Level with our gate he turned his head and looked at the house. It was Ninian. I had never seen him in our road, only out on Minto Street sometimes, on school mornings. He kept his face fixed in my direction till the curve of the crescent bore him away. Our windows looked black from the outside. The table was not right up against them. Although there were no net curtains to screen me from view the shadow of the interior might have done so. I switched on the lamp. Our road was not a short cut to anywhere. You turned off earlier to get to the swimming pool or Arthur's Seat. I glanced at my history book and the picture of John Knox. Long noses both. Ninian's lips were like that too, sensual. A movement in the street. It was him again – not on his way to anywhere but me – sailing this time, stretched up, steering with a fingertip on the top chrome point of the handlebars, the breast of his white shirt bared before the wind, tie flying, jaw tilted, jaunty now, this usually so shy, downward-gazing youth.

I knew then that he had seen me in the pool of yellow light behind my mother's window panes, the reflection thrown up by the pages beneath giving gold to my face. I could see it. I had arranged it, all vellum and candle and glow, like an oil painting. I leaned my chin forward on my hand. I could stare and stare. No need to look away. This was my castle. He had come to the brambly hedge. With a push of his foot on the up pedal he made a wide swerve like a flourish and vanished once again. I was left sitting there, charged and still.

The telephone was ringing in the hall.

When I got there my voice came out with a struggle, 'Hello.' I cleared my throat. 'Hello.'

'Mrs Brown?'

'No. But can I take a message?'

'My name's Rose. Tell Mrs Brown I'll be there to see the room on Thursday.'

'Rose,' I repeated. Needing to take extra pains because I felt remote from this, I wrote the name on the pad. It was a funny name for a man. 'Morning or afternoon?' I asked.

'Afternoon.'

'Afternoon,' I wrote it and said, 'I'll tell her.'
'Who am I speaking to, please?'
'The daughter.'
'Goodbye, Miss Brown.'
''Bye.'

I rushed back to the dining room, sat under my spotlight and waited. A woman came by walking a Cairn terrier. I got up and stood some time beside the curtains looking out. Miss Brown awaits . . . Miss Beatie Brown . . . Miss Beatrice . . . an Edinburgh accent made my name into a mixture of beetroot and liquorice. I liked plain 'Beatie' better. But there was another way to say it – an Italian way which made it sound like vowel practice at a school singing lesson, or like a poem – Bay-ah-tree-chay Mar-ee-ah Bor-nah-tee. I mouthed this to the glass. 'Miss Beatrice Maria Bornati awaits . . .'

CHAPTER TWO

When you hear footsteps running along the pavement behind you, you never think you are the one pursued. That Monday morning going up Minto Street I knew differently. I did not glance back, draw aside or even miss a step: I just knew. And from the moment of knowing I felt this tingle travel from the base of my spine up under my laundered blouse, to the school-tie noose, where it spread to my ears and the roots of my Sunday-night-shampooed hair. He drew level. The tingle flowered into a fiery blush. Ninian Orr.

The shock of having him there so close, panting, glancing at me, then the pavement, his long hands seeking the refuge of pockets in his confusion, wordless, helpless, made me falter. He turned back, puzzled. I made my eyebrows puzzled too. And we laughed. His hand came out to comb his forelock back. 'Hello.'

'Oh, hello.'

'I just—'

Just nothing. My eyes went up to his again. 'You're out of breath,' I said. 'You'd better get it back.'

'You walk fast. For a girl. Did you know?'

'Is this your way now?'

'What do you mean?'

'I've seen you here recently.'

'You've seen me?'

'A few times. There's my bus. I'll have to run.'

'Come to the pictures with me.'

'The pictures?'

'The Cameo.'

'Not the pictures. Sorry.'

'Whatever . . . anything, then.'

'Just not the pictures.'

'Come tonight.'

'No.'
'Friday?'
'Friday.'
'Friday. I'll call for you at seven.'

Borne aloft away on the gentle roar of the Number 5 bus that November morning I left him standing alone wearing a lop-sided smile at the crossroads at Salisbury. I slid into a top-deck window seat. My heart was thudding like a hammer in my chest. I hugged my schoolbag. I tried deep breaths. I could not still it. The mossed stone walls of Grange Road passed below, boxing in the green squares of winter grass, the trunks of trees. Inside me was all leaping and riot. Friday. Friday. And Thursday my birthday. I would have my black polo neck.

My desk under the window in the English lesson was where I studied for momentous moments: first kisses, caresses and sex. It was, I believed, obscure, a perfect brown study of a corner. The panelling in the room rose all round to sill height and the windows, which climbed tall, did not begin till well above eye-level. But looking out of windows is not the only way to dream. That day, for me, the view inside my head drew me as if the fair had come and camped on Bruntsfield Links. It was not exactly inattention. English was where we were educated in the passions of life. Mathematics and Chemistry afforded no such scope. But between the leaves of Palgrave's *Golden Treasury* we discovered joy and love, lust and grief and more. Thus, with my schoolbag shielding my open left, my knees tucked under the ink-ingrained oak desk, I could put my two elbows on the lid and lean my head forward on my hands and make a cave to shelter Keats's nightingale and Ninian.

And what would we do on Friday? I did not want the darkness of the picture house. I did not want the not talking, the sitting helplessly while your feelings were snatched and taken soaring to the heights or plunging to the depths. At the end this bucket of emotions dumped on your lap had to be brushed off like the sherbet or absorbed by the single quick dab at the welled tears with a knobbed hanky you hoped no one saw. When the velvet seats clunked up you had to emerge under the house lights and the tatty gilt out into the plain grey of Edinburgh's too tidy streets. And, there was this business in the pictures of the back row. Was Ninian the kind for the back row? I was not. But where would we go? And should I tell Dorcas?

'Beatie. Beatrice. Bay-ah-tree-chay!' In a voice that seemed to come from a long way off and not just three rows of desks, the English master hailed me. His quizzical eyebrows were up. He was waiting. 'May I interrupt to enquire of you, Miss Brown, "Was it a vision or a waking dream?" – as our poet, aptly, has it here?' Such play on words was typical of him but it was not an amused pause which followed. 'Tut. This is not like you, Beatie. Come on, now. Come on.' Had there been a question? I scanned the page for clues. With a sigh he granted my reprieve. 'I shall repeat: with what is the beaker filled, Beatie?'

'With what . . .?'

> 'O for a beaker full of the warm South!
> Full of the true, the blushful Hippocrene,
> With beaded bubbles winking at the brim,
> And purple-stained mouth.'

His voice dropped on the last words, his eyes were gimlets, not stars. (Sometimes they were stars.)

'Wine! Wine, sir. Sorry.'

'And why does he drink it?'

'To escape from reality, sir.'

And that did for the moment.

' "Fade far away, dissolve, and quite forget . . ." '

Remember the feeling of walking side by side, matched with a straight-limbed boy, dark heads together. And, on parting, that smile on his face – like the one on mine now – relief that the moment of asking was over and the real meeting fixed.

Dorcas was waiting for me. Beneath her straight-as-straw fringe, her eyes glinted like aquamarines. That year our timetable afforded us this regular meeting point on Monday afternoons. With some minutes before the bell went, we would lean on the radiator on the upper floor at the end of the art-room corridor and look out the window at the Bruntsfield Links. Since she was 'artistic' and I was a conscientious bursary girl we did not share many lessons. We had met as new girls at McGillivray's High when we were twelve and she had invited me at once to stay with her family in Dewar. The Drummonds lived in a flat in Bruntsfield during the week. At

15

the weekends – and in the holidays – they always went out to this place in the country south of Edinburgh, about forty-five minutes' drive distant. That weekend was the first I ever spent away from home and was momentous for many reasons (one of them the bullocks). When my mother discovered Mr Drummond was called Guthrie and was really an artist and that Mrs Drummond was an actress she had not let me go away again with Dorcas. She had this thing about what she called 'people like that'. Dorcas chopped and changed in her affections but in the end she still was friends with me. She was precocious. I loved her daring . . . but I was wary of it too.

I had decided the encounter with Ninian was too new to share. Other girls were with me as I turned at the top of the stairs. The bell was about to ring. I shrugged a signal of regret and made a beeline for the door. But she was on me in a flash. 'Come on! Come here a minute!'

'There isn't time.'

'There's time for *this*!' Such urgency! I saw life or death in her expression. One arm was elbow-deep inside her bag. She pulled me to the window. 'I've something for you from Dad; he said you've got to know. There!' She whipped out a magazine and laid it on the ledge.

'*Art Forum*,' I read: 'What's that?'

Dorcas spread it open for me at the place.

'Bruno Bornati . . .' She stabbed the page. 'It's your father!'

I think I laughed. Or made some kind of snort.

'I don't have a father, Dorcas. You know that.'

'Beatie!'

'Och! I make up things. I . . . I fantasise. That's all.'

'That weekend you came to stay you told us his name.'

'That was ages ago.'

'The name's the same. Bornati. That was it, wasn't it?'

I followed her index finger. There were several columns of text broken up by reproductions of some very strange-looking cubes and shapes. I flicked over the page where I found only more of the same.

'Isn't there a photo of this . . . artist, sculptor or whatever he is?'

Dorcas shook her head. 'What was your father like?'

That was the question. I pursed my lips. I could not tell in words. I had never tried but I knew if I spoke aloud the pictures in my head would just vanish. Their being there at all was something I just caught. If I charged myself to pin down the actual mouth, eyes, nose, hair, stature of my father, the image faded. But if I turned to him quickly, sneaked up on him from behind, took him by surprise, I got him. No matter what, I could always find his hands.

'What makes your dad think this is my father?'

'The name, for one thing.'

'The name's probably like Brown, Dorcas. Have you ever looked up a Brown in the phone book?'

'It says "Scottish born".'

My mouth closed. I tried to find it in the text. But my doubts were off again. 'Why would you even think he was an artist though? I never said anything about that!'

'Dad seemed to know.'

'Guthrie – ah!'

That look of Guthrie Drummond's was with me still. It was five years ago but it had come to me often in the years between. It was a blue Viking look, not cold but slow and I remembered particularly the attention in it. It was not the same kind of look he had for Dorcas: I envied that look, that fatherly look – the warmth, amusement, the love in it – for it was the look I ached to recognise in a father's eyes for me. The way Guthrie had looked at me was different.

His eyes had crinkled up. 'Beatie what?' he had asked when Dorcas introduced us.

'Brown,' said my friend.

'It's Bornati really, actually.' I had surprised myself. Then the words came tumbling out: 'Beatrice Maria Bornati . . . I used to be.' I had a middle way of saying it without the full Italian thing. 'Bornati was my father's name.'

'Was?'

'Was,' I had nodded. 'He's . . .' Usually I said he was dead. I don't know why but that was the moment that weekend when I gave him the possibility of life again. 'He went away when I was four,' I said.

'Bornati.' Guthrie Drummond's head had tilted like a bird listening to some subterranean disturbance imperceptible to other ears. 'It's Italian, isn't it?' His eyes had been a shafting blue.

'Yes. Afterwards my mother made me just Brown.'

★ ★ ★

17

Now Dorcas was drumming for my attention on the page. 'He . . . Read! Read it! This Bruno Bornati's a success!' Her eyes were large and anxious, eager for me. 'He's got a London agent. Cork Street. Dad says that's the best. And an exhibition coming to the Edinburgh Festival.'

The bell rang like a drill. He was not lying in a ditch then. Or in that Bowery place I had read of. 'Can I have this?' I snatched the magazine.

In the art room the navy blinds were drawn and the white screen was there for films. The lights went out. I waited, glad of the receiving dark. The projector whirred. Flecks jumped on the bright rectangle and threads danced in from the perimeter. My own pictures came up. There was an absorbed stillness in the childhood place I found. The sickly smell of poster paint on wet sugar paper refined itself to the aroma of rare resins, of linseed oil and beeswax. I was kneeling on a floor. My small fingers drew sawdust into cones, holding it high then letting it trickle back and down the pinnacles. Beyond was a choppy sea of woodchippings which I must not touch because of skelfs. Rising from this dangerous spot a tall man bent over something in a vice. Both his hands were fists, one, white-knuckled, clenched a chisel, the other held a pale mallet big as a balloon, and the sound of wood striking wood was in turns urgent and lively, sometimes tender, sometimes, in diminuendo, soft.

This man was my father.

Was this the same man as the Bornati in the magazine sent to me by Guthrie Drummond? It was too dark to read the article. I would keep that for when I was alone in my room.

'Well?' We met again outside. We leaned on the radiator by the window looking over Bruntsfield Links.

'Why is it always you, Dorc, who are the instrument of all my revelations?'

'Are you referring to your long-lost father or to – that weekend?'

'You're—' She had shown me sex and slaughter.

'Well, I don't get to church much – unlike you. But with parents like mine what do you expect?'

Church was my excuse for not ever having gone to stay with them again.

'Thursday's my birthday, you know.'

'Send him a letter. You'll be able to get his address from the agents in London. Say: "I wonder if this date means anything

at all to you by any chance?'' Get him to give you a present for
once. Ask for something *big*!'

I looked at her in disbelief. 'Presents are not what I want.
How can you think that I want *presents*?'

'I would.'

'You've got a father. You've always had a father!'

She gave a pinched-up shrug. 'Not much of a mother though
– or should I say *too* much of a mother. Not one who's ever at
home. It's funny, really, when you think of it. You have just a
mum and I have, mostly, just a dad.'

I did not see the joke. And I saw only the difference. 'But you
do *have* a mum, Dorc.'

'When she's at home they fight.'

'If I had a dad – if I had a dad at home, I mean – I don't think
I'd mind anything, even fights.'

'You would,' came like a double pistol shot.

We turned to the window. The march of trees along the
upper walk had gleaming black trunks, for storms had come in
the night and driven the rain at them, tearing off the last of the
leaves and driving them into gutters and the base of walls in
oiled and inky heaps.

'You've got to stand up for yourself, Beatie.'

'I know.'

'So you'll have to write that letter. He just went off and left –
he owes you a lot!'

'You're at it again – money, you mean?'

'Yes. Money. Things. Look at Jeanie Tait. She's just been
given a new Raleigh bike by her dad and it's not even her
birthday! Moira McCaig got a record player.'

'You don't understand.'

'I do. My family's not perfect either!'

'You don't!'

'Write and ask. Think of all the birthdays he's missed. You
see you get something *big*.'

She had pressed the trigger. I looked at her and hated her.
'Don't you dare tell me what to do! You don't know! *You* don't
know a thing about it! You just don't!'

Her mouth fell open. Her hands hung by her sides in
disbelief.

I struggled with the buckles on my bag.

'Are you telling me, Beatie Brown, that I should not have
brought that magazine in for you to see? Is that what you're

telling me? You can just hand it back then.' There were specks like iron filings in her eyes. 'Give it here. Come on!' She made a grab.

I pulled my case away from her and ran.

I had a right to the magazine. It was my problem. It was my father. I was the only one who knew what I could do about it.

The bus swung round at Salisbury and I jumped off. It was quite different from the morning, when Ninian had come running up behind, his footsteps seeming to point the way ahead. Now the past was catching up.

Four thirty and it was almost dark. Winter had started in earnest, a dismal rain falling. Should I tell my mother? The Remnant Shop window was garish with fans and swags of cloths, dress tartans, shot taffeta and tweed. She found bargains here. I crossed the road to Cooper's, the grocer she used, on the opposite corner. They had put cardboard down for an extra doormat in the wet. Row upon row of cans of soup were stacked against the front glass: Baxter's Cock-a-leekie, Heinz Tomato, Campbell's Barley Broth. The wind gusted up from The Bridges and blew my coat against my back. I turned up my collar and tied my school scarf round my head.

Like a long liquorice strap the length of Minto Street sloped southwards. I always walked from here. When I got in I would ask my mother for all she knew. The high-spinning sound of tyres whipped the wet surface of the road. A bus passed throwing spray at me. I brushed my coat and watched with a sense of injury it bear away behind steamed-up windows its ballast of cosy folk. Rain dripped from my hair.

The illuminated façade of a hotel on my left cast a wide glow on the pavement. One window drew my gaze like a spotlit stage. It was the bar. I paused. There were rows of glasses twinkling, bottles of amber, diamond and ruby spirits, sparkly taps and tilted, Brylcreemed heads. It was the kind of place men went to get away from women. Men like my father? From women like my mother? I had begun to see my mother – not my father's absence – as the trouble. I even suspected her of driving him away. I would get away. Soon. If. When . . . I clenched my fists inside my sheepskin mitts. At that moment my father might be sitting there like that in some bar . . . in some much more interesting bar, of course, if he was an artist in New York or somewhere . . . just sitting there easily, smoking, drinking, talking, laughing.

My numb paw-hands pushed up the flaps of my revers. I bowed my head and walked on. I made a brisk turn into our road. My footsteps began to mark with a more and more insistent beat the litany of questions running in my head: Where . . .? What . . .? When . . .? Did he ever . . .? Mother, do you . . .? But I would say nothing about the article.

The houses in our crescent were respectable sandstone villas built over a century before. Our neighbours left their main doors open till everyone got in at night so that a cheerful light from the glazed hall doors fell on the umbrella stands, Victorian tiles, doormats, brass sills and boot scrapers. At our end only the high-up, half-moon fanlight shone dimly for my arrival home. The number and the name 'Parklea' were on it. I pushed the gate. He must have done this. He must have come here with me when I was little, when it was my grandmother's. What did he think of me then? The latch clicked. I went slowly up the path.

On the step I stood and fumbled for my key. I was afraid of that dark threshold. I had been afraid ever since I saw the marks. Above the old bell pull on the right the stone had been hatched where some former visitant had customarily struck a match. I could not see this at night, of course, but I always remembered it when I stood there like that (Mother preferred me not to ring): the figure on the doorstep arrived – pulling the bell, waiting, striking, lighting up, pulling again – an inevitable presence, at my back.

My mother was in the kitchen doing the ironing. There was a smell of toasted linen.

'It's cosy in here.'

'It's a night for Scotch broth.'

She clapped the iron down and with two hands rearranged the folds of sheet. My mother was tall, long-boned, angular. Watching her now, it struck me how unsuited she was to a kitchen and those fiddly, fond, repetitive tasks: the straining and skimming, blending, creaming, the sprinkling, touching to test, the little sip, the measuring the merest pinch, the toeing of the iron into tucks. To see her with her arms outstretched matching the folds of a big sheet corner to corner was more like it. Ideally, she should have been striding forward somewhere with a banner. But in folding sheets she came near, her height an advantage, and nearer still when she pegged them out on the line against the wind.

But in spirit she was like a tree whose sap has crusted up. Branches spread from the fine structure but the leaves, if they budded, rarely opened. I had never known the true luxuriousness of all that burgeoning green, the extravagance of any flower, the ripening of any seed or ever slept easy in the comfort of her protective shade or been confident of her resilience in a storm. I knew her to be brittle and was afraid on that account.

I sat with my mug of tea in the corner by the Rayburn stove and I began, in spite of all my plans, tactlessly.

'We could make our house more welcoming – for it being home as well as being a guesthouse.'

'Vulgar, you mean? A neon sign? I'm surprised at you, Beatie. It is private. The neighbours wouldn't like it.' She was only too painfully aware of her commercial status in this residential street.

'The big door could be left open. That's all.'

'For all and sundry to traipse in!'

'It would be nicer.'

'Nicer! We can't afford to be nice. A woman on her own, like me, Beatie, cannot take risks.'

'Did my father take risks?'

Her red hands stopped their sweep across the folded length of white.

'What do you mean?'

'What was he like?'

She gave me one curt glance. Drawing the finished sheet over her forearm, she hung it away behind her. 'He . . .' Her neck stiffened. With a shimmery movement of her head, she reached for another piece of linen and spread it on the board. 'I told you,' she pushed the iron at it with little thumps, 'tall, dark and handsome.'

'Mother!'

'In an Italian way – he was.'

'Did he speak with an Italian accent?'

'No. Scottish, if any. He was second generation. Yes,' she said, mastering the creases, 'since you ask me, he did take risks. He had drive. Lots of "get up and go",' she said bitterly, 'as he did.'

'Why did he—'

'I left him.' In syncopation, her retort.

'Why—'

'He did not leave me. I left him.'

'Why did you leave him?'

'That is not your business!' She set the iron down.

'But, mother, it *is*.'

She creased the pillow slip, edges in, and folded it. 'I left him because I shouldn't ever have got married to him in the first place. My mother and father were right. A bank manager's daughter brought up in a respectable neighbourhood like Morningside and educated at one of the best fee-paying schools, the Muriel Wotherspoon School for Girls, had no business going off and marrying an Italian who lived above a fish-and-chip café away down there in Portobello. Because his family were immigrants – good grief – he hadn't even fought with the Forces in the war! My parents were right. I made a mistake. And I paid for it.'

'But there was me.'

'Everything I did was for you.'

'Were you never happy?'

'We were together five years. The first two we stayed with his mother above the café. And I tried. I'd serve. I didn't like it much, mind you, not having been brought up to that kind of thing, or among those kind of people.'

'What kind?'

'Italians.'

'Were they . . . what were they?'

She folded another pillow case. 'Nice . . . really. I have to say that. Clever with babies. With you.'

'So?'

'But it was no good.' She broke off and reached into the pile for the next thing, a school blouse of mine. She stretched the yoke flat in preparation for the iron. 'No. He hated working in the café. He was always going off even then. Up to the Art College for the night classes. He had this thing about being an artist, a sculptor. There was nowhere he could work; we only had two rooms. So I got my mother to help – Father never did come round – I got this wee flat near The Meadows, close enough to the Art College, I thought. I still went all the way down to Portobello sometimes to help out at the café if they needed me – though some cousins had lost no time in moving in there again with the mother. Then one night I came back and found he had gone out leaving you alone.'

'How old was I?'

'Three. He'd gone to the pub. Just a quick drink, he said. You were fast asleep, he said. There was I slaving and scrimping and getting this stink of frying in my hair and in my clothes and having to spend all the next day washing, and he could go and do a thing like—' She faltered. She pushed the iron at the blouse in agitated thumps. 'After that . . . well, after that I . . . I just wouldn't have it.'

'What, Mum?'

She tugged the sleeves straight.

'And he got stronger and stronger about his art, you see. His ART! I never went out again at night as long as I stayed with him. He went out every night – to the classes and to bars. And I discovered he went with other women.'

She fell silent then. I was very still.

Her ironing kept up its quiet runs and bumps.

I heard her take a deep breath. She seemed to draw herself up. 'It was your grandfather's death that decided me,' she said in a stronger voice. 'Mother was my ally by then. We sold the big house in Morningside Drive. To be away from our old neighbourhood was easier for Mother . . . I went back to my training in Domestic Science. Granny looked after you. It was for the best.'

'What happened to him?'

'He was in Glasgow for a while, working in the shipyards of all things, then I heard he was going to America. I had one letter which said he had found "someone to help him".'

'And?'

'A postcard of the Statue of Liberty.'

'An address?'

She shook her head.

'Was he still an artist?'

She did not know.

'Aren't you curious about what happened to him?'

She did not answer.

'Have you ever wanted him back?'

'I know my own mind, Beatie. If I'd have been able to stand for that kind of thing, I'd never have gone in the first place.'

'Did you love him once then?'

'Och, I fell for him. Hook, line and sinker, I fell for him. We met at a dance, a student dance. There was a great urge to get on, not to waste any more time after the war. Everyone was a student of something then, getting a training to get a job, to get on with life. I wore that dress . . .'

'Which one?'

'Cousin Jean had just got married. I made it to be a bridesmaid at her wedding.'

'Have you still got it?'

She leaned back and hauled a sheet from the pile.

'A red dress. It was a long time ago.'

She held the wide yards of white under her chin and out on either side. I glimpsed in her momentary profile the hopes and dreams of years before. She pursed her lips, though, and her concentration came back to the neatness of the fold and her answer.

'As I said,' she began plying the iron to and fro, 'it was just after the war. Everything was different. He wasn't really my kind. Love's a sort of trap. Then there was you.'

'And now, Mummy, do you . . .?'

'I never think.'

'I do.'

'Don't.'

'Mother!'

'He knows where we are, Beatie. I've changed the name. Your name too. As a baby you were known as Mary – Maria was what his mother always called you. My mother never liked it: she said it was Catholic name. When we moved here you started off as little Beatrice Brown, a clean slate. But he knew the address. The address is the same. It is downright inhuman that he's never written to ask for you. Don't think I haven't thought that. But he was a self-centred kind of man. Daft about his art. I never understood that properly when we married. But I cannot abide deceit. I cannot abide it. So . . .!' She flicked water from a bowl. Drops hit the face of the iron which spat back.

'Didn't he have other family?'

'The old mother was poorly. She died.'

'Was he a good artist?'

'I don't know anything about these things. He never made any money at it. The things he carved in wood were quite nice sometimes. He went off that though. I don't know what came after. *He* thought he was good. *He* thought he was Michelangelo!'

'But did he really never write again?'

She crashed the iron down, planted both fists on the board and spoke with passion.

'Beatie, I have slaved and saved and worked and prayed for you! Been a mother and a father both. No letters ever came. After that American postcard, no word of any kind. I wish they had. Don't you think a little money, a word of interest, of love for you, would have lightened my load? Of course it would! But none came. Ever.'

'Mummy—'

'And when you say to me, "Why don't we move to a small flat in Marchmont near the school, with no big rates to pay, no garden to maintain, less work?" I always think: no. No, he might not ever find us – you, *you*, I mean; I don't mean "us". I don't care, for myself. He might not ever find *you* if we moved.'

All this for me. This great stone house, this dismal guest-house, all for me. I stopped my ears.

Her iron scored across the board. 'I do not want to clap eyes on him again,' she said.

'Oh, I know *that!*' Our eyes locked. Then mine wavered. 'But I want to see him just once . . .'

'He could be dead.'

I leaned against the stove's warmth. 'But, Mummy, if he saw me now, what . . .?'

Quietly she put the iron down.

My mother was close. She took my empty mug. 'Let's heat that soup,' she said.

CHAPTER THREE

I listened for my mother going to bed and heard the click as she turned the key. She did this every night – even when we had no one staying in the guesthouse.

My hand slid under my pillow. I withdrew the magazine. This is what I read:

> The work of Bruno Bornati is an uncompromising exercise in the redefinition of sculpture. The forms he uses are shorn of the usual external correspondences. He has rejected his earlier interest in the human and the animal and any belief in the role of universal archetypes for conveying fundamental truths of an emotive or intuitive order by means of association and metaphor.
>
> We may be forgiven if the stark metallic constructs of his pieces trouble or puzzle, shock or appal. This is what he seeks: that we be aware: that the object before us commands our perception, demands examination in a new way. This, Mr Greenberg, the American critic, insists is the 'higher way' – for those like David Smith and Bornati in the States, Caro, Tucker, Turnbull in Britain who strive towards an appropriate creation of pure form are elitist.
>
> *In Out*, *Back to Back*, *Cells 9* and *Root Nine* are all large constructs, averaging two to three metres in size, the materials are sheet steel and aluminium and illustrate the debt Bornati owes to his training in welding on Clydeside.
>
> Of Italian extraction but Scottish by birth, the sculptor has been living and working in the United States for over a decade now.

It fitted: an Italian Scot, 'over a decade' away, a 'training in welding on Clydeside' – 'working in the shipyards of all things' was the way my mother put it.

> His work is generally acknowledged now in the United States. It will be interesting to see how he is received in Britain. His first exhibition there is planned for next year's Edinburgh International Festival.
>
> This is a bold cold show: barren. There is something of the bald mountain top about its finality – if one may be forgiven the reference to a natural object. It is awesome in that way also. The question that troubles the viewer is whether it is indeed 'the ultimate' (as Greenberg would have it) – or is it the end . . . a dead end?

This conclusion made me uncomfortable. I squinted at the pictures and even held them at different angles. They made me uncomfortable too. I could make nothing of them. In no way did they resemble the wood sculptures I remembered. Perhaps I would have to see them in reality before I could judge – and I would be able to do that: the exhibition was actually coming to Scotland. To my untutored mind – for we were only skimming the history of Fine Art on those Monday afternoons – they were unlike anything I had ever seen, or been told was art before. This difficulty was a kind of comfort. 'Difficult' was close to 'different' and 'extraordinary' and these words made my father's unnatural desertion of me and my mother easier to take.

I hid the magazine again and switched off the bedside light.

But not once in all those years had he tried to contact me. My excitement and my admiration at his success ground up against this grudge – glanced like knife blades against the dullness of a Carborundum wheel and sent sparks needling round the darkness of my room.

The words of the letter I would write began to form in my head. It was simple at first. I wanted to know him. I was grown-up now and I wanted to see who my father was. It would help me understand who I was. I did not know why he had left. Not exactly. If it had been my fault he went away I was sorry. But I could not accept his never having written; I was sure there must be an explanation and when I heard that I could forgive him. Perhaps I could say I forgave him already. Perhaps not. I could leave that out. All I wanted was to see him and for him to see me. I was as tall as my mother – could he imagine that? I did not look like her except our eyes were the same . . . But here the missive in my head arrived at danger-ous territory like a full stream running suddenly upon a desert. If a little rivulet of inspiration slipped free over the sand it was soon to hesitate. Such lines dried without a trace. In the end I decided not to say a word about my mother. Perhaps she had settled her score. I had not.

The next day from a public phone box I telephoned the London agent, said I was a student with particular interest in the sculptor Bruno Bornati and asked for his address in the States. The woman who answered was cagey. I invented a spiel about our sculpture club at college wanting to ask if he would speak when he came to town at the Festival. She was doubtful. Which college? The Edinburgh College of Art, I lied. He was not much interested in that kind of thing, she said. Besides they were not even sure he was coming over. Then the woman sighed and said, well 'they' couldn't do anything for me but she supposed I could try myself and she read out the address. She said it so quickly I had to scribble and hoped to heaven I had got it down correctly. It was in SoHo in New York. I thought only London had a place called that. I hoped she had not fobbed me off with somewhere that did not exist.

I put pen to paper the following night. I was quite confident about my skill at letter writing. They had been among my most excellent school exercises: the Formal (Dear Sir/Madam ending Yours faithfully), the Less Formal (Yours sincerely, small s), the Job Application, the Letter to a Friend (be natural). Had I not been given A for all of them, had them read out, displayed? There was no model in my loose-leaf notes for Letter to an Unknown Father. I did hope the ending was right. It gave me trouble putting down 'With love'. I forced myself. What else? 'In anticipation of your accelerated response' or some such officialese? That would have been protection, of a sort. I saw him laugh at that. Since I had exposed myself so far why not completely? I sighed it 'Beatrice', then added 'Mary', remem-bering what I used to be to him. On the back of the envelope I wrote: 'From: Beatrice Mary Bornati, 18 Dalkeith Crescent, Newington, Edinburgh, Scotland, Great Britain.' He had never known me as Beatie or as Brown.

I would not tell my mother anything about the letter or the article either – not until I received my answer.

She was up before me on Thursday and had bacon rolls and coffee waiting. A parcel lay beside my place. Even then I looked – in case, at last, he might have thought of me. But it was my mother's gift. She had bought me the black sweater and had finished the purple wool skirt. There was also a pair of tights: American Tan.

'You need them for the short hemline, they tell me.'

'Mum!' I hugged her.

'Happy Seventeen,' she whispered and kissed me on the lips which was an unexpected claim and moved me to cling for a moment. 'Did you get your Physics done then? You were up late.'

'Eventually.' She knew about my date the following night. She even approved because she knew something of the Orr family from church. She thought that because Ninian was an Academy boy he must be a gentleman. She did not know my 'Physics' was the final draft of my letter to Bruno Bornati Esq. It was in my bag now, written in my best italic script, sealed and stamped, safe between the pages of *The Golden Treasury*.

'I have this Dr Rose today.'

I had forgotten.

At the corner of the crescent, I put the letter between the jaws of the pillar box and heard it slip down inside. Done now. I could not call it back. Our journey had begun. There was no sign of Ninian on the broad and upward-sloping street. He had disappeared from my morning route. Having a chance of him, I reflected, had made it easier to risk pursuit of this progenitor of mine.

'He's coming.' My mother was by the sink when I got in from school.

'Tomorrow. He'll call for me at seven.'

'I mean Dr Rose, Beatie. Our new guest.'

'I thought you meant, was Ninian collecting me?'

'The room seemed to suit.' She turned round. 'Well, but of course he should call for you, Beatie.'

I had once been kissed by a boy. It was in my junior school, when we were having films on Friday afternoon. His name was Ian Robertson, a bully, who marked me out, and who planted his fleshy lips, surprisingly, on my face just before the lights went up on the *Life History of the Dragonfly*. I was flattered but the kiss was peculiar – badly aimed, too sudden, warm and wet and brought with it a smell of grubby knees.

There could be nothing like that on a proper first date. 'Just talk to him naturally,' my mother said. What was natural about it?

He rang punctually. I snapped on the porch light. I looked up at him, and away, and felt inside a frantic disturbance like wing beats. He glanced at the hall behind and hesitated as if he expected a parent to appear. But my mother was in the kitchen out of sight. She was leaving this to me, which helped. Uttering words about being sorry for not being ready though I was, I caught up my coat from the banister end and shrugged into the sleeves. Too late, he withdrew his hands from the depths of his navy duffle. I pressed my coat pocket to check my purse with its small change was there although my mother said she expected him to pay. That was the way it should be done.

It was simple, this physical attraction drawing us together as surely as magnetised poles. And it was mysterious. And it was strong. The small space of the porch was crowded. He brushed past, close, and I smelled damp wool and a strangeness: him, or the male in him. I paused, wondering. I felt tenderness too. Why that for a young man, a stranger? Perhaps it was tenderness for our plight. It could well be his first date. Did he guess it was mine? He was waiting out on the path. Yes. And how he stood apart: I was drawn to that.

We made our way along the crescent. His coat hung askew on his big shoulders. Leaning over towards me, hands safely tucked again in pockets, he asked questions and watched my face when I answered. The questions did not follow on. Perhaps he had rehearsed them beforehand. He was nervous, scared of pauses, not really listening to what I said.

'There's a café up here. We could have coffee.'

'Brattisani's. Yes.' But there would be crowds of others there. Surely he had better plans than this?

'So you don't like the pictures?'

'I do go sometimes. Very occasionally. *Breakfast at Tiffany's* with my mother.'

'*Last Year at Marienbad*?'

'No.'

'*Jules et Jim*?'

I shook my head.

31

'Very French. You should see that. I'll take you. If you'll come,' he said.

I inclined my cheek. 'What's it about?'

'Love. All that.' He pronounced the key word in a low, truncated way as if it confused him yet would not even let itself be dismissed decently. 'It's about a woman, Jeanne Moreau, and two men.'

'A triangle then.' I sounded pert.

'But not the usual.'

'No?'

'Well . . . you'll see.' He was listening to me now.

We arrived at the café's red façade and peered through steamy windows at the blurred heads and blotched mouths behind. Ninian took my elbow: 'No,' he said. 'Come on.'

We hopped on a bus. Everything happened lightly and quickly in those moments. We sailed down The Bridges into Princes Street.

He took me to The Chocolate House. I had never been before. The plate-glass door with its fluted bronze handle swung shut closing off the Edinburgh night. Warmth engulfed us. We climbed up the carpeted steps of a gold-scrolled staircase and arrived at an upper floor where there were lines of tables bedded in deep coffee pile and spread with pistachio linen. Copper-hued mirrors framed with geometrical segments of frosted glass overlooked each table. It was Edinburgh's latest thing. Girls at school had talked about it. Only two tables were occupied. The waitress appeared as if by magic, soundlessly. I ordered a Coupe Japonaise which I saw I could afford. Ninian asked for a Banana Split.

He hauled himself out of his coat and pushed it behind his back. But I got up quickly and hung mine on the wooden stand two tables away. Coming back, I was conscious of the new length of my skirt and warmth in his watching eyes. 'You look nice,' he said. I felt a blush.

He wore a navy fisherman-rib sweater. His hands moved around a great deal now that they were deprived of pockets. One ran through his forelock, one rubbed the back of his neck. The fingers were long but blunt. They were the only rather clumsy thing about him. He clasped them, clenched and spread them as we discussed what we had rejected on the menu card. This eating ice-creams was a happy solution. I had been nervous of being taken to a pub for I had never been in one. How to stomach oysters or handle asparagus loomed among the pitfalls I imagined might be set to trap me on my first date. But this was no obstacle course. My escort was friendly. We were nearly having fun. Ice-cream was easy, although the spoons were rather long. When Ninian's banana skittered off the plate we laughed. I tried my tiny paper parasol. There was the child in each of us. He more than me in that, I thought, watching him scrape the glass dish and lick his spoon again and again. The cherry ran around. Suddenly he scooped it up.

'I see you do that too.' My cherry lay waiting in the well of the dish.

'Go on!'

'All right.' I ate it.

'Let's have another.'

'I couldn't! Didn't you have any tea?'

'I had to leave before the meal tonight.'

'Dinner. Ah.' As I suspected, a difference between the bursary grammar-school girl and the private schoolboy: her tea at six, his dinner at seven.

'What Highers are you taking?'

'Three A levels.'

Those were the English exams which were not offered at our school. 'So you're very clever.'

'English, History and Latin.'

'You'll try for Oxford or Cambridge then?' I collapsed my little parasol.

'It's that or Law at Edinburgh and then the family firm.'

'You don't sound keen.'

'I like acting. I'm to be in the big production this year. We start rehearsals next term.'

'What for?'

'*Hamlet*.'

'What part?'

'Hamlet.'

I pushed up the paper shade again and twirled it. I could see him spotlit on the stage in black velvet slashed with snowy lawn, and in the darkness of the auditorium all the sisters and family female friends swooning at the sight. If his acting were as good as his looks, my chances might be short-lived. I would be up against all the girls of the town's sixth forms, a full predatory force, once the word was out. Quietly, for the moment, however, I had him to myself.

We had frothy chocolate drinks.

Ninian asked for the bill, got my coat, did the tip and paid for both of us. Glowing, we went down the stairs and into Princes Street.

Keeping an eye out for buses coming, we went up The Mound. It was a big dark Scottish night with high stars. My cheeks felt cold. I put my collar up. We climbed quite fast, close, not touching, his mass shielding the chill from me.

'The family's getting up a party for a ball. Would you like to come?'

'Me? Oh, I'd like to . . .' It was Cinderella time. I could do the dances. We were well taught at school. Except the foxtrot. I worried about the foxtrot. 'What ball is it?'

'The New Club.' My ignorance was bliss. 'Just old fogeys. That's why I want you there.' I knew his parents to say 'hello'. His mother took her turn with flowers at church. I had helped her once. She was the type that manned soup kitchens and ran Girl Guide rallies. 'Will your parents let you? It'll go on into the wee small hours. There'll be champagne.'

'I've never had champagne,' I said. Then: 'There's only my mother to ask, by the way.'

'Don't you have a father?'

'Everyone has a father, Ninian.' My parry confused him. I relented. 'Mine's . . . away.' I had never banked upon so much before. Just because I had something about him now in the magazine beneath my pillow, I was speaking as if I could summon him at will, as if he would definitely be back, like other people's fathers, after a trip.

At that moment, Ninian was walking up the hill in front of me. Beyond him, railings topped the slope and the ancient tenements loomed, their windows, randomly lit, hung like cut gems invisibly suspended against the blackness and climbed to mix with stars. Suddenly, he turned, looked inspired. 'A bus!' he cried. He pulled my sleeve and ran.

We leaped aboard, went upstairs and made for the front seat. Our rapid breathing slowed. He sat looking out at the night. His weight crushed my arm. I could not tell his thoughts. Edging out from under him I squeezed to the side and studied the pavements running along below. He moved away half off the seat, one leg out across the aisle. Was it because of what I had said about my father? I turned and found him watching me with a soulful look, the kind you allow yourself alone. I smiled. In stages his expression broke and warmth beginning from his eyes spread carefully. 'Sorry.'

'Why?'

'I squashed you.'

'Not unpleasantly,' I said.

We got off the bus on Minto Street and walked round into the crescent. Our footsteps slowed. His hand caught hold of mine and I felt the warmth of his wool jacket pressing the length of my arm. His height screened me from the streetlamps and extended to giant size the shadow I was used to seeing of myself moving aslant across the low walls and the familiar garden plots. This hand holding mine was dry and warm. But it restricted and was clumsy too. It was what he thought he should do. Had he planned it on the bus? I looked up at his face, trying to show without words that I liked him, had not been disappointed, had not found him a rugger-playing insensitive oaf. And I withdrew my hand.

Giving that small turned-down smile, that tragi-comic look, he found his pockets and said, 'Afraid your mother sees us?'

It was not exactly that. It was not dark enough here, certainly.

'She's shut the door.'

'It's always shut.'

'Will she be waiting up for you?'

'In bed, listening from her bedroom, I expect.'

'Did you . . .' he searched, took a great breath, and plunged, 'like – tonight?' No bully, Ninian.

'Yes.'

'You'll come out again?'

I nodded.

'Good,' he smiled, relieved. His hands were clenched inside those big blue pockets.

CHAPTER FOUR

That night I lay awake a long time going over Ninian's words and mine and what I might have said. I draped myself in different coloured satins – in orchid pink, amethyst and ultramarine – and whirled round and round a ballroom under brilliant chandeliers. Sleep, however, shifted more sand than my conscious mind could do and cast up for me next morning the memory of a red dress.

It had hung deepest in of all the clothes in my mother's wardrobe. I discovered it years before when I crawled in over the shoetrees and laces and felt this softness hanging and tugged and brought it down about my ears, a river running over me. I pulled it to my cheek and sat among the leather uppers with my thumb in my mouth stroking the velvet.

'Get out of there!'

I wound into it and hid.

'You stupid girl! Never go inside a wardrobe. It could fall, trap, kill you!' My mother's grasp burned a bracelet round my wrist.

I woke to the realisation that she must have kept it, the red bridesmaid's dress, till then at least . . . But I woke, also, to a Saturday morning and a hockey match, an away game over in Fife. Enthusiasm for hockey was one of the things I shared with my mother. Her school had been evacuated to Crieff or somewhere because a bomb fell on the Forth Bridge at the beginning of the war. One of the few things she told me about this was the great games of hockey they had had. Up till that moment I, too, enjoyed the sport. But suddenly I loathed the thought of chasing a ball about a pitch. It was the first time I had felt like that. Was this the beginning of the end? Having boyfriends threatened team spirit. I might become like one of them – 'the lorn', the lone girls, the girls with bosoms shelving out under their box pleats whose faces dipped deskward in lessons to avoid the teacher's eye, sulky girls who looked up in anticipation only when they quit the gates at four o'clock and met their destinies, the grey-flannelled youths who lurked by the railings on the other side of Gilmour Place. I flung the covers back. I did not fancy that either.

'You're late, Beatie!' cried ten of the First Eleven from their encampment of long canvas bags at Waverley Station. 'That's not like you.'

'I was out last night.'

'Beatie's got a boyfriend!'

'What's his name?'

'What school?'

'Kissed?'

But I gave them nothing more.

We won that day: three – two. And I justified my prized place in the team. Running on the wing out on the hard ground over winter grass, dodging the half-back, centre-back, keeping the ball bouncing ahead, then picking up the run again and arriving to swing with a clean whack and shoot a goal resounding against the rear board of the net was an exhilaration not to be abandoned lightly.

Mother was not in to tell. 'Lunch in oven,' said the note. 'Gone to tea with Cousin Jean.' It meant she had taken the bus to Corstorphine out on the other side of the town. I had the house to myself. Had she still kept that dress?

Outside my mother's bedroom door, I hesitated, suddenly afraid of disappointment. I would have my bath first. I wanted to shed all my St Trinian's trappings, to perfume and powder, to prepare.

The lavatory seat was up.

I looked across the landing. There had been nothing in the note. Mother would have said. That doctor man was not due yet . . . or was he? His was to be the narrow room with the table in it. That door was closed. Perhaps he had called to leave a suitcase. It could be standing on the other side on the green rug. I listened. The house was silent. I closed the bathroom door and slid the snib, in case. It was too bad: intrusion just at this time. I lowered the lavatory seat and at the basin ran a purifying trickle over my fingertips.

Bath taps full on, the last lavender cube, discovered between the Optrex and the syrup of figs, was dropped into the steam. I peeled off my clothes and stood naked on the cork mat. I shook out my hair, tested the temperature and went in facing the taps. Under the greenish water, my body flowed from me, foreshortened laterally, distorted for the moment. Sinking back I let my head go under and my hair float like weed. The hot tap dripped. I kept a wary eye: but nothing ever had come out. I lathered the soap and pushed the sponge down and round and under and lay back. I summoned up a favourite fantasy – being bound at the stake and rescued by a craggy male straight out of Hollywood. But I had a real face now and a real body. Gently, as the water welled about me, Ninian came: his long pale face; his body, under the thick duffle coat, I knew, also long and pale; and his hands, those restless, homeless hands, I made travel.

But not this afternoon with Mother already over there, already stretching for a scone.

You could hear the lions roaring. You sat in the front room sipping Melrose's Poonakandy tea out of china cups, pinkie cocked while Cousin Jean and Mother gossiped and all the time you heard the lions roaring in the Zoo over the wall just two bungalows away. Corstorphine would make anybody roar. Except Cousin Jean in her mote-free house, priestess with cake-stand of the afternoon tea.

These Edinburgh women suppressed all their roars. Both had had 'a past'. My mother had dared to marry beneath her. Cousin Jean's 'past' began further back. She had been brought up in Spain, unusually, because her father had been an engineer in mining there. This was still reflected in the way she wore her hair (a shiny bun smooth to the head), in the strong red she painted on her lips and her penchant for hooped earrings. The crimson dresses for her bridesmaids I put down, too, to this exotic start in life: their bodices had the same slender sensuous fit as a flamenco dancer's. She had married a young man who played football for Scotland. He wore his dark blazer with its badge of honour on the pocket for years afterwards to assist his sales of Coats's thread but his demise was a sporting first: he dropped dead on the eighth tee on the Eden Course at St Andrews after hitting a hole in one.

Cousin Jean was not troubled by the lions any more.

'Och, I never hear them, dear. Have a wee meringue,' she always said to me.

Now, while I lay soaking in the bath, they were feeding on

me over in Corstorphine, ingesting details of the Lawyer's Son, the First Date and the Invitation to the Ball. Also the New Guest. How nice he was. My glance rested on the lavatory seat. It lay inscrutably lidded. That the seat had been up was not 'nice', surely. The other tap was dripping now. You heard tales about medical students. Mother's 'nice' might have meant his accent. Curious how Received Pronunciation could confound us Scots, make our usually sharp judgement melt like tar in the sun.

I knuckled both taps hard. Dreaming was beguiling for a bit but it never made things happen. The moments I conjured for myself, lying in my bath and lying in my bed, were very different from stepping out on to the street with Ninian. The touch of his hand had made me freeze. The gap between my small experience of boys and what I gleaned from books and films and the sly lorn girls was a chasm dark and wide.

I used to plan the dreams about my father like a play, make them resolve and unresolve. But since Fate – or Guthrie Drummond – had made a move towards me and I knew he was alive, the blackness separating us was no longer a void like outer space, it was just an ocean and, by writing him a letter, I had stretched across. It would not arrive for weeks. Cautious reckoning told me not to look for anything till Christmas. Christmas, though, was surely a good time. Meanwhile I had Ninian.

I worked the shampoo into my hair, reached for the mug and got back to my real triumph: McGillivray's, three – Dunfermline High, two. I leaned back for a mermaid rinse and came up seal smooth, feeling as full of sweet success as when I whammed the ball. I used the mug for clean water from the tap, first cold then hot, and poured it over my head. I twisted my hair and stood up.

On the shelf above the basin there was 'Morning Rose' talc, a Cousin Jean gift. I did not like rose. It was the one fragrance never true to the delicacy of its flower. I puffed it on all the same. Then I cleaned the bath with Vim. I had not finished drying my feet – still, I did the bath. My rituals were full of such dilemmas: put out the landing light. I've not gone down the stairs yet. Put it out in case . . . Wash the pots. I've not eaten my dinner. Good to get them done . . . Stop your dreaming. I've just begun . . . Stop. You haven't time . . .

It was cold in the hall. Wrapped in a towel, I clutched my

bundle of navy serge and maroon socks and hoped my knickers were not dangling. This was always no-man's-land when guests threatened. I crossed quickly to my room and felt safe again only when that door was shut.

Kneeling on the floor in my old dressing gown, I brushed out my hair before the electric fire. Although breakfast had been rushed that morning, my mother had responded to the idea of the ball with an alacrity which surprised me.

'I've seen some kingfisher taffeta in the Remnant Shop. Just three-and-six a yard. Vogue patterns are best. How long have we got?'

'Mother!'

'What?'

'It's just – I didn't know . . . Do you haunt material shops devising my first dance dress? Have you second sight? Or what?'

'Tea?' The tilt of her shoulder.

I softened. 'Is there anything nice in red?'

'Red? I hadn't thought of red.'

Once she had.

My hair was dry enough now. As I remembered it, the fabric was some kind of velvet and watermarks would spot . . . if the dress was still there.

Her room was always tidy, 'never put it down, put it away'. The furniture was what she called 'decent', dark wood with carved detail running along the rails of the two narrow chairs and round the panels which flanked the mirrored wardrobe door. The matching dressing table had a twin clutch of small drawers and stood in front of the window where deep pink curtains, blue-shadowed with time, were drawn half across. Bald Edinburgh light struck down from above. I had watched it catch my mother full on the face as she sat on the stool accepting its harsh truth, applying Pond's Cold Cream, stabbing at her cheeks their punishment, their only chance of help.

I opened the wardrobe and stretched in to the left past an unpromising phalanx of sombre sleeves. I pushed aside scratchy tweed, stroking wools, sliding satin linings and with alarm cancelled by recognition met my grandmother's old squirrel coat. Deep in I felt my mother's heather-mixture skirt, her once-favourite 'art silk' afternoon dress, then her plastic mac which, come to think of it, I had not seen for ages – she had bought a new raincoat from the Robertson Rubber

Company. And the end. My hand was up against the wood. She must have rearranged them all. I did the right-hand side. But there was nothing. Then I tried from underneath, the way I found it as a child. I felt across the shoes. In the far corner my fingers caught a tangle of straps and pulled out a pair of old-fashioned high-heeled sandals dim with dust. A stroked line along disclosed red satin. They must be the ones. She had kept them. She must have kept the dress too. I reached up. A softness brushed. My other hand went in to help, past looping belts and inquisitive cuff buttons, strained up to get the hanger off the rail. She had covered it with the plastic mac. With distaste I took that off.

The dress lay across my arms. All moods of red moved in the silk plush. It was passive in its weight yet yielded. I held it up against me and kicked my foot forward at the hem. I was tall enough now. I shrugged off my dressing gown and raised my arms. It slipped over me, a sheath, assuming at once my warmth and shape. The material was cut cunningly on the cross. When I moved it swung and fondled my legs. It fastened at the back with a long row of tiny covered buttons sewn so close together that they touched. Loop by loop I began to do them up and was hugged by the neat fit. It was a struggle near the top. I tried from over my shoulder and from underneath again. I was larger than my mother. Lowering my arms, I turned and saw myself: a tall slash of red in the obscurity of the wardrobe mirror. My father once liked my mother in this dress. I smoothed round my breasts and down my sides. Would my father like me?

What would Ninian think? Was it too shocking for me, for Beatie Brown? I saw him blush.

Beatrice could carry it off . . . Beatrice Bornati.

With a quick turn I moved to the dressing table. My hair fell half across my face; my cheeks were pink; my mouth open in soft-lipped surprise at this sight of an unknown self. I hunched forward but this did not change the way my breasts were held by the binding, giving cloth except to hollow deep corners above my collarbones under the thin straps.

Beatrice. I leaned towards the mirror. 'Bay . . .' in Italian – 'Bay-ah-tree-chay'. She needed make-up. Some lipstick. Something roguish. Not the pearly pales that were in fashion. A real red. She reached for the tiny drawers and tried them one by one. Powder puffs. Knock that shut. Cotton wool. No. Beads.

Hairgrips. No. No. Nested things . . . stockings, a faded, crushed chou rose. No. Lipsticks, yes, a cache . . . 'Coral Reef', 'Autumn Glow', 'Sunset' – one called 'Crimson Lake'. A brusque line across was the mother's method but Beatrice bent close to the glass, wound the glistening ruby stick proud of its golden holder, and, like a film star, pouted out her lips.

A man was watching.

The lipstick dropped, rolled. His face was in the mirror. 'Who?' I tried to stand. I took a breath to scream.

He stopped my mouth.

I shrank down under the pale eyes, the pupils were mere points.

'For God's sake!' His forehead grooved between the brows. 'There's no need for these dramatics!' The intense look was fearful. He released me.

The crook of my arm went up.

He examined his offending hand as if it belonged to someone else, then squared the knot of his tie with it. He was not dressed like a thief. 'I thought you were a burglar,' he said. It was an English voice.

I twisted round on the stool. The tie was silk, shirt laundry-starched with deep cuffs and gold links; he wore a three-piece suit.

'It sounded like that,' he insisted, 'as if someone was searching for jewellery, ransacking the place.'

'Who are you?'

'My name's Rose.'

'The doctor?'

'John Rose. Yes.'

I heard relief in his voice. In the mirror I saw him offer his hand but I ignored that. My wrenched face burned. My pride had suffered graver hurt.

'You're . . . Miss Brown?'

I sat tight.

He bent from view. His tawny hair crinkled at the back. Then his curiously high forehead appeared again. He stood 'Crimson Lake' quietly beside me.

'It's broken.'

'It's just a lipstick.' There was irritation in his voice. Nevertheless, he recovered the greasy scarlet section and offered it between finger and thumb.

I kept my back to him.

'Oh, come along. I don't know about things like that.' He inclined his head. His features were small, fine – aristocratic, I remember thinking then. 'Look. There! I've stuck it on.'

'That won't work. It's broken.'

Why should his mouth fix in such an injured curve? I was the vulnerable one with my dress unbuttoned. I clamped my crossed arms up to my neck in front.

'I disturbed your dressing-up,' he said.

He was mocking me. Why not dressing? I was not a girl. I was a woman in this gown.

'I hate to see a lady in distress.'

I turned my back: I was not that either.

'Let me do up those buttons.'

My spine went stiff.

'I'm good at that kind of thing.'

'Get out!'

No answer.

'Just get out.' I appealed face to face. 'Please.'

His chin went up. He opened his mouth as if to speak then he thought better of it. He let a raised hand signal farewell and a plea for truce. With a light step, he quit the room.

On the floor the satin sandals lay apart, as if stricken. I bent for them, pushed one foot in and then another but my fingers had no patience with the straps and gilt buckles. I was quite unnerved but tried to carry on. Balancing on the heels I slid-stepped over to the wardrobe. My face had never looked back at me before like it did then. I leaned in close. The pupils of my eyes dilated fully black as if they opened to my core. 'A guilty thing surprised.' Words from the poem made my lips turn down in recognition. Get out of this, Beatie. Get out. Off with the shoes. It was not easy to hurry the dress with the finickiness of the buttons. Head down, hair curtaining my concentration, my elbows stuck out at angles that made my arms ache with the awkwardness. What if he came back? I lurched to the door and turned the key, as I should have done before, had I only thought of it, as my mother did every night because she never failed to think of it. Pull off the dress, put on the dressing gown, put the dress on the hanger, button the plastic mac over, replace both in the corner of the wardrobe. And the shoes. And shut. And smooth the bed cover. Then I remembered the lipstick. It was on the dressing table where he had left it, apparently intact. I wound it down with care. It behaved as if nothing was amiss. I hid it at the back of the small drawer. I listened at the door, opened, closed it and crossed no-man's-land and knew it for a mine field.

When my mother asked me later if I had scored a goal that morning I had to delve far back in time as if to some former age.

Chapter Five

'There's no need to wait up, Mrs Brown. I can turn a key and run a bolt home.' Cold air had entered with him.

'How are you to know if everyone is in, Dr Rose? And please, would you shut the storm door, before you open the other one, to preserve the heat?'

'Ah-hah! The airlock principle – you're a scientist, Mrs Brown.'

'No. It is just my way. Excuse me now.' There followed that embarrassing shuffle when two people try to pass and each steps to the same side. Something had altered the man from when I'd seen him last: his brow was smooth, his gestures almost laconic. There was a playful semaphore in the way he got out of the sleeves of his coat. Mother stood her ground. 'I wish to lock up now and get to my bed,' she said. When she moved I slipped out from behind her and started up the stairs. 'Oh, and, Dr Rose, meet Beatie, my daughter.'

'Hello, Beatie.'

'Hello.' With a half-look I acknowledged and checked. He unwound his scarf and the smell of cigarettes came out. He did not betray our first encounter. There was an easiness behind his eyes now as if he had just come from some warm place: the image of the nut-brown pubs whose glimmer lit the canyons of the old town came to me. I turned to go on up and in my confusion tripped, too late looking down to see the misjudged tread, my mug jerked askew, cocoa splashed beside the stair rod. I heard my mother drop the mortice lock: she had not noticed. Nothing would have made me bend just then to wipe it. I felt vulnerable enough.

'And when is breakfast, Mrs Brown?' The low, the oh-so-English voice.

'Eight thirty, if that suits.'

'If that suits' showed my mother liked the man. Eight thirty was when I left for school. At least I could avoid him on weekdays. I went quickly up, crossed to my room and closed my door, and heard his shut, very shortly, after.

I saw Ninian only once at weekends and John Rose all the time. No matter how I tiptoed on the stairs or made a swift traverse of the landing, he had a way of coming out, of asking for a shilling for the gas, or a match or a 'wee' drop of milk. He did not smile; there was something odd about his mouth, the upper lip was a little swollen on the right which gave him an injured look. He never referred to the day he found me in my mother's room but he made me feel uncomfortable.

The 'wee' drop of milk was tongue in cheek: I said it once and he used it ever after, seriously. Through his open door I glimpsed the green rug, another sign of mother's favour; it was an extra she sometimes granted, to take the chill off the linoleum. Beyond was his table stacked with thick books whose pages shone under the white ellipse of the reading lamp. He was studying hard for some sort of exam to be a specialist. Mother said he went off in the mornings looking very smart – the three-piece suit, I knew – for ward rounds with 'the big' consultants at the Infirmary. He had a car, a pale blue Triumph Herald. Although this relative of his, Mrs Jamieson, lived along the crescent, he did not seem to visit. He had his meals in the Men's Union over at the University. I heard the door just as I was about to settle to my homework in the dining room. Usually he came back early and worked late into the night. Sometimes I heard him go out again suddenly, about nine thirty, as if he had had enough. To the pub, I supposed. Mother made up the bed in his room each day and dusted what she could. She made no fuss about the cigarettes. She was a smoker herself. She counted his stubs and sympathised, and put it down to the strain of having to cram in so many medical facts.

A Venus pencil and a penny chew in a paper poke lay between my friend and me on the window ledge of the art-room corridor. I had just told her all about the letter, what I had said and where I had sent it.

'Thanks, Dorcas.' Her birthday present was late, of course, but she always did remember in the end. The pedigree pencil was a sophisticated choice. The toffee was the currency of First Year girls and all the dearer for that, being where our friendship started. It was not usual to give birthday presents. 'And sorry. Something just came over me that day. If it wasn't for you, Dorc, I wouldn't know about my father – I wouldn't know a thing!'

'You're telling me, you wouldn't.' Her response was a trifle too emphatic. Once more her eyes had that pure aqua glint, that slow insinuating sparkling cheekiness. I blushed. After all, it was she who, when we were twelve that first weekend in Dewar, saw to it that I knew about sex. The wee bulls she lured towards the gate for me that evening taught me the straight mechanics. Even now, their playfulness could take me by surprise at any time and make my face go red and my body suspend whatever it was doing in disbelief – as awesome as if I had been impaled myself.

That same evening, however, she had led me up another garden path, a farm track to be exact, and she had taken me through an advanced course, revealing, with the help of literature, the more bizarre titillations involved in this coupling business.

It seemed we had free run of the valley. Nowhere, nothing was taboo. She raised her hand to a woman at a cottage window then ducked beneath a hedge. A pheasant shot up with a squawk. I watched her crawl on her belly along behind a row of cabbages and crawl back with two feathery topped carrots in her hand. 'Food!' she said, rubbing them clean on her trousers. 'No need to go home. Could stay out all night.' I put my rations in my pocket and wondered.

The air was mild. We heard the river, sometimes near, sometimes farther from the road, hidden from us by tall hedgerows of hazel, ivy, hawthorn, beech. We swung our arms, leaped for branches, caught red rowans, brambled, hooted, listened to the quiet. The sun was already behind the Innerleithen hills. But they were high. We had hours yet. Dorcas cavorted like a dog, bounding from tree to dyke, darting ahead in and out of field paths.

'Bit clonkie, aren't they?' she said, suddenly turning round to me.

'What-ie?'

'You know. Clonkie. Wellies.'

'Noisy, you mean.'

'Not good for spying. But we have to have them for the farm, you see.' Dorcas tugged my sleeve. 'Come on. It's Jilly-Willy's.'

'Whose?'

'Jilly-n-Willy's. Jilly and Will-I-A-M's. Their farm. Their house. I often visit.' Jilly-Willy's was a mess. The dykes were mossy heaps, the gate stood half off, half open. Machinery lay about the muddy yard and malingered among the nettles. Under the universal coating of caked dirt I made out the shape of a horsebox and a tractor. But the bright teeth of the harrow and a plough gleaming like a row of scimitars just inside a dark barn did suggest real work was done here.

Dorcas encouraged me with a grin. We wove round the outbuildings and up the hill to an old, flat-fronted, stone farmhouse. Crusts of clay, wellingtons and a tin bowl were by the door.

Dorcas knocked. A dog barked inside. She beat an imperative tattoo. It barked again.

'Hello, Woossy. Hello. Hello, boy.'

The barking stopped.

She turned the handle, put her shoulder to the door and went in. A black Labrador wound round her, wagging. She bent to fondle him. 'Oh, Woossy, Woossy, Woosh.' She let him lick her face. I still stood outside. 'Come on. They don't mind.' She eased out of her boots.

'But you can't just walk into a person's house, can you?'

'You can in the country. Leave your wellies.'

The door opened on to a low room. At one end was a fireplace with a mound of ash and half-burned logs. Newspapers and magazines were strewn over a white rug and black leather sofa. At the other end was a kitchen corner with fitted cupboards in dark wood. A candle in a bottle climbing with wax drippings stood on the table beside some dirty plates and bowls.

'And who's been eating *my* porridge?' sing-songed Dorcas, skipping round, peeping over. She picked up a glass and sniffed, 'Ah! Wine!' She ran her finger round a plate and licked it. 'Mmm. Spaghetti was it, last night, eh, Wooss?' She flicked his black ear.

'Won't they come back soon?'

She shrugged.

'What time is it?'

'Och, Beatie!' she said. 'For goodness' sake! I told you it doesn't matter. Come on!' She beckoned now from the staircase opposite. The dog was already on the landing, tongue lolling, grinning, waiting for me too.

Upstairs, through an open door, I saw a big bed with a cumulus of navy-blue and white patterned duvet which was very modern in those days; my mother and I still slept flattened under layers of woollen blankets and taffeta-covered quilts.

'Jilly's Swedish or something.' I don't know if this was to explain the bedding or the tossed bed. Dorcas was standing there looking at it, her eyes half closed, a strand of hair across her face. 'What d'you reckon?'

'What d'you mean?'

'Did they, you know, *do* it?' One hand whisked the hair back to clear her rounded chin, bright lips, even teeth: her smile of relish.

'What?' I felt all stiff, confronted.

'Whatever you call it.'

Whatever did I call it? If it was what I thought it was it was something I skipped over, pushed away, skirted round, quickly.

'I . . . um . . .'

'Well, what *do* you call it?'

There was no escaping Dorcas.

'Whatever you . . . wha . . . Intercourse.'

There was her dimple. 'Have sex, silly. Make love.'

'Okay. Okay.'

'Last night . . . What d'you think?'

'That's . . .' I checked myself. Well, here was my chance. I wanted to know more about all this stuff. 'They're married, aren't they?' I was blushing now. 'You're supposed to do it then.' I eyed the bed.

Dorcas watched me oddly. Suddenly she said, 'Och, well . . . Beatie, your mum . . . maybe she never . . . you know. You won't *know* – not having a dad, I suppose.'

I knew for sure my mother slept alone.

'Mine do it,' Dorcas said.

'When?' It was my turn.

'Oh, I read in a magazine it was once a week.'

'Like going to church?'

Dorcas giggled. 'No, stupid. Not like that. It's supposed to be great fun.'

'Fun?' I thought of the bullock's extending fifth column. 'How?'

'Well . . .' Her grin became a grimace. She did not know what to say – rather, she did not know how to say it. But Dorcas was never at a loss for long. 'Come on. Come here.' Woossy wagged and came too.

She took us to the bathroom. One step and she was leaning over the lavatory pulling a magazine from a shaggy pile. 'Look! See!'

She handed it to me. It was open at the picture of a lady, two pages of her, bare skuddy. She was kneeling neatly on tight knees and back towards tightened toes. Her stomach caved inwards. She was pushing very hard to show her big breasts off and held them out like Christmas puddings. What I knew of breasts – for I had little to go on myself – came from the classical paintings I had seen once with school at the art gallery and from advertisements for the fashionable uplift brassieres with circular stitching and conical central points. Their neat proportions bore no relation to this swollen poundage.

'There's lots,' said Dorcas.

I turned the page. The pictures were all of rosy flesh, models posing with come-hither looks, lashes like furry caterpillars, beehive hairdos, nipples jumping out like eyes. My face felt hot. Part of me wanted to slam the pages down and run, but I found myself rooted to the spot. I slipped to the floor, my back against the fitted bath, so that I could stare and stare and leaf through steadily page after page.

A wet tongue took a swipe at my cheek.

'Woossy! 'Way!'

The dog toed over to Dorcas. He nuzzled her ear.

'Noochy-woochy.' She put her arm round him and rubbed his furry neck without lifting her eyes from the magazine.

Woossy's tail thumped against the lavatory seat.

'God!'

'Show!'

She held the picture up.

I nodded, speechless.

'What tits!' she said. I could not even manage 'breast' out loud.

'What d'you think it feels like – to have . . .?' My mother always said 'bust', usually in a home-dressmaking context. Dorcas gave a sort of secret smile.

We sat in silence considering the bottoms, lengths of thigh, black strings and things pulled up while the dog slumped between us and lay his muzzle along the linoleum. His brown eyes watched for any sign of action but we disappointed him. Stiletto heels made a stance like exclamation marks. Suddenly I smashed my page shut.

'Hey, don't tear them!' Only Dorcas's lips moved.

Woossy got up, watching me and wagging.

'Take another,' Dorcas said.

Curiosity overcame apprehension. I reached across and fell absorbed again.

At last my friend said, 'It's better without boys – you know, like George who was at the village school with me.'

'You mean, a boyfriend?'

'He *has* kissed me.' Her eyes shone. 'But. You know . . . Sometimes I bring boys. We just sit here like this.' I looked at the lavatory brush, the squint pedestal mat, the bath towel fallen in its heap below the rail. The floor area was about two square yards. 'It's embarrassing with them though. 'S better just girls.'

We settled again, companionably, with the Sabrinas and Samanthas, Cindys and Claudines.

After a rapt interval Dorcas put her copy on the pile. 'Better not leave evidence.'

I relinquished mine.

She pulled herself up by Woossy's collar. 'It's hard to stop when you get stuck in like this but I want to show you something else now.'

And she did. She introduced me to slaughter.

She was always one step ahead of me, however far I thought I had come. 'What did you get for your birthday then?' she grinned.

'I got—' Should I risk it?

'Come on.'

'I got, besides other things, a boyfriend.'

'Beatie!'

'A nice one.'

'What's his name?'

My chin went up. I was reluctant.

'His school then?'

'The Academy.'

'Oo. Posh.'

'And he's an actor.' I thought she would like that.

'An actor!'

'And he's asked me to a ball.'

'A ball! Do actors go to balls?' She wrinkled up her nose. 'If my mother could hear this!'

'Why?'

'Because Hamish and I don't do anything . . . proper.' She had the grace to cover her smirk.

I laid my Venus in my pencil case and zipped it up. 'Who's Hamish?'

'*My* boy – no *man*-friend. Mother doesn't like it.'

'Why not?' I unwrapped my toffee like a consolation prize.

'Well, *you* know.' So we were back to that again. 'He's much too old for one thing, *she* says. And he's poor. Farm workers get low wages. It's dreadful.'

'Is he like George then?'

'George?'

'Yes, you know. George.' I had met George too that first weekend. I imagined him now, grown bigger, still in wellies, driving cows home with a stick.

'George! God, no!' She leaned her elbows on the sill and smoothed the paper bag which had held my birthday present. When it was quite flat she said, 'Hamish comes from the Outer Hebrides. He's like a man from another planet. He's not an ordinary farm worker.'

'I thought you said he was.'

'No: he's a shepherd.' Her fingers stroked the whiteness. 'But he was a landowner in his own place. A kind of king, he always says. A crofter. He's proud. Proud and fierce.' Her fingernails shone white. She gave a little growl of excitement, 'Ggrmph!'

She made him sound like the romantic hero of a Scottish novel. I imagined him on a heather moor in a thunderstorm sheltering a half-dressed Dorcas by a grey rock – as in the song 'Come Under my Plaidie' – with Mrs Drummond coming up behind leading a squad of redcoats with blunderbusses, and bayonets fixed.

'You must meet him. And Dad says – I say – please come out to Dewar. Do. Please. This weekend? Things have changed a bit. Mum's in with the man at the Big House. You can meet Hamish.'

'I might. I'm going off church. What does your dad say about Hamish?'

She folded the paper bag into a neat strip, held one end, splayed the rest and fanned herself.

'Says I'll grow out of it. Got me on the Pill.'

The contraceptive pill hadn't long been available and I couldn't imagine any of the other girls taking it. Only her eyes showed above the demure mockery of the fan. I felt her smile at my amazement. So she *had* done it. The split between us gaped again.

'We've a doctor in the house,' I blurted out.

'I've seen one, silly.'

'A lodger, I mean.'

'Oh. Good-looking?' Her lashes flew up. It seemed she always 'cawed' the feet from under me, even when it was my turn 'in' at skipping.

'I suppose,' I said.

'You'd better watch it. You know what medics are like.'

'You're telling me!' I said with a warmth that surprised myself.

Dorcas liked that. She grinned. I felt, briefly, upsides with her. The bell rang then for lessons.

'Hey,' she said, 'you never told me *his* name.'

I was thankful for that. I had kept Ninian tucked away, dark, like a kernel safe inside a nut.

The satin had a sweet smell. But cold. It cut with the noise of skates across ice and moved with the swish of water. The dining-room table was draped in the pink of it, pink shadowing a blue bloom, the colour of the small cyclamen I had noticed in some gardens which uncurled themselves just as everything around them, leaf and fern, returned to brown.

'I'm glad we found the pink,' I said. I watched my mother's bent back as she, intent upon the task of cutting out the dress, snipped and snipped, stopped, turned the cloth and snipped again.

'That's it then,' she said. 'It's too late now to change your mind anyway.'

'But we decided. Short, like Audrey Hepburn's in *Vogue*.'

'It was always long in my day, of course.'

'But this is the sixties. It's not with it to wear long – we agreed.' Softly I said, 'And it was cheaper.'

'It'll be different. The latest style.'

'Not too different?'

'No, no. Don't be too conventional, Beatie. Nothing ventured nothing ever won.'

This was new. Perhaps this encouragement to be daring was a spark of her old self. I thought the red dress was a wonder. I had put its exciting colour and sensuous fit down to Cousin Jean's inheritance from Spain. But my mother was the one who had made it – that showed skill and flair – and she had worn it to dances afterwards. My father first saw her in that dress. I tried to picture the moment.

'You made the red dress too. When your hair was dark you must have looked so wonderful in that.' Then, because she had come down early, refreshed from her nap, to do this for me (I had ironed the tissue pattern pieces, checked the selvage and the grain, matched the layout in readiness) and because there was promise in this sweet pink cloth, I ventured, speaking softly, 'Was it love at first sight?'

'That was what he said.'

'What did he say when you met?'

'We talked about food. I was learning to be a cook at Atholl Crescent. I complained about the rationing and I remember him telling me the names and describing all the shapes of the different types of pasta. And all the different sauces. Macaroni and cheese was the only one I knew till then. He opened my eyes. He certainly did that.'

'What else did he say?'

'That I looked haughty. I was a challenge. The cheek of it!'

'Were you?'

'I was nervous. It was one of my first dances. I'd not long left school. When I learned dancing, I'd always taken the man's part.'

'So do I. It's because we're tall.'

'But you're a good dancer, aren't you?'

'How did you do, then, Mummy, when he asked you?'

'I did fine. He led me wonderfully, you see. You can do anything then. He swept me off my feet.' She did not sigh though. 'Gather up the scraps, Beatie. Roll them up for the rag bag. We've just the facings to cut now.'

We were almost happy there together.

'Look, Mum. These dressmaking pins are called Dorcas,' I said.

'They've always come in a pale blue tin like that.'

'Some things you're so used to, you never really look at.

What are those on it? Dandelion seed puffs. See! I'd never noticed that. It makes me think of shepherdesses.'

'Wasn't Dorcas a seamstress?'

'This tin makes me think of shepherdesses though . . . which is funny.'

'Why?' Mother straightened up.

'Oh well, Dorcas loves . . . little woolly lambs. She told me she helped that couple, Jilly and Willy, at lambing time. They lamb late up that valley. First week in April – how did I remember that?' This came out in a rush. I took a breath. 'And, it's her shade of pale blue, that tin.'

'You enjoyed Dewar, didn't you?'

'She's asked me out again.'

'Oh?'

'But with all this,' I meant dance dress and boyfriend, 'I can't go at the moment, can I?'

'No.'

'But – sometime?'

My mother smiled. It was an ambiguous expression. But surprising progress had been made.

CHAPTER SIX

Dorcas was lying on the sheepskins. She was bare skuddy and was being rolled over and over upon by her Highlander who had eyes as fierce as sapphires, and black hairs, like fur on his limbs, but matted on his breast and on his groin.

This scene was in my head. I did not know how it arrived there. I could not get rid of it. Perhaps it was my first glass of champagne that was responsible. Or was it all this?

I was in the centre of the circle in a reel. The dancers all held hands and slip-stepped round me, round for eight and back for eight. They gave sudden eldrich shrieks. It was a demon ritual with me the human sacrifice. They were lords and ladies dressed in silk and jewels, cummerbunds and black bow ties. It was no haunted kirk, however, but the Georgian pomp of Edinburgh's Assembly Rooms with the big band up on the stage behind the potted plants. More figures moved beyond the cream pillars or sat around on small gilt chairs beside the wall. A sleight of thought and I had them all involved. But the pairs of eyes that watching, watching, circled me were worst for, though the bodies turned one way then the other, the eyes never left my face, my chest, knees, bare back, toes, even. It was an act of will just staying there, making my neat setting step keep me on the spot as I had learned it should. I looked at Ninian but he failed to see my panic. I summoned Dorcas and found her, disconcertingly lascivious, upon the sheepskins.

'*What* – a pretty shade!' Mrs Orr had said in the cloakroom when we arrived. She tried not to notice the shortness of my hem and my long legs underneath. I smoothed my gloves and looked her in the eye. She wore pearls and a smile like the Duchess of Windsor.

'And pink shoes too,' said Ninian, looking at my knees.

When I first arrived that evening, I had felt conspicuous enough in my school navy nap. Mother had offered Granny's squirrel: maybe she knew. The other women all wore furs, even furs that dated back some generations too. I thought to recover my poise when I revealed my lovely pink. And I did stand out then as strikingly as the model in the *Vogue* fashion plate – but what note struck in such a short backless evening dress, such a spare flare, when the other women were all belled to the floor in pastel satin?

I had been warned. Mrs Orr had briefed me when she asked me to their house for tea. It had been too late to change my dress.

'And, my dear,' she had said, on the doorstep as I left, 'we wear gloves.' She mimed the length hand over wrist.

'Do you?' Her regal imperative made me cross.

But I did wear them. I did because I had always wanted to. Audrey Hepburn wore them too. I withdrew them now from the clutch of a big male who cast me off after the setting and turning, and let me go weaving a neat chain with the rest, trim hips, trim feet, trim shoulders which came brushing back to back at last with Ninian. His face had a secretive excited look. Champagne was working. With his dark hair and height, he was handsome in his dinner jacket.

'I'm surprised your mother didn't put you in Highland dress,' I said.

'The moths got it. And I'm happier in Moss Bros.'

'She's furious I'm not wearing long,' I hissed.

'You're lovely.'

'She doesn't like me. She doesn't approve.'

'You're lovely.'

'I like your dad, though. He's so old-fashioned. Makes me feel a lady. He's nice to dance with.'

'Better than me?'

'He's had more practice, I suppose.'

Ninian looked rueful.

'Dorcas has never been to a ball, you know.'

'Your friend, you mean? Well, nor had I till this.'

'Or me. It's just . . . she usually does everything first. But she hasn't done anything like this.'

'Never danced?'

'Not at a proper ball.'

'Proper! Those reels are barbaric.'

'This isn't.' I meant this suit, his black bow tie, his too big double cuffs.

'Are you enjoying yourself?'

I smiled. I liked the champagne. I liked Ninian to be close to me. But I had not enjoyed the Dashing White Sergeant though I had him on one side of me and his father on the other. Each time we progressed under the arch of arms to meet a new trio I met three more sets of cold eyes. I had it in my head that most folk here were lawyers, sons and wives and affianced of lawyers, and that I was under scrutiny. They were all thinking what an awful mistake the girl in pink made wearing a short dress and a backless one at that: I might as well have come in navy gym pants.

We linked up with the most stunning couple in the room. She was a slender woman with hair like honey naturally waved, eyes soft as violets and she had a tan – goodness knows how at that time of year. Her breasts, like tawny apples, crested the bodice of her scarlet dress. Yes, it was a scarlet dress, not as dark, not so dated as my mother's but flowing more gracefully than most of the others in the room. Her partner was also tall and fair. There were yards of good wool in the heavy swing of his kilt. His jaw was as square as a loaf. I could not help thinking of the children they would make between them, progenitors of a super race. Then I overheard her say 'Yah' and 'Absolutely' and something about 'Dahn to the kuntry' and had that sinking feeling Scots feel at the invasion of the English.

'Ninian, steer into the middle.' It was a waltz. We were managing quite well. But if we stuck to the perimeter we would come to Ninian's parents sitting out just a pillar away. I saw the tall blond couple had stopped to speak with them. 'Come on,' I begged.

'Don't think I can. Wait. Two, three. One, two, three. Don't push, Beatie. I'm the man.'

'Well . . . don't if it's too tricky. Don't – ouch!'

'See.'

'Nian.' The intercepting glove of Mrs Orr. 'Nian, dear, come and meet Rolf and Michaela.'

Michaela was saying, 'Jus' could not beck the bloody trayla. Now a double haws box is that little bit moah . . . H'llah.' Her eyes moved to me before her mouth stopped and then they dropped to the hem of my dress as they had done once already in the dance.

'Michaela . . . Beatie. Beatie . . . Rolf.'

'May I have the pleasure?' The big feet, skean-dhu, strong hips, wide shoulders, teeth like a Hollywood star's.

'Yes.' My gloved hand went into his.

The Gay Gordons. Good. A romp. Fun, always. No chat possible. But it was. He was as boisterous in his questions as his dance.

'What do you do, Beatie?'

'Finishing school.'

'Which?'

'No. I mean I'll probably leave school this year.'

'Which then?'

I shook my head. In Edinburgh classification of the individual is done by school. I had hoped in adult life it might not count so much.

'Let me guess. Something intelligent – St. G.'s?'

'McGillivray's.'

He made a mental and sociological adjustment. 'One of the one's at Church Hill?'

'You mean Langmuir? No. That's a corporation school too. I'd have gone to that if I hadn't got a scholarship to McGillivray's.'

Schoolgirl information was prattle suddenly. I turned things round. 'My name's not Beatie . . . it's Beatrice – Beatrice Maria Bornati.' It was a wild bid. I made it with my best Italian accent. It was self-defence. But my father was on his way to me. Even if this lordly Rolf had no interest in art, he might recognise the name this summer. It would be talked about at the Festival. I did not know that his type rarely go to galleries, that they quit the 'tan' for the 'kuntry' during August, certainly after the Glorious Twelfth when the grouse shooting has begun.

'You look Italian,' he said.

'I'm half-Italian.'

'Doesn't that make life complicated?'

Birling now round and round under him, the brilliant ball-and-socket human engineering of our joint hands just touching, I looked up into the face that was so handsome it was ugly, and I shook my head.

Time flew at a ball, I discovered.

There was another dance hall which played jazz and rock 'n' roll and Beatles songs. Under a spangled turning light and away from Mr and Mrs Orr, we enjoyed ourselves. As if to prove himself, Ninian went at this with a will. His big cuffs grew longer till they sat on his thumbs like a clown's.

'You dreadful children,' called Mrs Orr when we joined them in time for supper. 'Where were you? We needed you to make up our set for the Duke of Perth.'

'We'll dance the next one with you.'

'Oh, Nian!' Her call was a caterwaul. 'It's too late. There's only ever one. Look at you. Where's your handkerchief?'

Ninian's forehead shone with sweat. He mopped it hastily.

We went in to supper. It was cold turkey and lettuce and potato salad, then jelly with fruit set in it. We had wine. At the end the parents left us to ourselves. A waiter offered us liqueurs. Ninian said Drambuie.

One sip set me on fire.

'Tell me about your friend then.'

'My friend Dorcas?'

'What does she do?'

'She goes where angels fear to tread.' It was the alcohol talking. It was where Drambuie might take me too. Ninian was lighting a cigar. He leaned back to watch me under near-closed eyelids like a caliph surveying his hareem, puffing smoke in a smouldery way as if he had something exciting in store. He had a little cough occasionally. In my head I kept Dorcas and her Highlander nesting in the sheepskins. I had caught Rolf's eyes wander over to me during supper and had pretended not to see.

'Where's that?'

'Into the dark. Into danger. Into the arms of men.' My eyes went round: I surprised myself.

Ninian raised his glass.

'What kind of men?'

'One man.'

'What kind of one man?'

'What old school tie, you mean?'

'No . . .' He looked surprised. 'Not that. Why?' The room was noisy.

'People here set all their store by that.' This din, these guffaws.

'Do they?'

' "Do they"?!'

'I don't.'

'You're too close in to see it. You have to be on the outside to see it, like me.'

'You're *here*. You're not on the outside.'

'No?'

A large hand was on my shoulder. It was big Rolf. 'Did you enjoy your supper, Beatrice?' He said it with emphasis the Italian way.

I blushed. I waited till he had gone.

' "Bay-ah-tree-chay"?' Ninian was motionless and dark.

'It's my name. I told him.'

'But it isn't your name.'

'It is. Didn't I tell you?'

'No.' Ninian was emphatic. And angry.

'It is. "Beatrice" is my name.'

Ninian gaped.

'Beatrice Maria Bornati. I wonder why I never told you that.'

His loose bottom lip twisted. 'You didn't tell me because you've just this minute made it up. That's why.' His sudden laugh mocked me.

'Beatrice Maria Bornati,' I repeated. I was shaking my head at him. 'Didn't you know?'

He was still laughing at me.

I got up from the table. 'I need to powder my nose.' I pushed my way past the elbows sticking out along the backs of chairs. He had spoiled things. Did the drink do that? . . . Or was it me? I had not wanted to spoil things. I ducked from the watchful eyes of the waitresses.

I could not find him when I came out. The tables in the dining room were being set again with clean cloths.

Back in the ballroom the lights were less bright. Ninian was embarking on a waltz with his mother. He wore a strained expression, brows just meeting, corners of his mouth stretched out. He was failing to be amiable. She made him adopt a hold with one arm extended and the other elbow tilted high like Ginger Rogers did with Fred Astaire. Her hand tentacled across his back but from the front she was serene with her curved smile and bright eyes, eyes only for her only son.

'Beatrice,' this Italian murmur, deep, with mockery in it, from behind, 'may I?' The magnificent Rolf was asking for a dance.

He swept me off around the floor, his big hand on the small of my bare back pressing me against him so that I could feel

64

the buttons of his jacket. He led so strongly it was impossible to miss the beat. I fairly flew with him. I could not catch my breath. He made no attempt at conversation this time, seeming to be totally taken up with dancing. But at the turns he leaned and breathed 'Beatrice', diving deep into the third syllable in a way that made my ear tingle. When he whisked me round he took a firmer grip; his hand grasping my skin so tightly that it nipped.

The whirling stopped. Ninian was there. Like the next runner in a relay race, on his toes, leaning forward, starey-eyed, he covered every possibility of a slip in the changeover. When it was safely done he kept a proprietorial hold. But he was awkward with me now.

'What's this about another name?' His hand was clammy on my skin.

'Didn't I ever mention it?'

'Never.'

'I don't know why . . .' I lied.

'Why did you tell *him*?'

I shrugged. His mouth pursed up. His hand dropped away to my satin waist. I was disappointed. 'Do you want to know?' I whispered.

He nodded grimly.

'My father's Italian. My mother's conventional and Scottish. She wanted Brown.'

'But I want to know why you told *him*!'

He must have felt my body go stiff in his arms. He searched my face. He did not ask the right questions.

The night was coming to an end. Lights dimmed. Across the darkening heads, through the mass of men in black and the swaying women, the hue of their satins subdued to a moonlit mode, I saw Rolf and Michaela in a clinch. That man, I thought, eyeing his back, the foursquare shoulders in the black dress jacket, was like an ox. What must it feel like to be held like that? Crushed. But this stiff hold of Ninian's left too much room for me to move and think. Why did I not lay my head against the breast of his bibbed shirt like some of these other women were doing, and close my eyes and lose myself, feeling only, and wanting to feel, him close?

I did try to lean a little. He looked nervous. The band sent the notes of 'Moon River' wailing over our heads. A romantic mood engulfed the room. Dancers moved as one like the waves at night. Satins glimmered. Jewels came out like twinkling stars. I brought Dorcas into things. I laid her there on the sheepskins. She lured her lover with her come-on smile. Her pale bare arms came up and twined about his neck.

I shut my eyes and felt the movement of the dance. We were not going anywhere. We were rocking to and fro like all the other males and females round us. Above the forest of legs and deep below the twining arms, I felt that middle darkness stir.

Dorcas and her shepherd met there. In the whiteness of sheepskins, her Highlander's skin was like beechnuts. The black hair curled on his chest and in his groin. From below there that thing, the long pink searching leg, was growing between them and finding its way.

But I could not picture it exactly. I had never seen a real live naked man. Girls at school had been heard to recount sightings of their fathers – fleeting, naturally, the Scots being private in their habits. And some had brothers. I had neither. Only small boys presented to the pavement's edge by their mothers had ever flashed at me, their penises pale, limp, dribbly little members, inspiring pity, poor wee things, unpredictable and, judging by the mother's careful, if speedy, tucking in and zipping up, vulnerable to hurt.

'Beatie?'

'Sorry.'

'What are you thinking about?'

I had used Ninian in my dreams – his head, shoulders, ears, his clumsy fingers. I could picture his long legs but they dissolved to vagueness at the groin.

'Bodies.'

'Grisly.'

'Not the Burke and Hare kind.'

'What kind – astral, car or live?' His face was in blue shadow. 'Do you like being all dressed up, Ninian?'

'I'll see I get a better fit next time.' He shook a cuff. 'Big run on DJs this week at Moss Bros. Next time I'll book one ahead. Perhaps my mother will buy me my own shirt for a start. My tie's my own.'

'Hello, tie.'

'It's real. Difficult to do. You can tell, can't you? Is he squint?'

'Mm-huh.' We swayed like weed under an inky sea.

'Shows I'm a gentleman,' he whispered.

'You'll need to own the whole paraphernalia if you're to be a respected Edinburgh lawyer and a member of the club.'

'Indeed,' he said. He was not teasing. Under his black forelock his expression was guarded.

During 'Auld Lang Syne' we were near his parents once again and that was how the evening ended. We had a cup of Bovril, my navy nap rubbing shoulders with the furs while Mr Orr went out to fetch the Humber. Ninian held my hand in the back seat. It was a statement. I longed for something more explorative. Perhaps his parents were to blame. The car stopped in the crescent. I was glad that night there was no neon sign outside. Ninian came with me up the path and waited while I opened up. Then he gave me a quick peck on the cheek, said, 'Lovely. Thanks. Exhausted. What a night!' and went back to his parents who had kept the engine running. He could have slipped behind the storm door for just a moment. He could have looked at me properly. Stroked my cheek. Slipped a hand round under my coat. No one would have seen him.

I slid the bolt.

My toes hurt. Off with my shoes. Relief of my feet flat on the cold tiles. Off with my coat. Carrying these I tiptoed up the stairs.

A line of light under his door told me John Rose burned the midnight oil. I was slipping past. I heard a click.

'Beatie!' A whisper, half-voiced, as if silent hours had made him hoarse. He was in his dressing gown and slippers, hair mussed up as if he had been wrestling with problems.

'Hello.'

'Good dance?'

'Quite.'

' "Quite"?' His frown was rueful. Behind him, the lamplight fell on the white pages of the books, the corner of the bed, the green rug. 'Let me see it then.'

'What?'

'Your dress. Let me see you in your dress.'

'Oh.' I put out my arms, one hung with my coat, the other holding the pair of shoes.

'Give . . .' He leaned over and put his hand on my shoulder, firmly. He withdrew my coat from me. 'Now.' The same touch urged me, pushed. 'Turn.'

I did. And back. Was it because he did not smile? A clichéd

compliment and I could have gone easily. But it was not his way. He stood staring with those blue pinpoint eyes, and the small injured look on his face. I made for my room.

'Don't you want this?'

He was holding out my coat.

I came back, snatched it, and he caught my wrist.

'Don't you want something . . . a nightcap, a drink?' With a slow smile, 'Cocoa?'

I pulled away.

'I liked you in the red dress better.'

I got to bed. Instead of stretching out in grateful relief, I felt bound up as tightly as the rubber wound inside a golf ball. Why did John Rose do this to me? I tugged the covers and clenched them to my chin. And I was angry with Ninian.

CHAPTER SEVEN

The boy was standing in the middle of the road outside the farm. He was about twelve, like us, with ruddy cheeks, curly brown hair and a crumpled face.

'George, meet my friend Beatie.'

His glance flicked up.

'George, Jilly-n-Willy're out. Come and go hunting with us.'

He considered the proposition with hands deep in his pockets and eyes on his wellingtons. 'Could,' he said.

'Won't it be dark soon, Dorc?'

'So?'

So I trailed behind them through the yard and into the black maw of a tall barn. There was a warm sour smell. 'Ssh!' We heard animal breath and the sound of straw. A bovine nose put itself on the top rung of a stall. 'Must be sick or something.'

We went past. Away in to the back a corrugated-iron tower stood the height of two floors. It seemed to inspire awe in Dorcas. She exclaimed, 'The grain bin!' and gawped as if we had arrived at Sleeping Beauty's castle. We advanced on tiptoe. George's hands were still in his pockets but Dorcas's were outstretched as if she balanced on a tight rope. 'Ssh!' she said again.

She stopped and pointed George to a flight of stairs. He picked up a piece of wood from a pile near some sacks then he climbed to the top. I watched Dorcas choose a stick for me. It was like a paddle. She motioned me to wait. She was making her selection, testing for weight, for grip, like a golfer – or an axeman. She stood up. 'When they run, brain them.' I heard a scutter from deep under the bin to the back. 'George!' Her teeth flashed.

George swung the wood, his hands and face pale smudges above me in the brown dark. Crash! His paddle rang against the iron drum. The din reverberated bang-bang-bang.

'They're coming.'

Our sticks went up.

The camouflage of rats at dusk is perfect. It's the running that betrays them. One flowed out, a shadow drawn on pulled strings towards our feet. 'Gotcha!' No. The tail wired. Yes. 'Yippee!' The very first. I was amazed.

'Beatie!'

More came. My side. Her side. I reared my stick, shut my eyes and struck.

'Yah!' cried Dorcas. 'Yah! Yah!'

The drumming filled our heads and filled the barn. Then the rats faltered. I saw one stop and cross from Dorcas's side to me. It hunched over the toe of my boot. I jumped and struck. 'Ayee!'

'Two!' shrieked Dorcas.

We paused for breath. Dorcas wore a grin. I knew the difference now: the crack and jolt if you missed, the thud and crunch if your blow struck home. I was panting like a dog after a run. The waiting was ages. Then George began again. The din swelled to an apocalyptic thunder roll. Our eyes were circled white. With halts and runs, zigs and zags, the rats came out again, flowing along the shadows. The flails whammed down.

But soon we could count only two. Then one. And it escaped.

A thrumming lull hung round.

'George!' Dorcas railed at him. 'Beat the drum, George! George! Come on!'

But the boy, now, wanted blood.

'Hey, Thingummy,' he yelled. 'You down there, you, The Friend, go on and come up and let me have *my* turn. Beat the drum for *me*!'

'Och, George! Let her—'

'No. It's no' fair that!'

Lack of rats and lack of light did stop the sport at last.

Dorcas played her torch beam round. On the floor lay the brown heaps with worm tails and small stains that must be blood. 'Don't!' I cried when I saw Dorcas stretching out a hand. 'They're dirty! They could be plague rats!'

'Och, we'll "wash handies" after.'

'We hiftae operate,' said George. He produced a sharp stone and began to saw the tails off. The furry corpses rocked.

'Can I do mine?' Dorcas took longer than George. 'Now you, Beat.'

I had come far that night. I clamped the creature firmly under my boot and sawed away with my caveman's tool. The tail felt like string.

'They're our trophies. We make a bunch and hang it by the gate to frighten people. Got anything for tying, George?'

I went to the door of the barn. A sound from the stall surprised me: I was thankful it was a dumb beast. Outside, night was ink already. I took a step and felt the ruts underfoot. I remembered the nettle beds and rusting iron traps.

'Dorc!'

'Co-om-ing.'

The sound of wellingtons and Dorcas's voice.

'The torch is getting faint,' she said.

At last, five years on and in a different season I went out to Dewar once again. It was the beginning of January and I travelled on a green country bus. The adventures of my first weekend came flooding back.

That time they had collected me in town and driven me out. 'We have sheep and goats, dogs and horses, hedgehogs, pheasants, hares for your delight.' Mr Drummond spoke like that, poetically.

'And bulls and rats! *Dad*, she's *my* friend!' Dorcas had slid him a look and raised an eyebrow at me as we sat opposite each other on foam cushions and rugs in the back of a little green van.

Now the bus roared off up the hill and out of sight. I stood alone at the Dewar junction. Snow was falling, small but steady flakes which had already covered the landscape with a thin coat of white. There was the abandoned railway station and beside it the wooden hut, once apparently a tiny shop, now boarded up, the enamel Horlicks advertisement eaten by rust still hanging on below the sill. The road into the valley was deserted. Hills held their folding arms around. The twentieth century seemed unsuccessful here. Dewar had let it go, accepting the return to nature. The red telephone box under the embarkment was the only sign.

Suddenly its door swung open. Dorcas had come to meet me after all.

We flung our arms out, our mittened hands clasping at our

71

wool coats, scarves swinging. Her fair fringe needed a trim. Upturned to catch the falling flakes, her cheeks were pink and dimpling.

We had to walk the mile to their house. The cold land lay about us, fields ploughed back, the once-warm clods of the furrows turned to face the winter sky and the breaking by steel frosts. The road wound into the valley where the land was steeper and fit only for sheep. These animals stood watching from their narrow paths like spectators in the stands at a badly supported football match.

'Had a good Christmas?'

'Quiet.'

'Don't you have guests?'

'Not at Christmas.'

'What about that doctor?'

'He left suddenly. Failed his exam. He'll be back, he said. Sheep are funny.'

'That's not what Hamish thinks.' There were dog hairs on her navy jacket. His sheepdog hairs, I guessed. 'He gets very worked up about his sheep. They make him curse and swear. He does it in Gaelic. And in English – *that* makes me laugh: "Pukker this" and 'Pukker that"!' Her eyes shone. She tucked her chin into her collar.

The dykes climbed in grey lines dividing up the hills. The grass was drained of colour. Beech trees were bare as pebbles but, just here and there, and in the crisscross of the hedges, were copper hints, the dead leaf clinging, the new bud pointed as a pin.

We walked on side by side. The scene was changing all the time. I hoped Hamish was not going to spoil everything. We got to the 'big' farm gateposts that I remembered – the sharply right-angled bricks, the cattle grid, trim hedge, trim tarmac drive that made our schoolgirl trespass now seem marvellously bold.

'Is Big Daddy still in there?'

Dorcas did not think so.

I supposed he must be past his prime. Big Daddy was the prize bull which had been kept in a pen at the back of the 'big' farm. His eyelashes were curved and white. His head seemed small because his neck and body were massive. His tufty bit was thick and hung down with a strand of straw trailing from it: earthed. Dorcas had nudged me in that way of hers. She was peering round, under, pointing. 'Big as tennis balls, see.' And hanging, bagged in skin. This bull's weight was such that I could not imagine how he got himself off the ground sufficiently to climb on any cow.

Now the clipped hedge became the tumbled wall.

'And Jilly-Willy?'

'Jilly's gone. She went off with someone else.'

'Someone Swedish?'

'No-o. Someone in the next valley. People seldom leave Dewar, you know, once they've come. It's all a bit incestuous . . .' She tailed off with a half-smile that lingered on her dreamy face as if these were old ways and were tolerated.

I stopped to examine the twigs of the tree by the entrance. Then the ground. 'Look!' I pointed to a wormy gobbet, liverish and intestinal, not yet covered by the snow. 'The rats' tails?'

'Or something Willy's cat sicked up.'

There was little trace of her old relish. Scraping my hand along the parapet of the church bridge I made a snowball and flung it at her just to see. She squealed and stooped to make one too. But just the once. She was mellow now. No struggle. No spying. No kicking at the door. No need: she knew.

The snow was falling faster. The sound of our wild halloos, the clunk and run of our wellingtons on this same road years before that late September time came back to me. Big soft drifting flakes. It was as if someone had lifted up the glass bubble of a toy snow scene and turned it upside down. I was inside, upturned too.

'It's snowing faster. Look behind. See our tracks.'

They were being quickly covered up.

'Beatie, has your father written to you yet?'

'No.'

'Perhaps the letter got lost.'

'Perhaps that's what he wants me to do. Again.'

'Dad keeps asking if you've heard.' Our boots trod quietly. Then Dorcas said, 'Deirdre's here at the moment. Dad says it's important not to breathe a word to her about your real name and Bornati being your father.'

'Why?'

She shrugged. 'You have met Deirdre, haven't you?'

Dorcas called her mother by her first name. She was the only person I knew who did. Perhaps it was 'trez artistique', as she put it. I thought it was an affectation. I could not imagine calling mine by hers. Dorcas was not very nice about her mother.

She was remarkable to me for not being there. Rattling along in the green van that first time, I had asked innocently, 'And when's your mother coming?'

Dorcas had shaken her head.

But her father had volunteered, 'Perhaps Sunday. Friday and Saturday are her big nights. But I'm cook, Beatrice. Am I not, daughter o'mine?' Mr Drummond had taken a deep bend rather fast and swung me against a box of groceries. A spaghetti packet poked my ear. I smelled cardboard and onions. He'd accelerated up the hill, making the van roar. Dorcas, who had retained her balance, had shaken her head again but was smiling at her father.

And at tea he'd taken the mother's place. 'We never worry,' he said. 'There's not much mischief you can make here. Hunger'll drive you home eventually – usually before dark. I hope your mother won't object to this primitivism?'

'Oh, no.' It would have horrified her.

'Eat up, Beatie.' Dorcas was shovelling baked beans with a fork.

My eyes had been on her father's plate. Two eggs, punctured, were fried flat like pancakes. My mother would not let anything but a perfectly fried egg pass. He had done me a good one, though. 'Is Mrs Drummond in a play at the moment?' I had ventured, lancing the yolk.

'Yes, Mrs Drummond is at play – *in* a play, as you would have it.'

'What play?'

'Mrs Drummond is at present playing Lady Macbeth at Pitlochry.' He stabbed his sausage, cut it and impaled the section. 'One of her most renowned parts. Good at the "Out, damned spot!" and all that kind of thing, you know. A most theatrical woman. Pass the ketchup.'

'Her Macbeth's too short and has bandy legs.'

'Is that so, Dorcas? Your mother has trouble with her leading men.' Guthrie thumped the bottle hard and sent a gory spurt of sauce across his pale plate.

But she never had made it out to Dewar that weekend.

Deirdre Drummond, the quite-well-known actress, wife of Guthrie, had been experienced by me just the once when she came to judge our House Plays Competition two years before in the Upper Hall at school.

Her hat, black with a wide brim, and her mouth, also wide, were what I remembered. A vermilion gloss emphasised her lips, which slid out to the edges, thinly turning down or up in quick doubt or approval. Her smile was a revelation of strong teeth and fine crinkles. When she spoke, her voice rang clear to the wall bars at the back. Her enunciation was ruthless. She showed no mercy for the little syllables at the ends of words ordinary people are happy to let go. Her small body was draped in scarlet wool on that occasion.

A mile into the valley, over the bridge and under the church trees, we came to the long high wall that marked the boundary of the estate. Just before a bend in the road there was the imposing pillared entrance. 'Alas,' I remembered Mr Drummond's words that first time, 'we are but keepers of the gate.' The Drummonds' house was just inside, the original gatekeeper's lodge. It was a quaint stone building with narrow gothic windows and crow-stepped gables, miniaturely grand.

Mrs Drummond welcomed us at the door. She was clad in hyacinth this time but wool again, incorporating as before the flowing historic, histrionic dimension which allowed for sweeping gestures and the artistic pose. 'Darlings!' she gushed. 'What a night to arrive! We shall always remember the New Year that blew dear Beatie in!'

'Hello, Mrs Drummond.'

'Deirdre. Everyone calls me Deirdre.' She gave that phonetic cluster full value. 'Off with those wet garments! Come along now. Someone will soon be seeing to the fire.' The small sitting room was all greys and white, taking its cue from the scene outside, but brushed with a charcoal wash already, for the afternoon was moving into evening. A pile of ash lay in the hearth.

'Make yourself at home. No formalities are meet in my book. No formality is right for Dewar. Gatehouse or Big House. This is Out of Edinburgh. Life's too short for niceties. You'll find we say what we feel and do what we want here.' She bent to gather papers and a dog-eared book from the sofa. To Dorcas she said, 'Do fetch me my mackintosh, darling. And I'll need that big sou'wester I hung behind the kitchen door. That should do it.' She squinted out of the window, raised her hand to her forehead, and exclaimed, as if she was upstage, acting in a play. 'Good Lord, look at it! Well! I might not return tonight. But don't you young people worry about me. I shall be back when I'm back. Enjoy yourselves!'

Dorcas closed the door on her mother, who made her exit dressed like the man on the pilchards tin. We listened anxiously to her revving up the car. It juddered off.

'Where's she gone?'

'The Big House. Where she always goes. Sorry about "the niceties" – that's food, you know, and heat! Means she hasn't done anything about the fire or the dinner. She carries on all the time as if there was a whole supporting cast – imaginary cooks, maids, butlers – ready at her beck and call. Food and drink is "pretend" too, like props. She lives off hot air or inner fire . . .'

'Or some such vapid substance,' said Guthrie, who had appeared silently and now stood under the arched lintel leading from their bedroom.

'She's so different from my mum . . .' I shrugged and smiled. I could not even begin to explain.

'Has she gone?' He wore that very still expression you see on those who have just emerged from some totally absorbing occupation, or from sleep. He was just as I remembered, the same fine fair hair as Dorcas but it winged back from a high brow. His moustache and beard were not large but they masked his features and made you watch his eyes. His big sweater had the same Icelandic browns and greys as all those years before.

It was amazing, Dorcas said, that her parents stayed together. Apparently there had been separations. Always it was Deirdre who left, after some terrible row or other. But Guthrie kept to his routine of school teaching – it was just some corporation school, not one of the posh ones, because Guthrie had been a Marxist and was straightforward like that. At Dewar at the weekends Guthrie got on with his own painting. He knew what he wanted. He was comfortingly staid for an artist – perhaps he'd have been more successful if he had had some of Deirdre's drama in him. But she was enough of a hysteric for the lot of them. There were 'lovey-dovey' reunions, Dorcas said. Deirdre would always have to depart again, though, sometimes with a valid, but sometimes with a suspect theatrical excuse. But she always had come back. Like a desperately naughty child, Deirdre needed Guthrie and Guthrie knew it. He knew children. His style was not to smother them. Just to be there. He gave Dorcas a lot of rope. More than my mother ever dreamed of giving me. More than any mother would.

'Welcome, Beatie. It's cold in here. Let's light the fire. It's been too long, you know. I've wondered when we could spirit you back. I knew the time would come, of course.' There was a quietness about his speech and manner, and that look – warm with some knowledge, that I remembered so well – was there behind the blue. He kneeled on the hearth. We put our coats to dry on a clotheshorse beside a paraffin stove in the kitchen.

The light was becoming blue outside the window. White flakes still fell. We drew the curtains. Soon the smell of kindling filled the house. We brought a tray through and settled round the fire to enjoy our tea and buttered toast.

'I must go soon and tell Hamish,' said Dorcas.

'Tell him what?'

'Tell him I can't come tonight.'

'I thought you'd have told him you had a friend to stay,' said Guthrie.

'But I didn't know it was going to snow, did I? I'd planned to take Beatie there tonight to meet him.'

'Well, you can't.'

'I know. But I'd better tell him.'

Guthrie's face was impassive. This was old terrain, I sensed.

'So I'll be back soon, Beatie. Just . . . he gets angry, you see.'

'I get angry too,' said Guthrie in an even voice.

'I promised. I'll take the torch.'

I was uncomfortable only for a moment sitting there alone with Guthrie. The firelight and the cosy tea eased the transition. I had waited a long time for this.

'So your father hasn't written, Beatie?'

I shook my head. I made a move to get up: 'I'll just get the art magazine you—'

His hand stopped me. 'Keep that.'

'I know it.' I pointed to my brain. I knew it by heart.

We watched the fire. The heat pushed at us. We leaned back in our chairs.

'He may just be nervous.' Guthrie's hands were eloquent,

the fingertips touching, moving apart then meeting at the point again. 'He's coming to Edinburgh in August – at least we think he is.'

'Coming here?'

He nodded. 'It's usual for the artist to be present at the opening of his exhibition. If he can.'

'Coming here!'

Guthrie said, 'We *think* he's coming. It's delicate. Suddenly the gallery people – by the way, it's Deirdre's pal up at the Big House who hears all this – suddenly these people heard from Bornati's agent that he was threatening to call the visit off, which was strange because he had agreed. Artists generally enjoy appearing in public on such occasions. There are exceptions, of course. Their agents like them to – especially when there's a deal involved as there should be here.' He looked at me, his fingers steepled to his beard. 'But there's been some hitch.'

'It's because he got my letter!'

This was terrible. Seeing him was all I ever wanted. I was hearing now that my letter might have chased him off for good.

'No one else knows of this dimension.'

In the warmth of the firelit room amid the homely debris of the tea things I froze. 'Is this what I am – a "dimension"?'

Guthrie's eyes were a painful blue.

'A "dimension"!' I repeated.

He tried to find words.

I did not want to hear. I clamped my head between my palms.

Guthrie's hand was on my knee. I was shaking. I let it stay there. I felt its weight.

I burst out: 'My fault! Sorry! My fault his triumph should be taken from him! My fault the agents'll be disappointed! My fault I've been born at all! I wouldn't have done it if I'd known!'

Guthrie's hand tightened. We sat like that for a while, taut. He withdrew his hand then but leaned over, bringing his arm round me. Coming through the oily wool of the thick sweater I felt the comfort of an animal warmth. Words were not needed.

The fire made a purling sound.

'Would the exhibition go on anyway?' I asked.

'Yes. All that is in progress. Works are being flown or

shipped here from all over the place for it. These things are planned years ahead.'

'I could see his work – properly, I mean. Those wee pictures in the article don't—'

'You shall see him too, Beatie.' I tensed round at this. Gently Guthrie moved away. With his eyes still fixed on mine he settled back in his chair. 'There is a way.' A log collapsed with a faint sound. 'Have you been to the Big House?'

I shook my head. 'I remember the cars going up the drive to it. I remember Dorcas mentioning it – "the Big House", but we didn't explore in that direction. We did farms and fields that weekend, I suppose.'

Guthrie's eyebrow went up. 'Well. Dewar House is its proper name. That's where Deirdre's gone now. It's owned by an impresario by the name of James Ingram. Or Jimmy. Jimmy inherited it from his father who had woollen mills in Galashiels. He's a clever chappie . . . with money, a collector, a patron of the arts. An enthusiast in a tidy Edinburgh way. Avant-garde – almost. He greatly enjoys the company of artists and performers. Which includes Deirdre . . . He's generous. He even provides a retreat for The Select.' Guthrie's wry smile moved under his moustache. 'So you see why my wife feels at home.' He stroked the palms of his hands together – not quite a washing action. 'Ingram has now invited Bornati to Dewar House. He could even work there for a bit. There is a studio. Anyway, his whereabouts will be secret.'

'Secret from his nosy daughter, you mean?'

'He will believe exactly that.'

'Are you sure?'

'I'm sure. And Deirdre'll keep up the pressure.'

'What does she have to do with it?'

'She can persuade Jimmy Ingram there's no show without Punch. She's very set on seeing Bruno Bornati visit Edinburgh. She's just . . . well, curious, I suppose. I told you we were all acquainted in the old days.'

My eyebrows went up.

'We were contemporaries. I did not know your father well. We were in different departments. I was in Painting. He was in Sculpture. A year or so in age between us too. But I knew Bruno . . . a little. He would join our group in the café, at the bar in the evenings. There was always a big event at New Year. A fancy-dress night. I remember him at that. He came as

Michelangelo's God for the first half and switched to Adam for the second.'

'But—'

'No clothes. No. Just that baleful stare, the curly locks and his hand with the finger out. He didn't give a damn. You students of the sixties don't have a prerogative on "happenings", you know. Deirdre offered to be Eve, I remember. That's quite in keeping, of course.' He bent suddenly and threw a log on the fire. Then he poked at it till a blaze flared up.

'Deirdre still has no idea who I really am. And you don't want her to know, do you?'

'I don't, no.' He turned round to face me, still kneeling on the hearth rug. 'I'm glad Dorcas remembered that. I think it's best just we three know, don't you? Deirdre's so damned melodramatic. She'd be sure to let the cat out of the bag.'

'And scare him off?'

'She might.'

'Is he a coward?'

'Not from what I remember.'

'What do you know about him now?'

'Nothing . . . now. I do know the Festival Committee had it somewhere that it was to be his first visit since he left for the States in the early fifties. I do know the City is considering the purchase of a major work.'

'Should I write to him again?'

Guthrie stroked his beard. 'I'm trying to imagine what it must feel like to receive a letter like that out of the blue.'

'You're a different kind of man.'

'I'm a father.'

'Yes. And care for Dorcas. You feed her, watch out for her. He's a father too. He just abandoned me!'

'There's more to it.'

'The mother?'

He raised his eyebrows then looked thoughtful. 'He had a very strong talent. He was a driven man. We knew that even then.'

'You're an artist too.'

'In a humble way. Compromised. Three-fifths school teacher. Someone has to be the bread and butter person. Bruno Bornati was not the type for that.'

'I want to write again.'

'I understand.'

'What should I say?'
'Just . . . give him room.'
'To get off the hook?'
'That's the way to catch him in the end.'

The following morning such a quiet lay about the house it woke me up. The warmth of my friend's body was close. But she was not. So heavily asleep, she lay on her back, one arm flung up, her lips apart, rosy against the white pillow. I watched her closed eyelids and in their tremor, in the small tilt of her chin, the urging breast, the movement of her hand, I read the kept secrets of a sexual night. I held to my mattress edge. She had not come home till late, to Guthrie's fury. We were in the small room in the roof we had shared on my first visit. We were sleeping in the same bed but it seemed much smaller this time. It was a Scottish double, narrow, needing close sleep habits, strange to me. I was alert. The light pressed through the weave of the unlined curtains making them the colour of parchment.

I slipped a leg out. The floorboards were cold. I lifted a curtain corner.

Above the snowbound landscape the sky was an endpaper tint somewhere between yellow and grey. A foot of snow topped the boundary wall. White turrets crowned the circular stone posts. The gates, which always stood open, were rimmed with a soft highlight and the spearheads along the top were white-tipped. The brown river, the only line, and a broken one, wove under cover of hummocked banks. Once-strong features like the flat road and the high hedge were quite blanked out.

There was no sign of Deirdre's mackintosh beside my coat on the back of the kitchen door. I took the crumpled newspaper out of my boots and pulled them on over a double pair of socks. I let myself out of the house.

From the branches, birds made small whistles which tilted like darts into the cold air. Their movements displaced featherings of snow. I followed the car tracks up the drive. These were deep enough but if I stepped out to the side the snow came over the tops of my boots. I knew I was destined to follow this road. The gloom which had oppressed me since the arrival of Christmas without an answer from my father was lifted by the brilliance of this scene. Utterly quiet. Utterly white. I had been relieved, too, by my talk with Guthrie. I was not fooled. There was still some secret in his pocket. But I was comforted by what he had explained to me and felt I had an ally. I had gained him and I was losing Dorcas. She was in a different world where neither sun, nor snow, nor drizzle made any difference; the sheepskin nest, as I imagined it, was her axis now. Later she was to take me up to meet her shepherd. I wondered when she would wake. Noon, perhaps. That look was one I had never seen before, that abandonment to sleep and sensuality.

Great trees rose to my left. They were the conifers called wellingtonias. Their branches leaned towards the ground, weighted down with snow. Every so often, for the sun was there climbing too behind the screen of cloud, a soft fall of white broke the stillness and the twigs swung up. Rhododendrons on my right gave way to a low two-railed iron fence, traditional for such parkland boundaries, and a white field stretched to the far vista of the house. It was built of apricot stone, Georgian, with a pillared entrance, not as large as I had thought. It was symmetrical. I realised, though still distant, how conspicuous to anyone looking out from there my small figure would appear against today's landscape. I turned.

Guthrie met me at the kitchen door. He wore his sweater over pyjamas. 'Coffee's on.'

'It's wonderland out.'

'Planted the first footprints?'

Indeed I had.

Dorcas did not fuss about what she wore. She gravitated towards garments. She browsed. If she took a fancy to something she slipped it on. I caught her stretching an arm towards my Christmas Shetland, an air-force blue. 'Can I?'

'I'm wearing it.'

'Have one of mine. Which d'you want?'

'A warm one.' The Gatehouse felt besieged by cold.

'This red double-knit. Or that old Icelandic then.'

'That. Wasn't that your dad's?'

It was like her dad's. Of the same ilk. I felt warm at once. And animal. It smelled of Dorcas and her father. I wondered if it had ever been washed. Wearing it, I was hugged by both of them yet had room to curl up in it and stretch.

We took the road running westward. From the distance I noticed how a hill rose steeply up behind the Big House.

Dorcas told me there were rings on the top, the remains of an ancient fort.

'Can we climb up?' I had never seen anything like that.

'Not in this weather. And we've to meet Hamish. Remember?'

'How big are the rings? How high? How old?'

'Guthrie likes that kind of thing. Ask him. Did you know that Hamish's ewes are all in lamb now? In the storms he has to make sure they're all off the hill. Sheep do have an instinct about bad weather. They come down. Some get stuck, though, in gullies and odd places.'

The shepherd's cottage was half a mile farther up the valley and stood on the shoulder of a south-facing bank. Two black and white Border collies came to greet us. Dorc bent and fondled them. The asymmetry of ramshackle sheds, black planks leaning, the scored ruts made by a small tractor signalled the working man's patch.

'He'll have been out early scattering turnips for extra feed,' Dorcas told me.

A pair of overalls, stiff and snowy, hung from a line suspended between a downpipe and a bare tree. Solitary man, poor but accommodated.

Dorcas opened the door into a side porch. The smell of sheep fat was palpable.

'Hamish!' called Dorcas.

From hooks driven into the yellowing tongue-and-groove, greasy dark clothes hung. I edged past. Crooks and sticks were in a corner. We stood in the kitchen. Did live sheep smell like dead sheep? Or did Hamish deal too with the carcasses of what he cared for?

'Hamish!' she called again. To me, she said: 'He must be in. The dogs are here. And his coat.'

He appeared silently from the other room. He was as dark as I expected, his hair straight, thick, oil-black with a cat's lick at the front which made a lock of it jut out and fall across his blue eyes. His hand jerked up to push it back but it fell across again at once.

'You haven't shaved yet,' Dorcas said, regarding him with some pleasure.

The same hand came up again but slowly and passed across his chin. He had the lean looks of his own Border collies. 'I tid not shave pecause I had more important things to do this morning.'

She drew her finger experimentally across his cheek.

Standing very still he let her do it. His eyes were shiny. His chin went up. 'Ach, woman!' he said. She desisted, stepping back with a quick intake of breath.

'This is Beatie.'

'Hello, Peatie.'

The fierceness of the handshake was a shock. His eyes had a cold glint. Aquiline fine, his nose scented for danger.

'Meet Midge and Madge,' Dorcas introduced the dogs now settling by the stove. 'These two are the only ones allowed in the house. The others stay out in the kennel. Poor things.'

'Nonsense. That is the place for dogs, woman.'

To hear Dorcas called 'woman' like this depersonalised her. Girlishness had truly gone.

Hamish cooked for himself. I suspected Heinz Tomato Soup and Mother's Pride. Apparently, though, he butchered his own mutton as his family had done on their croft in Lewis. He explained this curtly at Dorc's request as if what else would you be expecting him to do. Dorc even showed me the knives he used – not huge but black with age and bright along the blades: the flip side of the pastoral idyll. Hamish must have prized them and honed them with care but in front of me he feigned disinterest. Dorcas fussed around. Suddenly she said, 'Show your gun to Beatie, Hamish. Please.' I said not to trouble. Really. Dorcas insisted. Her eyes were shining; she pressed her breast into the angle of his arm. 'He shoots rabbits with it. And foxes – for bothering the lambs. He's a very good shot, aren't you, Shamus?' She liked using the Gaelic version of his name. With that look and a black beret he would have passed for a member of the French Resistance.

I did not see the shotgun. I saw candles made from mutton fat instead. Perhaps those gave off the nauseating stink which would make it a relief to get out of there.

The shepherd was not demonstrative with Dorcas. She had leaned towards him, laid her hand on the warmth of his ribbed sweater but he remained aloof as if in his country that kind of familiarity in front of strangers was not seemly. But he had not deceived me. When they were alone, when they abandoned themselves to each other in that unseen other room, in that sheepskin nest I had imagined for them, there was passion. And that passion, now I had seen Hamish, I knew must be fierce.

CHAPTER EIGHT

You do remember what you had on and where you were when something awful happens. You would think the awfulness would blot out such trivial things but instead they stick together, transfixed in time as by a photograph.

On that last day of school I was wearing the McGillivray summer frock. It was lily-of-the-valley-green rayon with a round collar and a tab front, unfashionable, uncomfortable (mine was too small), a sick contrast to our maroon blazers and thus only ever worn by any girl after First Year on the single public occasion of the school Prize-giving at the Usher Hall.

Wearing this garment was what was distressing me, ironically, when I found the letter on the mat in the porch. Mother was in the kitchen getting breakfast for some guests. John Rose was also in the house for he had returned to have another shot at that difficult examination. His presence had compounded my chagrin: I cared how I looked when he was about. The letter was a blue airmail from the USA, postmarked New York, addressed to Beatrice Bornati.

I ran upstairs to my room. I was about to tear it open. Then I saw it said 'Cut here'.

> New York
> NY
> June 23, 1965

Dear Mary,

You have given me a big surprise – two letters and I do not know how to answer them. I gave up on fatherhood a long while back.

You sound satisfied with your success at school. If you are anything like your mother was, you will make a good school teacher. She always took the strong moral line.

Your mother and her parents wanted me out of the way.

I embarrassed them. They could not understand the kind of freedom which is a necessity in any artist's life. I could not support their narrow views. When the chance came I left Scotland for this country not intending to return.

I care only about my work. One day you may come across it. You say you want to know what I am like now. See what you can from my sculpture. It will have to speak for me.

Do not try to contact me again. Believe me – there's no point.

Bruno Bornati

The best days of an Edinburgh summer are often spoiled by the arrival of a sea mist. It is called the haar and it comes in from the Firth of Forth. That June morning I stood at my window with this letter in my hand and watched it insinuate itself upon the city. The sun dimmed to opal. Clean-cut shadows blurred. Hot tears were standing in my eyes. My throat ached, full and sharp. This marked the end . . . the end of the fine weather we had been enjoying. While the rest of the country still basked in sun, we would lie under a dank blanket for some time. The clear light of the capital in sunshine is always poignant for this reason. Glints on the crown spire of St Giles, the coral of the Crags, the garish bedding plants of the Flower Clock at the elbow of The Mound, the city buses, maroon and white, passing round and down to Princes Street, gleaming as smartly as a businessman's starched collar, are dulled by the chill coming of this Old Norse mist.

'Beatie!' My mother was calling from the top of the stairs. 'Are you in your room, Beatie? Do you see the haar's come in, and I was planning to wear a silk frock.' She opened my door and put her head round.

Doubling the letter against my stomach, I concealed it with my hands. 'Wear it, Mum. I don't get prizes every day,' I said.

'I'll take my light wool coat, then. The hat will match.' She paused. 'Are you all right? Have you a pain?'

'No.'

'Standing like that – you've not had any breakfast.'

When she was safely across the landing I folded the letter and put it inside my Bible. I considered hiding it in *The Golden Treasury* but suddenly stopped myself, feeling it might contaminate the poetry. The letter from my father needed to be filed away beside God's laws. Both were texts of insoluble difficulty, texts which I could not accept: unfinished business.

I was shivering. It was the rayon dress. I drew on my navy cardigan and pushed my arms into the sleeves of my blazer. That evening was Ninian's *Hamlet* and dinner with him afterwards, a farewell, for he was going off to France on holiday.

'You're quiet,' my mother said as we walked together round the crescent to the bus.

'Last day, Mum.'

'Your future begins tomorrow.'

'Ninian goes away.' To put her off the scent.

'Is that what's the matter? But you start your job at the library. You'll meet new people.'

The haar had drained colour from the outstretched hands of the chestnut leaves. Pale heads of roses offered themselves above the low coping of the garden walls.

We sat side by side downstairs in the bus and travelled through subdued traffic to Toll Cross. People waited at the stops with their shoulders hunched, brows knit, frowns on their faces. They stood under hats and perms and pressed their brogued feet together. They had braved the biting east winds of the winter. They tucked their chins in. They deserved better than this of the so-called Scottish summer.

'And we're going to McVitie's, dear, at the West End, for our lunch, afterwards. That'll be a nice treat, won't it?'

The Usher Hall was then a blackened circular edifice built by beer to house culture. We were familiar with the place. Every year we had come for this event. I saw my mother to her seat in the stalls and went to find my fellows. When we were younger we had watched with awe the big girls, whose last year it was, bite their lips and burst into tears at the final filing out.

The organ console was centre stage towards the back. The choir banked steeply up from this to the soaring organ pipes. It was a dizzying experience to be seated there. Your feet were level with the shoulders of the girl in front and when you stood up it felt like being strung out against the face of the Eiger. The cavernous auditorium gaped.

We were in a glare of yellow, our heads of soft washed hair, the tawny browns, the fair, the wavy black, ranked above the cheeks of our ripe girlhood, our eyes brimming this culminating day, our women's bodies masked by our uniform frocks, the brassy unicorns on our blazer pockets standing staunchly out. We could subsume our individuality this one last time to this farewell. I, for one, knew real gratitude. School had opened doors for me. We sang our songs. We sat through speeches. We clapped prizewinners till our palms burned. When our own turn approached we left our places and waited in the wings. The names were called. Dux in Art. Dorcas went walking out, shook the hands, bowed her head and returned with a rosy spot high on each cheek. 'Well done!' I put my arm around her.

'Beatie' – a warning from a person with the list.

'Dux in English. Beatrice Brown.' I walked out across the stage. My English master's eyes were stars today. He wrung my hand. And wrung again. 'Congratulations. Congratulations, Beatie. Oh, very well done. Very well done.' I was touched by his emotion. It was too late to see him as a focus for all my effort. I had put my father there. The English teacher had been some kind of lieutenant. Clapping surged around the hall. I received three books. Inside I read my name inscribed three times. Beatrice Brown. Bornati was not there at all. We filed back to our seats.

With a major chord from the organ 'Jerusalem' began. We prepared for the usual effort, lusty always, though this was the last rendering for some. The imagery of battle glinted:

> Bring me my Bow of burning gold:
> Bring me my Arrows of desire:
> Bring me my Spear: O clouds unfold!'

In the parting clouds I saw my father come from a Blakeian sunburst. He had thrown his thunderbolt. There was no break in our full-throated song. My own voice was clear. I would fight. The organ pealed. The chords came down. Pipes trumpeted above us. Girlhood was ending. We ducked our heads.

I was not happy. I did not cry, though, like the others.

I saw Dorcas standing with her parents and I pulled my mother away to avoid having to talk. Dorcas would suspect. Deirdre would gush. Guthrie would see.

We walked down to Princes Street through the damp air. My tall mother clicked along, one hand holding her gloves and her handbag up against the breast of her white coat. She wore a look of satisfaction on her face. Of pride. I hugged the small pile of books: my *Complete Shakespeare*, *The Letters of John Keats* and *Waiting for Godot*. Every so often I opened one, examined the clean print and the smoothness of the paper, stroked, sniffed, closed it. I had to run to catch her up.

McVitie's was full of housewives having lunch. I watched them snap the clasps of their handbags and make commas with their napkins at the corners of their mouths. My mother was proud of our celebration. I was the first of our family to be going to the university. I had no appetite. She pressed me to have apple pie. The defiant mood that had surged up when I sang 'Jerusalem' had ebbed. The pie lay on my stomach. Back at the house I said I would like to have a nap.

I slept deeply for hours. I woke feeling tragic but calm. I had to hurry.

Ninian's rehearsing for this play, and before that exam pressure on both of us, meant that we had not been together much in recent weeks. Our relationship had reached the level where we arranged the next date and parted with a good-night kiss, dry, brief and quick. I felt cheated. Ever since the regal imperative on evening gloves, I held his mother, in a vague way, responsible.

I made my own way down to the school. Ninian, as Hamlet, appeared in black velvet doublet, white shirt open at his breast, spotlit on the darkened stage: a paragon of tragic virtue. I watched him brood. I saw him scheme and strike. The production was a classic one, the cast all male, of course. Ninian's voice carried. There was more confidence in his rendering of Shakespeare's text than in any utterance to me. He had that command of words, grasp of their very root which enabled him to play their meaning to the full, to make them flower.

Afterwards, in the dining hall, orange juice and sandwiches were set out on long tables covered in white cloths. Ninian's face glowed. All the actors were like that. Their colour was up. It was more than just the incomplete or too-vigorous removal of make-up. Their eyes were too wide, too bright, and roamed. Response to questions was disjointed. I could spot the players throughout the room. An increased human voltage coursed from them in an invisible but near-palpable field. Getting out of one's own skin I observed to be an extraordinarily exhilarating experience.

'Hello, Orr,' I said to Ninian. 'What does it feel like then? To lose yourself? You did, tonight, didn't you?'

'I can't believe it's over.' He had had us all in thrall.

I did not want this Ninian to go either. 'You must do more acting. You were good. Really good. You'll not forget Hamlet. Not ever. Those lines are yours. They'll keep cropping up in your head.' His eyes were fixed on mine. It was disconcerting. 'I imagine . . .' I tailed off.

He gripped my arm. 'Your school days ended today.' He put down his glass of juice. 'Have you thought what that means, Beatie?'

The restaurants Edinburgh students frequented then were often in cellars like the one in the lane behind Princes Street where we soon found ourselves. You never quite forgot the old vennels with the cobbles and leaky downpipes on the other side of the roughly plastered whitewashed walls. The smells were of damp and candle wax mixed with rough red wine and garlic. Guitar music played in the background – in this case a wheedling Greek equivalent. I sat opposite Ninian near the back at a small table with a red-checked cloth. I picked at the candle drippings on the bottle and remembered Jilly-Willy's uncleared supper table years before. Ninian held the carafe of house red by the neck and poured me out a glass.

'Are you sorry I'm going off tomorrow?'

'Ninian!'

'Well. How am I to know what goes on in your head? You're . . .' he paused before delivering the excellent word, 'inscrutable. Often. I feel—'

'Yes?'

'I feel it's *full* of things. Things I wot not of.'

'No it isn't,' I lied, shaking my head.

He shrugged, in some way disappointed.

'Hamlet, you were brilliant!' I raised my glass. 'Congratulations, oh most noble Prince! To your future and all that.'

'You're in a funny mood tonight.'

'No I'm not.'

'Anyway . . . Hamlet didn't have much of a future. Make that toast to *me*, Beatie. No. To *us*.'

'Us.' I sipped obediently. He took a large swallow and watched me all the time above the rim of his glass. I drank to us as individuals. I suspected his wishes were for our united front.

We considered the menu next. Ninian insisted on explanations from a hirsute Greek. Black olives came and little dishes filled with food I had never tasted in my life before. We broke bread and spread on knifefuls of the stuff and washed it down with wine. My stunned spirits revived. Ninian had grown in my eyes tonight. The rendering of Hamlet made him hero-size. Even his control of this moment, his confident handling of the order, his hunger as he sat with me and we gorged ourselves, cheered me. The inhibiting framework of his family which had come to constrict my view of him in the past months faded.

'So. Will you miss me?'

The wine glass was at my lips. I would miss this young man's earnest look searching for my soul by candlelight, the feast spread at our fingertips on a scarlet cloth.

'You must have a good time when you're away.'

'You sound as if you don't care one way or the other.'

'You might find someone else, you know. I could feel them all out there in the audience tonight, all those females longing to get their claws on you, to rip open that lovely shirt – tear it bare to your torso.'

'I thought only statues had those.' Self-doubt became amazement. 'But really?' He went back to the thought. 'Good.' His smile grew. His eyes did not leave my face. 'I'd like that.'

'They will.'

'Let it be soon. Please.' He leaned across the table close to the candle in its green bottle. The light reflected in his eyeball. He was trying to see inside me. But what he read in my face made him put his big hands to his head and rumple his hair in desperation.

'Motorists only pick up tidy-looking hitchhikers,' I warned. 'When you get to France, you'd better have one of those very short cuts.'

Tousled, dazed, he looked at me: 'And risk losing my following of females?' He was not one who thought about his appearance, usually. 'Would *you* go for me in a continental cut though, Beatie?'

With his confidence up, as it was tonight, it might be possible. 'Perhaps.'

' "Perhaps!" Why aren't you nice to me, Beatie?'

' "Nice"? That's a silly word.'

'Are you accusing me of being inarticulate?' He shot me a Hamlet look. 'I'm willing to put it another way . . .' he nodded towards the black Greek wiping the bar counter, 'later.'

'What way?'

'My parents have gone to St Andrews for the weekend. I've got the house by myself.'

My eyes dropped from his.

'More?' He poured. We were very still. He was waiting. 'Beatie?'

The bus roared up The Mound and delivered us with indecent haste at the district of The Grange. It was almost midnight. Each house slept deep behind its high stone wall. Ninian pushed the gate, penetrating the fastness. We entered between the sentinels of holly bush. Spikes of jasmine curved out. I put up my hand. I remembered they owned the classic Edinburgh beast, a black Labrador: 'The dog?' I said.

'He's gone too.' Ninian's voice was a near whisper also but low, breaking. I heard him clear his throat. He went ahead. Then he was holding the door open.

Mr Orr's bowler hat hung on the hall stand.

'In here.' Ninian switched on the light. It was too bright for me. I looked down towards the low swing of the pendulum in the grandfather clock. It was the drawing room where we had had tea.

'I can't be too late,' I said.

'Is your mother waiting up?'

I shook my head. If all the guests were in, she went on up to bed and left me to bolt the big door. Maybe she listened for me. Maybe not. She trusted my good sense.

'Well, I'll walk you home. Take your coat off for a minute,' he said, indicating my cotton mac. 'Have a seat. What can I get you?'

'That light's like an operating theatre.'

He gave me an interrogative look. 'Wait. Wait . . .' he said. He switched on a small table lamp beside the mantelpiece and loped back to the door to put off the centre bulb. Then he relieved me of my coat, flinging it over on a chair. He turned and grinned at the sight of me smoothing my yellow mini dress. We were by the sofa. All of a sudden he was not grinning but had loosened his tie, whipped it off and was unbuttoning the top of his shirt.

'Is this for my benefit?'

He did not answer.

'Hamlet stripped to his shirt sleeves?'
'Be nice.'
'I am nice!'
'Let me . . .'
'What?'

Watching me his brown eyes were warm. He pushed his lips forward as if considering then quirked his mouth. 'What's that out in the garden?' he said.

I turned. We took a step towards the window. The curtains were drawn back. The yellow lamp's round reflection glowed in a bower of bushes. I pressed up against the sill. 'What was it?' I strained to see. 'A prowler? Or what?' I could make out only the dark forms of the beds and the espaliers with their leafy arms outstretched. I felt Ninian press against my back.

'Ninian . . .'

'Mm?' The length of his body was up against me. His arms came over my shoulders, making me stay like that. They crossed in front. His breath was in my ear, dry lips worked along my cheek, but it was not my mouth that he was after. One hand took my chin and then, a mixture of stroking and fumbling, inched down under the front of my dress. I stood transfixed by that intimate invasion. His hand delved and probed and at last held one breast in an awkward clasp. The surface of my skin contracted, from my stomach to my toes shrank in awe at the awefulness. He let out a shuddery breath. His hand shifted. I felt the zip jerk down my spine and his fingers at the hook of my bra. I could not have looked him in the face. Both hands had me now . . . just held. I waited, nervous for him, nervous for us both. Then he made me twist my neck to kiss him fully on the lips, which was masterful but not comfortable.

Stitches ripped.

His mouth, his hands deserted me. Stranded, I stood exposed to the shadows in the glass. The yellow disc of the lamp went black. I was pulled to the sofa. He tugged clumsily at my dress.

'No.'
'Be nice.'
'I am. I was. Wasn't . . .?'
'Be nicer.'

His hand was on the inside of my knee.

'I go tomorrow.'

'I know.' An orange glow reached into the room from the sodium streetlamp beyond the wall. It was enough to show his long body sprawled against the cushions, legs wide, his ruched shirt spread-eagled, arms angling, one reaching for me. His dark forelock hid half his face.

'No, Ninian.'

'Think what I've been through today. Be nice.'

His dog eyes pleaded. His mouth drooped in a dissolute pout. My knees buckled. He touched me higher up. I pulled away. 'Anyway,' I was scrupulous, 'I thought you said you had other words . . . than those. That you'd explain.'

'Love me.'

'You go away tomorrow.'

'But this is tonight.'

The grandfather clock by the door measured all the seconds equally and sent each mellow tock and tick for them out into the room.

'Love me.' His face, shirt white.

'I can see for you it would be a culmination, Ninian. After *Hamlet*. After your successes. Before you set out on your travels. To know.'

'But it's the same for you – successes today. You told me. Your prizes!'

My hands were on his shoulders. He looked up at me eagerly. He thought he had won the point. But he did not know about my father's letter. Today had been the worst day of my life. For a boy whose father's hat hung there on the hall stand overlapping by a genteel inch his mother's Guide Captain beret, whose carpets smelled faintly of dog, whose family rose bowl held in June and in September the crimson blooms of Ena Harkness pruned, manured and sprayed by the father for the purpose, plucked, de-thorned, arranged each season by the mother – such a young man could not ever understand – even one who had been the Prince of Denmark, who had acted mad and had come back again.

'How many dead bodies are there at the end in *Hamlet*?'

'Why don't you wear stockings?'

'How many bodies?'

'Stockings are much—'

'How many, Ninian?'

Ninian removed his head from against my thighs. 'Four.' He looked up. I saw that mobile mouth, the flash of his strong teeth. 'Six if you count the news of Rosencrantz and Guildenstern.'

But my tragedy was no play. A real murder had been committed. As good as, anyhow. My father might as well have wrung my neck as sent me a rejection such as that.

'What would your father and your mother think,' I asked, 'if we did . . . what you want me to do,' I could not say the words, 'here, on their sofa, where they sip Earl Grey tea and nibble shortbread?'

His eyes gleamed. He pressed his chin between my legs. 'But that's the point: they won't ever need to know!'

'I know that!' I was the only one who would not remain intact.

'What would *your* mother and father think?' he asked.

'My mother, you mean?' It was really too awful to imagine. Yet it was not my door she locked at night – but her own. 'She's terrified of it.' By 'it' I meant sex. Ninian thought I meant me having sex.

'What about your father? My *father*'s better. I can talk. Just. What about yours?' Moisture glistened on his lip. He was moving his hands upwards to the top of my tights.

I should tell. Perhaps I could. I only managed though: 'Mine doesn't care.'

I heard him draw in his breath. 'What?' His voice was muffled.

'He doesn't . . .' His fingers were between my legs, distracting me. 'He doesn't . . . care,' I said faintly. He was stroking me, pushing a bit, but gentle. If I was spurned by my father and locked out by my mother did it matter what I let him do?

'What?' Ninian whispered, a nervous, unfinished enquiry. His fingers faltered.

'He doesn't care.'

He had stopped stroking me. His shirt-sleeved arms were by his sides. He was getting to his feet. He just stood there. Very close. I waited for him to speak. But he had no language for this need. Bullishly, he pushed against me. I felt the sudden strangeness of his penis grown and large. 'What?' He tugged at my dress. 'What? What?' breathing that word in my ear as if it were an endearment. He did not know what he was saying. He did not know what he had said, what he had asked. He was repeating it automatically like a child does when he is already playing something else.

That I had a father or not meant nothing to him. And this . . . this and Ninian's nuzzling was like an animal's. I pushed him off.

Sex would have brought the end of term to a splendid climax for Ninian but I was afraid it might precipitate a whole nightmare action for me.

I knew this meant he would probably lose his virginity with someone else. I did not care about that. I would rather he practised on another female first. I had rejected his lovemaking. He thought I had rejected him: I cared a little about that.

CHAPTER NINE

'Tucked away, aren't you?'
'Ssh.'
Dorcas dropped her voice to library pitch. 'Does anyone know you *exist*?'
'We're *the* Central Children's Library.'
'But down all those steps . . . there isn't even a sign.' She ducked to see past the piers of book stacks in the long low room. 'Are you alone?'
I shook my head. My boss, the librarian, was nibbling sandwiches in her sanctum at the back. I was supposed to be writing reminder postcards. My fingers snicked through the overdue tickets in the box.
Dorcas made an 'O' with her mouth. Then she grinned. 'Be a librarian and see life, is that it?'
I bit on a smile. 'What have you been doing?'
'Waitressing at Crawfords. But I've just left.'
'Why?'
'Servitude. Hated it. And cockroaches in the locker rooms. If those Morningside ladies eating cream cakes with their hats on and their pinkies sticking out knew what went on in that kitchen they wouldn't set foot in the place ever again.'
'It's not as bad as that here,' I said, soft-voiced. 'I don't feel like a second-class citizen or anything.'
'No?'
'No. Books are comforting.'
'There must be *something* you don't like?'
'There are no windows. If I go out at lunchtime and the sun's shining I don't like coming back. It's easier when it's raining. And busier. The old men from the Grassmarket come in to shelter. We shoo them away. They smell.'
'You meet some queer folk out in the world, don't you?' She leaned her elbows on the counter. 'At Crawford's there's a

woman called Lizzie on the tea urn – a gap in her teeth, thin, and her neck's all black and blue with wee bruises . . .' Dorcas narrowed her eyes. 'Do you know what marks like that are, Beatie?'

I did not.

'Lovebites.' Her nose wrinkled up. Her eyes flew wide. 'Imagine! God! What must go on in Leith!'

I wondered how you did a lovebite.

'Leith's where all the sailors come in,' Dorcas informed me and left a pause. 'Tell me, how's your boyfriend?'

'Away hitchhiking.'

'Too bad.' Her face changed again. The question was coming: 'Have you heard from your father?'

I extricated a tricky ticket with a frown. 'Tut-tut, here's a Scot who knows no thrift, James MacKenzie of Ramsay Gardens: five weeks' overdue fine to pay – and on four books!'

Dorcas sighed. 'I don't know how you can stand it here. When's your lunch break?'

I had had it.

'Well . . . I'm off. I'll be out at Dewar for the rest of the holidays. They need me to help up at the Big House. There are visitors. The Festival's near now, you know.'

As if I did not. Already at home there were queues for the bathroom, endless bacon breakfasts and bundles of pink nylon sheets outside the landing doors. 'Won't that still be "servitude"?'

'It's different at Dewar House, Beatie. It's the difference between prison and Liberty Hall. And I'll see Hamish every night.'

'Is he . . . fine?'

'Fine.' She hugged her cardigan across, thus roundly defining her large breasts. She bestowed on me a smile of bliss.

I felt a pang. I started on the first postcard.

'I hope Master MacKenzie of Ramsay Gardens appreciates the excellence of your italic script, Beatie.' I went on writing. She still stood there. 'By the way,' she got it out at last, 'Guthrie says to tell you Bornati *is* coming.' My pen poised on a full stop. 'Also . . . there's a job for you at the Big House. If you want it.'

When I found my voice it sounded prim. 'It's too late. I signed a contract with the library to work till the end of August.'

'But, Beatie!'
'What?' I was fierce.
'You must be free for the Private View!'
'Why?'
'You want to *see* him. You want to *meet* him. Don't you?'
My lips puckered. 'Not now. No.'

Right there in the silent listening room she pleaded and expostulated. But I could not bear to tell her the facts of the letter. The librarian approached along the strip of carpet to see what the fuss was about. At the sight of her Dorcas turned on her heel. But one backward look showed her pale eyes wide, awash as swimming pools with enquiry and disbelief.

Working at the library suited my mood those first weeks after school, Ninian and my rosy dreams of having a father over. I felt cloistered there. I liked the distance from real life. Footsteps and voices approaching down our steps hushed at our varnished half-glazed door. It was a children's place. And their world was different. Not that many children came. The families who used to live in the old buildings around had moved out to the new estates like Craigmillar and Insh.

The library was on George IV Bridge high above the black canyon of the Cowgate. Pigeons flapped from the bridge to roost on the sills of the tenements far below where the windows were all blank or barred. Even the tramps, shut out of the mission hostel during the day, did not linger. They favoured the open width of the Grassmarket and sat on the benches there watching the birds peck at the cobbles. If it rained they came up to us.

Agnes, my boss, was a middle-aged dormouse. The library was her nest. When she was not holed up in the tiny room at the back she was at the counter, whiskers twitching. Even my arrival down from the street brought her mouth to a pensive point. In her mud-coloured eyes fear lay waiting.

When my first Grassmarket tramp shambled in I asked in the usual way to see his tickets. He shook his sheep's wool head and pushed forward in his broken boots. 'Get Mr Turnbull!' Agnes squeaked, darting out to stand in a quiver of anxiety, barring the wicket that gave access to the stacks. I fled downstairs and fetched Mr Turnbull up from the basement. He showed the culprit off the premises, this act, for him, being as routine as plugging in the kettle for our tea.

Next day I passed one of these old gents leaning against the entrance pillar to the main library. He had the usual look of having just been doused by the contents of the ash bucket. Low in front of him, his fingers, sausagey and mobile, worked at what I thought must be a roll or bottle. He had his rheumy eyes on me. Then I saw he was busy with his flies. It was my first glimpse of the grown male member and its strangeness was a shock.

I backed Agnes to the hilt after that. I saw what a fright a child would get if she met that kind of rascal behind the bookcase when she went to fetch her Enid Blytons. Nor were these characters to catch a whiff of the methylated spirit with which we cleaned the plastic covers of the books – Agnes kept the bottle locked away with the petty cash under the counter.

Days passed. Then weeks. The sun shone on the swept pavements. The library grew quieter. Even the tramps left us alone. I remembered Dorcas's question and I felt the pattern of my life becoming as pale as an inscription written in invisible ink.

I began to miss Ninian. I went to church to see if that would help. Scanning the canny congregation I realised what a focus for my thoughts his long dark head had been. I began to regret pushing him away because he had put his hand down my bodice and up my skirt. Under the curtain of my hair I made his palms come rounding on my breasts again and I felt him tremulous against me and held him there like that. 'Blessed are the pure in heart.' Could I then be blessed? I took a peek. The Orrs' pew was empty. The parents were away in Mull. The Moggachs, all four, sat slumped obediently. What was 'blessed' anyway? Would a man, I wondered, ever fondle Wilma's heavy breasts or walk his fingers up between those solid knees? At night Ninian came to me as Hamlet in the full-sleeved snowy open-breasted shirt, a dark lock across his anxious brow, and we tussled in restless sexual fantasy.

This hankering for Ninian stopped abruptly when his post-card came from France. The picture was of '*Les portes et les remparts médiévaux d'Avignon.*' I liked that: it was romantic. But his message read: '*Les femmes françaises sont très sym-pathiques.* XXX, Ninian.' In front of the signature was a scribbled box, midnight-blue biro, so desperately hatched it made an indent on the other side. Had he written 'love', then crossed it out? My cheeks went hot. He had botched it: yes. But he was cocking his snook. He had got off with a French girl.

Like a sign, the next day, parked at the top of Candlemaker Row, was the pale blue Triumph Herald belonging to John Rose.

I had come as usual on my lunchtime route, my escape as I now saw it, which took me down the West Bow with its little shops to the Grassmarket and back round up the hill by Greyfriars Bobby. I stood beside the drinking fountain with the statue of the little dog on it and gazed at the car. He must be in the pub. The little dog had waited, so the story went, I could keep a vigil too . . .

But it only took a moment.

John Rose came out. Alone.

'Hello.'

He swung round. 'Hello there!' He put his two hands into his trouser pockets and sauntered over. His eyes had that clear gleam – they seemed to search ahead of any words. After an age he said, 'What are you up to here, Miss Beatie Brown?'

'Nothing. It's my lunch hour.' I watched the way his head went back as if he doubted that. 'Why is it you always say I'm "up to" something?'

'Do I?'

' "Dressing up", for instance?'

He smiled with his eyes, remembering.

'I'm working at the Children's Library.'

'Actually, your mother told me.'

'Oh.'

His eyes still smiled. He was not hurrying away or anything. 'How's . . .?'

'The studying?' He made a rueful face. 'At least it's nearly over. I'm going over to Queen Street now. Can I give you a lift?'

But I had to be back.

'Another time then, h'm?' He sounded genuine.

'Yes.'

'I've not had such a lovely smile from you before,' he said. 'It suits you.'

Which stopped me.

We said goodbye.

I watched him get into the car. At the back of his head his

hair was crinkly. The door closed with a low clunk. He gave me a wave, then pulled out into the traffic on Forrest Road.

Inside the gateway of Greyfriars Kirkyard I let that smile return. I still had ten minutes . . . I could have accepted a lift. Just to the foot of The Mound. I could have run back up and not been too late . . . No, it was better like this for, eager though I was suddenly, I did not want to be a fool.

My mother recommended this place to guests. The church rose rather grey straight ahead. There were Gaelic services the board said. The only person I knew who spoke Gaelic was Hamish. Somehow I did not see him in a church. It was peaceful in here away from the street. Another world that brought other ages near. Mature trees reached their shade lightly over the paths and the turf between the gravestones, memorials to the long since, the famous and the ordinary dead. I walked down the slope and back up round the hill. Up to the left there were august family vaults bearing names straight out of Scott and Stevenson. They marked unrest too: bones smashed by musket balls and great claymores, and the too brief resting places ransacked by the robbers Burke and Hare.

Like a tunnelling root my feelings worked towards John Rose. The soil here was as sooty as the fibre in which we had plotted up our bulbs at school. Nothing seemed as black to us then – perhaps because we planted them in the context of white paper and clean printed books – nor was anything as white and fierce as the roots of hyacinths. Grow them in a glass and watch the thick threads reach and coil below to bring the bell flowers into heavy bloom on top. In our classroom cupboards this network proliferated quietly in dark-bellied bowls. If too tightly packed the roots cut the surface by the rim's edge like a row of pointed teeth. There was something desperate about the contrast and the struggle there: you would think they could have kept themselves under. There is an indecency about a root, like a bare bone, or the glimpse of white petticoat.

My shears clipped the quiet of the Sunday afternoon. Snick. Snack. I was putting myself in the way of an encounter.

It was from behind this boundary hedge I had lured Ninian. That November dusk I had arranged myself under the lamp-light and waited. I snipped precisely at a privet sprout. Snip, to you, Ninian. Snicker snack.

As far as my mother knew he was still my 'boyfriend' but absent on holiday till September. I did not give her details. She locked that door. She knew love was everywhere. She had been caught by it herself. But she let him go, my father. Pushed him off. I clawed the hedge to free the clinging sprigs. Worthless. He was. To her. The shears weighed on my arm. Some worth as an artist apparently – Guthrie, the article, the exhibition, he himself in that horrid letter said it. I took a double grip, clenched and swung the shears up to cut the top. I heard my anger in the yapping of the blades and felt the good pain of it jar with every jolt.

Under the wall a terrier turned up his bramble eyes at the arrival of a twig. No dreams of Daddy in that wiry nutbrown head – but of a mate: maybe.

John Rose was having Sunday lunch at Number 50, the house with the chestnut tree. He had walked along. I knew that because his Triumph was still here parked by the kerb. If I leaned out I could touch it with the tip of my clippers. He never did that. Unlike the other men in the street who swabbed and polished most weekends, his energy was all for other things – text books mostly . . . but not exclusively, I suspected, recalling the way his eyes fixed on me that night he asked if I wanted cocoa. Cocoa! My arms collapsed on the spiky surface of the hedge. Still no sign. Not even of Mr Jamieson checking for greenfly. Perhaps they had all gone out together for a Sunday walk. I made slower, snippy clips. His exams began the next day, Mother said. I had very little time. Two more yards only were left for me to cut.

Tonight. It must be or he would be gone again. Each snip brought me nearer the boundary fence. I was ready for him this time. Ready for our eyes to meet. Ready to dare. Ready for anything. Not very nice perhaps – 'nice'! That lace doily! That redundant adjective! Nice. A word much debased, I know, dear Starry-eyes, dear English teacher mine. Nice comes from *nescius*, ignorant. Yes. And from the Old French meaning silly. And so in this day and age – look at Dorcas – surely, is being a virgin. I might not be nice but I would know. Dorcas knew.

Thus, to fortify myself I lay in wait.

Stood clipping.

From time to time hung over, looked along.

A cat dropped from the fence and slunk between the squeaky stems of the montbretia. From over in The Grange came the sound of evening bells. I swept the clippings up. I trundled the barrow through to the back and had to banish from my mind again that blundering advance of Ninian's which still laid in wait to ambush me. I tipped the bitter privet on the dump and put the tools away. My hands smelled of soil, sour sap and cat and my hair of tree dust. I went in to have a bath.

To set my cap.

To set my trap.

That rhymes.

One hour later and I had John Rose sitting in my Cinderella corner by the Rayburn stove. I had him for as long as it took to drink the mug of tea he was holding between his hands. I had him pleased I was there with my nose, he said, out of a book for once, and willing to iron a shirt for him for the exam next day.

'What's your charge, Beatie? Pullars at Salisbury want two-and-thrupence a shirt.' He added, 'I think.' So I knew he did not have to count the pennies. 'This one's clean but it's been crushed at the back of a drawer. I forgot to collect the usual lot last thing yesterday.'

'Did you enjoy lunch along the road?'

'It was fine. A nice bit of home cooking which I do appreciate – now and again. We walked it off going round the Hermitage of Braid. That's a gloomy place.'

'I like it. That passage through the rocks, trees towering, dim light, brown burn, Hermit's cell – it's straight out of a poem.'

He was watching me. ' "Brown burn." You're a romantic Scot, Beatie, aren't you?' I flourished the shirt from the board and made as if to drop it on the floor. 'Forgive me. But I am just an Englishman, you know. Seriously, I wish you had come. The Jamiesons saw the place quite differently.'

I made the shirt flat again. 'How differently?'

'They're not . . . They're rather narrow, let me put it like that. Their main concern was the disgrace of citizens who let their dogs off the lead to defecate at random, and what loud voices children have these days.'

'There's a great echo there!'

'Yes.' John Rose was smiling at me when I looked up. I ironed away. My hair was still wrapped up in a towel turban which I felt begin to slip. 'How do you like your job at the library then?'

'I don't know.' I tilted my head back to balance the turban. 'I thought it was nice at first. But it's boring.'

'I should have met you before at Greyfriars Bobby – taken you in for a drink.'

'Should you?' I smiled. I set the iron on its heel. With both hands I pulled the towel from my head and rubbed my hair.

'But you're not eighteen yet.'

I challenged him, wide-eyed.

'How's that boyfriend?'

'He's away for the summer.'

'Are you lonely?'

I smoothed a side seam. 'A little.'

I heard him swallow a mouthful of tea and the chink of the mug being set on the stove. My fingers slipped under the cloth and arranged the next section of shirt over the end of the board. Pushing the iron in long even strokes up and down I wished this could be the flat of my hands and the shirt smooth against his breast. Under my spiky hair I sneaked a look. He was leaning right back against the wall and eyeing me. I looked down quickly. 'Folded or on a hanger?'

'A hanger. Please.' Slowly he bent forward to get up. 'Thank you, Beatie.' Electric sparks went off in those blue eyes of his. 'Beautiful. How can I thank you? What do I owe you?'

I was insulted. 'It's nothing, Dr Rose.'

He was standing on the other side of the ironing board. 'Sorry,' he said. Then: 'Will you do something else for me?'

I waited.

'Call me John. I call you Beatie. You call me John.'

That seemed difficult.

'Try.'

I could not say it.

' "Good luck, John," ' he coached.

I nodded.

My mother said when she got home from church soon after that: 'But I could have done that for him! The poor man! Of course a doctor must always have a decent shirt. I hope you did it nicely, Beatie. Did you remember what I told you? Yoke, cuffs and collars first. Seven minutes it takes to do a shirt. Seven minutes. You cannot rush a shirt.'

I assured her I had not rushed that shirt.

CHAPTER TEN

The shirt looked fine. We shared an early silent breakfast table next morning.

For five days after that I saw no sign of him. At lunchtime I looked for his car outside Greyfriars Bobby but in vain. Even in the evenings, late, he stayed out. I rose early but found he had already been in the bathroom. He left it steamy and smelling of what I discovered later was an aftershave called Old Spice. Transported by its mystic vapours, I closed my eyes and made a wish. I tilted the mirror and wiped a clear patch.

Downstairs my mother complained he did not eat breakfast any more.

The longest hour in the Central Children's Library was Saturday afternoon five o'clock to six, the last hour in the week. The sun had shone all day; hardly a soul had been in; the stacks were tidy. Agnes was doing some new accessions in the back. I stood at the counter cleaning the plastic covers of the books, my cloth fumy with methylated spirit tipped from the bottle. I liked its pure violet hue and strange reek. It contributed a small excitement to the routine nature of the task. I wanted time to stretch. I did not want to find John Rose gone when I got home. Before, when he heard he failed he had cleared out of town immediately. Yesterday my mother said she found a suitcase open on his bed with books packed in it. Six days had gone. Four for exams, two to get results.

I looked up, surprised by the sound of a bright step. He burst open our sanctuary just as Burns's plough turned up the mouse nest.

'I was told I'd find you here, Beatie.' Excitement shone in his face. 'Now, who am I? Say it. Say who I am.'

'John,' I managed.

He wanted more.

'Dr John Rose.'

'MRCP. Member of the Royal College of Physicians. I've passed. I've got it! The hardest exam ever. I've bloody got it!'

I took a quick look behind me. This exuberance was near riot for our library. Fumbling, I tried to fix the cap back on the spirit bottle. But nothing was to trap this genie. John Rose leaned across the counter, took my face in his two hands and planted a firm kiss. I made a protest with my hands against his jacket. 'Come with me to celebrate, Beatie. No one can object to that.' The door to Agnes's inner sanctum clicked. 'Now. I'm waiting.' He did not let my eyes escape.

Trim feet made a pattering along the carpet.

'I'm not off till six,' I breathed.

'Ask.'

'Oh, no.'

'Ask.' His glance went over my shoulder.

I turned. 'Agnes, do you think . . .?' She had on her pointed face. 'Agnes, could you . . .?'

'Beatie's mother's taken ill. I'm a doctor friend come to fetch her home . . . Agnes, is it? You can spare her now, Agnes, can't you?'

Agnes's eyes shone round as bagatelle balls. She dipped her chin in an affirmative.

The clunk of the passenger door shut me in beside him. I had never been in the front of a car. The seat was low. It made me lean back. I felt luxurious and helpless. His hand on the gear stick between us made deft movements. The Triumph roared into life.

'*Is* my mother ill?'

'Is she?'

'You said . . .' I pulled at my short skirt to try to cover some of the exposed length of leg. He gave my knees a sidelong glance. 'You said . . .' I tailed off.

'Don't you worry your pretty little head. I'm in charge.'

The car swung out into the traffic, roared up Bristo Place and turned westward along by the Infirmary.

'We aren't going home then?'

'No. No. There's not much fun at home, is there?' He said it lightly.

'I'm usually back for tea on the dot, though.'

'Does she worry, your mother?'

'I shall have to tell her where I am.'

He sighed. 'We'll find a phone box.' He stole a look at me. For a dreadful moment I felt him weighing up the odds, deciding if I was worth the effort.

'My mother's taken to you. She doesn't usually take to guests, you know.' He did not say anything. When I looked, his mouth had contracted up. I climbed back on to surer ground. 'She'll be pleased you've passed.'

We stopped beside a phone box. I told my mother I might be late. I wanted that clear. I wanted to be free. When I returned to the car John Rose stretched across to release the door and watched me clamber in. He had lit up a cigarette and now inhaled deeply. 'OK?'

'Fine.'

'What did you say?'

'That I'd be late.'

'What does that mean?'

I did not know what to say. I looked at him.

He laid his hand on my knee, opened and closed it, then gave me a pat. The engine was turning again. He revved the accelerator. 'Pubs and parties,' he said. His quick fingers thrust the car back into gear and we were off. 'Pubs and parties,' he repeated above the noise. 'That do?'

Ninian and I had not gone to pubs. Strictly speaking we were both under eighteen, law-abiding creatures, and unused to drink.

That evening we began at the Golf Tavern. He was locking the car when I turned and saw at the top of the grass slope the school I had now left for good. From here it looked more imposing than from any other aspect, very wide and tall, the red sandstone madder in this light for the sun slanted low across the Links. At this warm day's end the people putting played their shots in slow motion, toyed with the small red flags, dropped them back and ambled to the next tee. But my heart was jumping. By the pub entrance, the pavement was in shadow. I hugged my thin dress close and followed him inside.

It was dark and brown and smelled of beer spills. I felt male eyes swivel round and look me over. Small stained-glass windows glowed high up away to the back.

'Martini,' I said remembering a tip from Dorcas.

'Sweet?'

I nodded. There were prints and drawings round the walls all of antique golfing scenes.

'It's early.' He surveyed the other customers. 'No one's here yet.' He led me to a dim corner with a small round table.

'Are you meeting friends?' I was nervous.

He shrugged. 'This was one of our haunts when we were students.'

'How long ago was that?'

'Five years,' he said.

'Are you . . . almost thirty, then?'

'Are you a calculating young woman, Beatie?'

My fingertip circled the rim of the glass. 'What did you think I was?'

'An innocent young thing.'

I took the glass by the stem and held it up, ruby against the light. The sweetness swam in my throat. My expression did not change. 'Which I am,' I said.

'Of course.' He gave me one of his cool blue-eyed looks. Then he got a cigarette from a new pack and lit it up.

'I thought all doctors were to show a good example and stop smoking.'

'I am not exemplary, Beatie. I'd like that to be known before we go any further.'

'But you are now – what is it? – MRCP.'

'I'm still only human.'

Perhaps I did not know how to speak to men. With Ninian we had this whole framework of school and study as a reference, and a mutual innocence.

'You never smile. Do you know that?' I said. 'Why?'

'I discovered not smiling was more effective.'

'But "Smile", "Say please" is what we're taught! What do you mean by "more effective"?'

'I get what I want. More.'

'You do?'

'I do.' Without a smile. Then: 'Do you know, I meant to get a haircut.' His hand brushed his head, the fingers finding ends turning up at the back.

'There's a curl like a duck.' My finger went to touch it.

'A duck?' He smoothed it again. 'But they can't have noticed. All they saw was the white face. Fifty per cent of the doctors today come from India or Pakistan or Africa.'

He told me about the examinations then, about multiple

choice questions, short cases and long cases and how the patients themselves gave you clues sometimes but they could be wrong clues so you had to watch. The more he talked the more serious and clever, ambitious and professional he seemed.

'How long will you stay in Edinburgh this time?'

'I may get a locum job. May go on holiday. I don't take up my next hospital appointment for a couple of months.'

'Last time you just vanished.'

'I wasn't very proud of myself.'

'How are you related to Mrs Jamieson?'

'Mrs Jamieson is my mother's second cousin. Any more questions?'

'Where's your home?'

'Yours, at the moment.'

'Don't you have any . . . things? Where do your parents live?'

'My mother's the matron of a hospital in Bletchley.'

'Your father?'

'He died.'

'I'm sorry.'

He looked surprised. 'That was a long time ago. I was ten. I don't remember him much.'

'Was he a doctor?'

'What makes you think that?'

'Doctors and nurses, you know.'

'No. He was a salesman. Often away. My mother hated the idea of me doing anything like that. She was the one who wanted me to be a doctor.'

Here was proof again of how much better it was to have one's father simply dead. He appeared untroubled by the absence. Strange how my childhood instinct had been sound.

No old acquaintances turned up for John Rose at the Golf. On our way out he disappeared into the lavatory. I felt deserted, quite unreasonably. I hovered on the pavement then walked over and leaned against a low fence. People were still dotted about but a disgruntled chilliness had fallen on the Links.

In the Greyfriars Bobby Saturday night was abuzz already. He sat me in a corner on the red-buttoned plush. Above a long bar was a twinkling frieze of glasses, the bottles of spirits glowed behind, jewel bright. Willing barmaids pulled the pints, poured 'wee drams', gave fresh smiles above frothed blouses, turned to ring the money in the till.

Now I saw him look at other women too. When the door opened from the street his eyes went up then steered without a sign away. The seclusion of our corner was interrupted by some girls, the kind who must brave pubs on their own: bold, bosomy, loud, with back-combed hair, mascaraed eyes, short fat calves and high stiletto heels. They held cigarettes, blew smoke from the side of their mouths and took drags down deep as if their lives depended on it. One turned from hitching her buttock to our table top, gestured her request then bent low to John Rose for a light. She inhaled a first igniting puff with eyes hooded, lips pouting, potential for ecstasy displayed. He returned her look with an ungiving stare, shook the match, drank his Scotch.

'Has it changed much from your day then?' I knew he still wanted some soulmate to arrive. I feared he felt, after all, that I was not the best company for his celebration.

'*It* hasn't. No.'

'This is a medics pub, isn't it? Is that why these girls come in here? There is something about young doctors in Edinburgh. You'd think they were all young gods. Is it the special knowledge that you have, access to the mysteries?'

His eyes were mocking. 'You're getting too deep for me, Beatie.'

'You take responsibility.'

'Oh, I don't know about that . . .' He drew on his cigarette.

'Medical responsibility,' I tempered. 'I really like that about you.' I gave a faltering smile.

He blew cigarette smoke upwards and with narrowing eyes considered. Slowly he said, 'Shall I tell you what I like about you?'

I took my glass by the stem.

'Shall I tell you what I thought that first afternoon?'

I took a sip.

'You were the best thing I had seen in a long time. I return to the solid elegance of the Scottish capital, walk into my new digs, and open the door on a young woman admiring herself in the mirror. I thought I'd walked into a cinema, that I'd just missed the roar of MGM's lion. That dress, that stuff . . . what do you call it? What is it? Velvet? It's . . . I could hardly keep my hands off.'

The martini was dark as garnets.

His voice changed. 'Did you *know* how you looked?'

'It didn't fit. I couldn't do it up.'

He leaned closer, blocking off the curious eyes. He took a large swallow of whisky. 'You cannot pretend such innocence, my girl. If you do, someone will have to teach you a lesson. You cannot bare such an expanse of virgin breast, let that hair of yours fall—'

'Ssh!' I hissed. I had never heard breasts referred to in conversation by a man before, let alone my own. 'I just could not do the dress up at the back – that's all! And you barged in, remember! I did not invite you!'

He ignored my protest. His elbows were on the small table, his hands held upright, one twisting within the other. 'Your skin glows. Most British people have pinkish, grey flesh but yours glows.'

'You barged in!'

'You're angry too now. Look at you! You were very angry then. Bright spots burning in both cheeks.'

If he had smiled it would have been different; I might even have enjoyed the game he was playing.

'You don't know what that does to a man,' he went on, 'do you, Beatie?' His outer hand still held the cigarette. The ash fell from it as he took a breath and put it to his lips. 'Obviously not,' he murmured. 'Beatrice in red velvet.'

I frowned.

'Next time, of course, you were in school uniform. You had a boyfriend too.' He made it sound ludicrous. 'I dared not touch.'

He had moved me from anger to some kind of pity; I mistrusted that.

The people in the bar behind were a noisy blur. His eyes were on me. It was very shocking what he had done – laid me bare but then stepped back. I pressed my knees together. I wanted him to touch me. My tense fingers toyed with my empty glass. I wanted him to stop looking and to touch me.

'Is it to be the party then?' His voice was harsh.

I could hardly move. The alcohol which had made me angry now filled me with a heavy warmth. I did not want a party. I wanted to be somewhere dark along with him. I said: 'It's your celebration.' I had wanted this. My terror was that he would drop me for the schoolgirl I so recently had been.

The party was up a stair in Marchmont. I climbed behind him, his navy suit, white cuffs, shining black shoes wickedly smart. Our tread on the flinty stone of the steps sent bleak echoes upward. I tried to summon up my other, my more exciting Italian self. Make me so that he will want me (I told myself) . . . Make me so that he will show me . . . But at the top, standing separate from him, holding the wooden banister, my print dress crumpled, I felt empty. I was afraid the magic failed.

The flat belonged to former fellow students. 'Long time no see, John.' A boy face fringed by honey curls greeted us.

'Harvey, this is Beatie.' He pushed me, urgently, forward. 'Beatie. Harvey McDougall.'

'Beatie. Come away in, Beatie. Lucky I heard the bell, eh?' The hall was packed with bodies locked in various kinds of communication. I could not see over their heads. 'Booze in here,' pointing up past the crush to a section of orange ceiling and pulley slats.

'I need food,' I told John.

He pushed a path between the people. Glasses were lifted, lighted cigarettes jerked back. 'This child needs food,' he said. Mouths smiled, encouraging us through.

Against the fridge door leaned a colossus of a man with straight brown hair hanging over his eyes. 'Rose, old fellow! Congratulations. Hear you've succeeded where many a good man's failed. MRCP! Well . . . do we bow?' He lurched forward. 'Last time I saw you . . . was at the Golf. R'member. Day of the final results. The MBChB is good enough for me. Swore not to sit an exam ever again. But you're a glutton . . . Ronnie's got it too. Did ye hear? Ronnie Whatshisname . . .'

'I saw Ronnie. Ramsay, you mean. Ronnie Ramsay. Where're you hiding the booze then, Archie? This child needs food. Where's the food?'

He squinted at me. 'Ah!' he said. A shiny red-lipped smile. "S a new lady friend I see. Fill 'er up, Rose. Fill 'er up.'

'What are you doing these days, Archie?'

"Nsthetics.' His head was back, chin settling on his neck.

'That should suit you, Archie. Bored out of your mind ninety-nine per cent of the time.'

'Shit scared the rest.' He swallowed his beer.

'Shift over, Archie. Let's get at the fridge.'

'Food's there.' He indicated across the hall. 'Must – bladder's up to m' umbilicus. 'Scuse . . . Hey, what happened to that . . . whatsher name, eh? Wait!' He pushed off into the crush like a whale.

'This way, Beatie. Food's in the living room. You should learn to drink like the rest of us.'

But of course he had had other women: I knew that.

On the small table in the living room were only crumbs of bread, crusts of cheese and the dug remains of a half-pound of butter. 'You're too late.' A dainty woman spoke in a high voice. Her pregnancy was football size and jutted out from under the empire line of her blue Crimplene maternity dress. Her nose was pointed as a pixie's. 'Congratulations, John Rose. John?' She waited for his attention to return: a blonde on the other side of the room had caught his eye. 'You know Sister Palmer, John?'

His puzzlement. 'She was a simple Second Year, as I remember.'

'Oh, a lot of water's flowed under her bridge, I'll be bound. I hear you've joined the ranks of the would-be great.'

'Thanks, Jean. You too, I see.' He eyed the belly. 'Congratulations!'

'This is as far as I go: the carrying. I'm not the maternal kind, John. Harvey's to take paternity leave. I've told my boss I'll be back doing all my clinics just as soon as I've dropped it. That's the bit I have to do. His daddy's to share the rest.' She patted her bump.

The blonde was signalling now, pouting and making big round eyes.

'Jean's a doctor too, you see, Beatie.' He was prosaic – but his glance wavered. 'Do you think she'll change her tune when she's had it?'

'I don't know Jean . . .' I did not care. The blonde looked despondent.

'So you're Beatie. Well, no I won't, is the answer.'

'Harvey and Jean met when we were freshers.' The blonde was dimpling again. He must have returned her signal. How did he do it? Conduct a conversation with two of us and another with this third person across the room?

'We're a boring old married couple – that was not your style, was it – is it, John? You favour variety.'

'Now steady on, Jean! I—'

'I was surprised to hear you'd come back to do the Membership. I always imagined you as a GP in a some pleasant rural town like Harrogate or Ilkley, somewhere with a bit of style that allowed you the good things in life.'

'Which are?' He bent his ear while he kept his eyes on Sister Palmer.

'Country house. Horse in the stable. Ponies for the children. Home-grown veg. Raspberry canes. Handsome armful of wife.'

He reeled his attention in. 'Oh? Those are the good things?'

'Yorkshire: yes,' Jean insisted, on a mystery note. 'Come on. So sorry, dear. What was your name again? Food.'

He slipped away across the room. Jean pulled me in the opposite direction. I felt sick, made an excuse and found the bathroom. On the other side of its locked door I closed my eyes. Should I follow like a dog at his heels or could I try to brave it out: stand like a dignified wallflower or break into other people's conversations? That would not be easy. Out there everyone was paired off dancing to some smoochy jazz. Had I drunk too much? Someone banged on the door. I would have to get out of there.

When I came out he was in the hall wrapped in a clinch with Miss Palmer. He had taken off his jacket. Her blue eyelids made the same curve of bliss as her lips. Her chin rested on his shoulder. They did a quarter turn so that I saw how his hands massaged the full curve and weight of her bottom through the tight white dress. Too proud to hang around, I fled down the black well of the stair out into the street, breathing fast, into Strathearn Road, a long way to Salisbury but a straight line.

I burned in fury at being passed over.

My first party – God knows how many hundreds he had been to in similar Marchmont flats similarly brimming with nubile nurses, easy conquests compared to the virgin school-girl daughter of an uptight landlady living in the same street as your mother's second cousin, a child who could not help aspiring to a little intelligent personal enquiry. He had balked at that. There were complications already in his life. Something in Yorkshire. He wanted sex, though. Men like that did not go without it.

I strode along the road. A bus swept past. And a car, blue, but not his Triumph. He was in the arms of the blonde. I'd been dropped. How dare he! He was not going to get away with that. Not with me. I would not have it. Not again.

Such respectability reigned in these houses of dressed stone, fine doors, foot-square brass handle plates, quiet gardens, pollarded trees. Such containment. My head roared with the injustice of my lot. The solid street was a reproof. I could scream aloud and not a window give a chink.

A car passed, pale blue – his this time! It pulled to a stop some yards ahead.

But this was not the way I wanted it. I doubled back, ran over the road and up a lane.

It was called Lover's Loan. I knew it from the bus. I did not look behind, heard only the thud of my feet, whistle of my breath, saw only the leafy, diminishing perspective, the length of the long cemetery wall to run. Ninian and I could have strolled here. Like the tradition of St Valentine's Day, though, the name had been too obvious for us. Old ladies walking dogs used it but not in this charcoal dark. A stitch worked like a spike into my groin. At last I grasped the single bollard at the other end and emerged under the welcome streetlamp with no man behind . . . my hand leaving the crown of the post, soft thud of a cat landing, skimming off . . . nor any car or human on the street in front. I crossed one more block before turning east. Lighting-up time and the pavements and walls of The Grange were moving into dusk. I was sure of my direction, determined on my way.

The sodium haze made the pale cars parked round the crescent each give off the same weird hue. His Triumph was not there. I lurked like a thief on the opposite pavement. Only the high fanlight was dimly lit, 'Parklea' just discernible. The house looked blind. I slipped across, muffled the gate, slunk up the path. My key was ready in my hand but that nightmare moment caught me – the opening of the door, the feeling – flitting inside me, swooping like a bat tonight – of a man there ready to pounce.

I was in. I hesitated, then left the door unbolted. A cistern was running upstairs. On the landing I nodded to a lady who crossed my path in socks and striped pyjamas.

In my bed I waited for all sounds to settle. I switched the bedside lamp off and hoped sleep would come. The odour of warm plastic hung near my nose. I could remember my mother making those lampshades, oversewing the flesh-tint grainy stuff to wire frames, pushing a needle through punched holes . . . with the covers up to my chin, I lay listening. I tried counting sheep . . . Over a Dewar dyke. Hamish and his woolly. One, two . . . A car slowed outside. Reversed. I lay stiff. Key in the lock. It was him. His step on the stairs. I hardly breathed. My fists knotted up the covers. A tap at my door. Then a pause. He was opening it. I lay pretending sleep. He closed it again.

Responsible to that extent.

I followed him in my mind back to his room where he got into bed, lay his head on the pillow, closed his eyes. Was it Sister Palmer who offered herself to him again before sleep came? Or did he play my scene? Did he break in on me when I was ready in the velvet dress? Did he uncover me as I, lying still as a stone in my bed, now had him do . . . discover me as I rehearsed it now?

CHAPTER ELEVEN

'One kipper. Two bacon, egg, sausage, tomato, mushroom. One bacon, egg, sausage, tomato, no mushroom. One poached egg. One scrambled. Why do they all come down at once?'

'Write it down now, Beatie. Jeanette does that. Put the plates in the oven. Prick me four sausages. Whisk two eggs. Slice some mushrooms.'

In the dining room were three sets of guests, all polite, up early with polished faces, exchanging comments about the weather over their cornflakes. I was glad Jeanette, the secondary modern school-leaver who came in to help, spared me this now on the other days of the week.

Later, I sat with a coffee in my kitchen corner while my mother scraped the butter dishes.

'No sign of the doctor yet. I thought he'd be down for a decent breakfast.' She looked at me. 'How were the celebrations then?'

'I came home early. Didn't you hear? He took me to a horrid party?'

'Why horrid?'

'People.'

Last night he had opened my door, which mollified me – but it spoiled the rage I had wrought on my run home, a rage so fine, so clear, so strong it was like a honed blade.

Our other guests were moving on that day, which left John Rose. His departure must be soon. I did not want to miss him. I did not want to meet him either – yet. I told my mother I would skip lunch. She said it was salad anyway. She was easier now she was busy. She liked my growing independence. I heard her boast on the telephone to Cousin Jean about my job at the library and that, on the strength of my Highers, I had got a university place, early.

I walked round into the Queen's Park. The Crags were red, the sky a morning blue. I took to the steeper slope and began the climb up Arthur's Seat. My hands were pistons on my knees. I forced myself to the very top and only there I rested.

The city lay below, its roads contracted into crevices, stone gables, windows, chimneys, roofs jigsawed to one complicated mass. The landscape spread from this in some relief, the Firth of Forth lazy with the green fringe of Fife beyond. To the south rose the shoulders of the Pentlands and away towards the Borders there was Dewar nestling in the folded hills. I thought of Dorcas, how she hugged her cardigan across . . . But here, beneath me, was Dalkeith Road: our crescent curved down in from that. Life crinkled up so in the city. Life shrank so in one house. In Dewar Dorcas must be laughing at my stuffy ways – if she ever paused in her embrace of life to think of me at all.

He had driven after me last night, though. He had opened my door.

I breathed in deep of the sharp Edinburgh air. The sky was huge. I stretched my arms out to my fingertips. I came down from the summit, zigged and zagged, leaped, sought safe tussocks with the sureness of a goat, strode home.

'Is that you, Beatie? Dr Rose was asking for you.'

'When's he leaving?'

'Not tonight, at any rate. He's got a farewell at the Jamiesons'.'

When my mother went to church, I stole the dress. Then I poured myself a cup of sherry from the bottle in the dining room downstairs. 'Fill 'er up' – that was what the awful Archie had said.

We each of us stood by our bedroom doors.

'Where did you run off to?'

'Where did *you* go?' Tying my dressing gown, I moved to meet him. He wore the injured look. My chin went up.

'What have you been doing?'

'Having a bath.'

'I've been trying to catch you.'

'You could have "got me" last night.'

The line of his lips made no expression, but his eyes had a glint. He said, 'I forgot how it was with schoolgirls.'

I recoiled and slapped him.

He caught my wrists. 'So you're not a schoolgirl then?' The

blood was climbing to his cheek. 'Is that it?'

The touch I had longed for, had imagined, hurt. I tried to pull away. My wrists burned. 'A-ah!' I whipped my wet hair but he held me off. I shut my eyes. Felt confusion. Wailed.

Then he was not hurting. He was holding my wrists in his upturned palms. I felt a gentleness come through. I raised my head. There was no smile. But I was not for fighting any more. The doors on the landing were ranged round as if they were on watch.

'Do you know where we are?'

My sudden question puzzled him.

'This is no-man's-land,' I said.

'What?'

'This landing's no-man's-land.'

'No-man's-land?' He looked round the square of linoleum, the thin rug, the phalanx of plain doors. The expression he brought back to me had sorrow in it. 'I'm not your enemy,' he said.

He released me then. Ninian had sought the excellence of bare skin – John did not need that. It was not new to him. He touched through the stuff of my dressing gown. A vein coursed his temple. It was daylight still. I wanted dark.

There was a sudden sound below.

'My mother's—' Open-mouthed, the kiss that stopped my schoolgirl cry promised – as we heard her step in the passage to the kitchen, jigger of the kettle, squeal of the pulley wheeling down – more for me. I stepped back. 'Later,' I said. But my tongue hardly touched, lips hardly moved to close those consonants. 'Later.'

He pointed to his door, pointed from me to it again. There could be no doubt this time.

The eternity of a Scottish summer evening closed at last. Leaf and stone lost definition. Lamps came on. I pulled my green rep curtains and made a sepia snapshot of my room: the card table in the window corner perched with its line of books along the back, my bed, small chair and, on the next wall, the wardrobe waiting with its secret.

I had dealt with Mother, said I had a headache, needed an early night, which she wanted too she told me. Dr Rose would 'put the house to bed', she said. I hid a smile at that.

I tried to read but kept having to begin again at the same

place. The sherry was sweet and smooth. The book slipped from my knee.

The sound of the gate: my cue. My one-act, one-scene play.

I pulled the wardrobe door and swung my simple nakedness to view. Clothing was crude, really. Even the most fine, especially that, too complicated. Below the face – a body had its own poetry: two nipples, triangle of dark hair, parts most private, quite lovely where they were, on the tips and nestling, better placed than any silly button, dart or pleat; the line of thigh and arm, the mellow tone of skin more delicate than any fine brocade. I lay my hand between my breasts and felt the surface cool and the quick warmth under. I reached for the rail. Silk velvet was the one exception. I whipped it out, cast it across the bed, rivering, rich as brandy now.

Clad only in the helpful dark I left the mirror wide to watch and moved about my room . . . my toes flexed on the cord rug, my legs brushed the candlewick. I bent on an impulse to tug it up, to have its soft weight round me – but I stopped. I must leave the cover there. I must practise, must move in this unfamiliar nudity, be easy in it. Fear in me might make him quail: he was a doctor after all, and though lusty, had, I trusted, scruples.

I stood tall to receive the dress. When I was struggling to fasten the buttons I saw my reflection – lit, somehow, not by the velvet, my bright cheeks or my hair, but by something in my eyes.

This crossing of no-man's-land was the most daring yet. All the doors were closed except for his which reeled me in towards its crack of light. I slipped inside. He was standing on the green rug with his back to me, a gown hanging from his shoulders. There was a tumbler in his hand. On the table was an amber bottle.

I twisted the key. He turned. I was the other Beatrice tonight – Beatrice Bornati. His throat was bare when he drained the tumbler back. Had he not expected me? 'Will you . . .?' I showed him the back of my dress.

'I'm to help this time, am I?'

I bowed my head. I waited. But he did not play the game my way. Instead, he was pushing off the straps, pinning my arms, bringing me to the table.

Whisky scorched my throat. He drank too then made me drink again and while I did he stroked my neck. He took the drink away. I wanted his touch. But he was in no hurry. It was all done without a word for, though the doors were thick and my mother's had been heard to lock, sounds would alert her. His palms rounded on my shoulders and then, making me start, on my breasts. When I saw his pleasure I relaxed. I slid my fingers under his lapels, under his arms, round his back, leaned against his length, his warmth. The gown came off. He stood naked. I was close against the mystery. I pushed him back to see. Those male parts were stranger, larger, darker than I had ever thought. I touched an edge of curling hair. Then my hand retreated to the safety of his thigh. He waited. He came close. The lamp shone on his pale flank, shone on his strength tensing into the red of my dress. He guided me to touch him. I was too tender and he taught me. He seemed not so vulnerable there now. He was growing under my grasp. He did not know how strange he was to me. I dared not show it. I did not: the animal was taking over. His creature part was rising, a strong and warm familiar. He pushed at the velvet folds. There was soon nothing timid about my need which joined his and made me urge against him.

He undid the dress, had me turn, let the fabric slip away. I tried to stand as I had practised.

His rare smile was curiously inverted. 'You're not so innocent, my girl.' The words should have made me bolder but all my strength went into standing still uncovered there, all the power of my will to keep my hands from flying to cover the places. He took my breasts. I held my breath. I watched in awe how he touched the tips, felt his fingers rasp me there and wished he would stop, wished he would . . . I gasped: he had lit some magic fuse and I felt pleasure threading through the outrage and I came climbing out of it, ripe for him. My legs trembled. His penis had a purple fist. I swayed. He caught me, stepped inside the circle of the dress, moved between my legs, rudely reached for that spot I thought my most secret, and played there so softly, so specifically, that only my determination to have this expert ravish me could suppress the anger that he was so skilled. My jerking hands crept up his thighs. He swung me over to the bed.

Our bare bodies rode against each other. All sense became one sense, hot and melting. Yet there was this something . . . this . . . this Thou Shalt Not. But it was so good, the looseness, the . . . He slipped from me suddenly and I reached out for him to have him back, 'Don't . . .' I heard the small sound of rubber snap. What was that? Was that . . .?

'You're laughing . . . Are you laughing?' Tense across the dark.

I bit on my lip, reached out for him, said, 'Come, come back. Come back.' My chosen *ravisseur*: he had not failed. He covered me again. I pulled the crinkles of his hair, had his mouth close, and stretched against him. His knee slid up between my legs. No more pretending to the rhythm and the rub of love for this was it, the scarce-impeded penetration, and there was nothing more in this world that I wanted now he had brought me to it than this sharp—

He had taken back his mouthing kiss. He had arched away. I wriggled for him.

'You bitch! You little bitch!'

In the teeth of his curse, I clutched for his buttocks, the hardness of his thighs. With a sound of rage he fell on me again and, this time, forced his way. I wondered how he could come in me so deep.

There was not pleasure after that. There was the muscling strain. There was the smell of sweat. Then he had heaved himself off and lay apart – only a hand's breadth perhaps, but because he had turned his back, because he lay so still, so dead still, it was as far apart as if he lay in someone else's bed. I grew cold, reached for the blankets. Found them trapped by his weight. I put a hand on my belly. I felt not much different. Really. I curled away from him. Sticky. Just. Wasn't there more . . .? Dorc had a glow sometimes . . . somehow.

Later I wrenched the sheet out from under his straight, slumbering body: small price to pay for ravishment, attention to such detail. With the dress draped round, the linen bundled underneath my arm, scarlet and white, I crossed no-man's-land like a camp follower. Returning with a clean sheet from my bed, I roused him, the man favoured by me, favoured too by my mother – she had granted him the Egyptian cotton kept just for us (guests usually got brushed nylon). To his – I suspected – deliberately deep, drowsy impatience, I replaced it. Next morning I would put the stained sheet to soak in the back kitchen and say my period had come.

I woke, aware of John Rose standing by my bed. He would not have administered that one dry kiss if I had not made a first involuntary nervous move. Old Spice was stale now on his cheek. 'Dropped off, didn't I, Beatie?' he whispered. Of course the way he said it told me. 'Last night . . . I didn't know. I thought your boyfriend . . .'

I was watching his face.

His hand loomed. He lifted my hair and held a hank looped across his finger. Then he let it drop.

'I have to leave.'

'I know.'

'I can't . . .'

The milk van whined outside.

'I have a wife and child, you see. Not a very happy arrangement . . . but there I am.'

The sound stopped.

'In Yorkshire?'

'How did you know?'

'And Sister Palmer?'

'Who?'

'That nurse the other night.'

'What about her?'

'Does she know too?'

He shrugged. 'Christ. God knows . . .' Impatient with me. 'But you . . . because . . . So that when I go you don't . . .'

'Don't what?'

'You know . . .'

'Tell my mother?'

'Not that, no.'

'Tell Mrs Jamieson?'

'So that you don't . . . you know. Hope.'

'I won't hope.' My lips were muted in a line.

'You are beautiful.'

How could I have seen in him aristocratic looks?

He laid two fingers on my brow, very medical, like taking a pulse. 'Are you all right?'

'I'll survive,' I said. He had the pinched features of a jockey. I humped the covers up and turned away. There was a gap where the curtains did not meet that showed a drab stripe of morning. My words came out clipped, 'I'd get out if I were you. Before my mother finds you here.'

He left the house soon after. From my upstairs window I saw him going with a case. I watched him stow it in the boot of the car and then return for another. Finally, on the front step, he struck a match – put another notch on the cross-hatching by the bell – and lit a cigarette. I watched him inhale deeply. Then he screwed his eyes against the sun and sallied out. He gave 'good morning' to Jeanette, arriving at the gate. From behind my green curtain I observed him turn his head to check the pert shift of her bottom in its mini skirt.

CHAPTER TWELVE

The gleam in Guthrie's eye was like the sun on water. His winter weariness had gone. 'You're pale, my Beatrice.'

'I've been cooped up,' I said. A Morris Traveller had long since replaced the little van. It smelled of petrol. My feet perched on a tool bag. I wound the window down and leaned my arm along the rim. The air was clean as a knife.

'Gosh, Guthrie . . . This feels so good.'

'You're different.'

'My hair's longer.'

'That's not what I meant.'

'It is like prison, having a job. That's why I gave it up. It's worse than school.'

'You stood it longer than Dorcas. It's hardly a job she's got here, but she's turned out good at the cooking.'

'I thought there was a cook.'

'Mrs Caird goes along, yes. Her husband's the gardener. But Mr Ingram likes more . . . *je ne sais quoi*. Dorcas provides that. Perhaps Deirdre taught her. You and she are there for the flair – and the bedmaking, tattie peeling, the laying of tables.' He gave a laugh.

We passed between the gates.

'Is Mrs Drummond at home?'

'Resting? No, no. That's not her style. No. She's got work: the Festival's coming. She's up in Edinburgh rehearsing this week. She's in *The Burdies*, a Doric version of a play by Aristophanes called *The Birds*. Just the kind of thing the Festival people like to inflict on foreign visitors.'

'Won't we Scots understand it?'

He looked doubtful.

'And Bornati *is* expected?'

'Tomorrow.'

We ducked under evergreens beneath the hill and emerged

from the shadow into a sunlight which, slicing across the drive, the low rail, the park beyond, smiled on our arrival at the house.

There was no sign of life. No car was parked where I remembered seeing them, their noses pointing outward, in the snow. The stone façade basked apricot in the sun. Stirring up the gravel, Guthrie drove on round the side. To our right was a sunken tennis court, net lazily adroop, one post askew, but quite verdant, innocent of markings. An ornate roller leaned at ease in a far corner.

We parked at the back and got out. White sheets were slung on lines across a courtyard. Beyond stood an open door.

'I knew you'd come!' Dorcas beamed at me, in her fair health lovely as an advert for Your Daily Pinta. There was flour on her face and on her butcher's apron. Around her were the white walls and scrubbed wood of a big old kitchen. Green apples ranged beside a mixing bowl.

'Where's Mrs Caird?' asked Guthrie.

'Toddled home. Back at five to see to dinner. Everyone left this morning. It's calm again.'

'A good day for Beatie's first,' Guthrie said.

'Perfect.'

'Did Mr Ingram *mind* me coming?'

'Oh no. It helps *me*! Hamish is getting difficult. Those musicians we had staying here were an awful trial. And they suddenly let their hair down last night so I didn't get off to see him in the evening even. I must go over this afternoon. He'll be livid.' Guthrie's moustache bristled. Dorcas did not notice. She went on: 'Mr Ingram asked what you were like, Beat.'

'And you said?'

'I said you were tall and dark, broody, with hang-ups.'

'You meanie! You didn't! What hang-ups?'

'*A* hang-up,' she corrected herself. 'If he knew who you actually were—'

'Quiet, girl,' warned Guthrie. 'Walls have ears.'

'He'd pack me off at once. Yes. Ssh, Dorc.' I met her eyes and made my point. 'And how "broody"?'

'You sit on things like a hen, not moving off to show what you're hatching – that broody.'

I felt chastened by her view of me but could hardly deny it. A slatted greengrocer's box was on the floor. 'What are these?'

'Aubergines.'

'Beautiful. And?'

'And courgettes. Peppers, salad, garlic, onions.'

'I know onions!' But I did not know such onions – so big, and as coppery as the timpani hired for the school concert. I fingered a papery plait of garlic. 'You don't see vegetables like this in my mum's kitchen.'

'Mr Ingram has them sent from town. That's for ratatouille,' Dorcas explained.

'Ratat— what's that? What's this?' A green oil.

'Virgin olive,' she explained.

'The first pressing.' Guthrie was suddenly close, his explanation warm in my ear. 'Smell it when it's heated, when it reaches the point of fragrance . . .'

'I didn't know cooking could be so . . . It's . . .' Well, was this food talk?

'Not decent?' quizzed Guthrie with his eyebrows lifted. 'Dorcas has always been precocious that way.' Guthrie cracked off a celery stick. 'Does it appeal then, *this* kind of cookery. Could you do it, Beatie?'

'If Dorcas can I can.' I played his game. He kept his eyes on me, chewing the green stalk: the mischief was exciting. To my friend I said: 'Is this apple pies?'

'Yes. Trad. But I like making them. Hey! See the sun.'

'Should I change? I brought a black dress. Do we wear frilly caps and aprons?'

'Of course we don't. We're to look pretty. As appetising as the food. That's what Mr Ingram says. There!' Her hands brought the dough together in the wide ironstone bowl, the bluish tinge of the white inside like the inside of her wrists. 'Into the fridge with it for an hour. Out to the sun with us.' She had turned to me yet she addressed her father. 'I'll look after her now, Dad.'

'You mean: Go away.'

'Yes. Go away, Dad.'

He had been about to say something. To me he said, 'Your case, madam.'

I blushed. 'Oh, Guthrie. Thanks.' He turned without a word. His abrupt departure flustered me. 'See you later,' I said in a rush.

Dorcas, from her cleaning up, said, 'You like my dad, don't you, Beat?'

He was the best dad I know. (And he flirted with me.) But I

said, 'What's he doing at the moment?'

'Scottish Water Colourists. He's exhibiting in that. Not *your* Dad's league!' She wrung the neck of the tap. 'Nice reliable red dot stuff. Always a proper show. He's got half a dozen in that this year. But it won't set the world on fire.'

'*My* father's stuff will?' I was cautious.

'What do *you* think?'

'I think it's monstrous. I hate it. Have you seen it, Dorc?'

'Just the photos in that article.'

'Those give no idea. The pieces are huge abstracts. I sneaked a look down at the Fruitmarket Gallery. Horrid. They'll think they're horrid.'

'Who?'

'Edinburgh. People. My mother.'

'They're feeardy cats. I thought she hated art. They don't count anyway. It's the dealers that count. There's big money to be made in art now. Great big money, Dad says. Cheese scone?' She unfolded a tea-cloth parcel and buttered us two each. With a mug of coffee, we were all set for the tennis court.

We slithered down the sunniest bank, nested our mugs in the tussocks and started on the scones.

'Lucky we've got it all to ourselves, isn't it?'

Around us green growth exuded the smell of sap. Insects bumbled amongst the grasses. We were sitting in a park within the bounds of hills. Trees made a dark accent at a pleasing distance. The mass of the house was a warm mid-tone. My head felt clear. Edinburgh, with its warren of cramped emotions, was far behind.

Beside me, her voice low-pitched and earnest, Dorcas enumerated my sins. 'You *were* avoiding me on Prize-giving Day. You *had* heard from him. You were *lying* that day I visited you in your library.'

'It's not *my* library!'

'Beatie!' Her mouth was stern.

I took a deep breath. 'Yes,' I confessed. 'Yes. Yes. OK.'

'Spit it out then.'

'He wrote saying he didn't want to know me and I wasn't to try to get in touch again.'

Dorcas's eyes narrowed. She swallowed her coffee with a gulp and stayed motionless.

'All fathers are not like your dad, Dorc.'

'I am learning that.' Her mouth was thin and grim, a way I

had never seen it. 'What did you do?' she asked.

'You know what I did. At first. I obeyed him, really, I suppose.'

'But you changed your mind?'

'Because here I am: yes.'

'Why did you change your mind?' Dorcas began to fiddle with her clothes. 'Why?' She pulled off her shirt. It was a man's – was it Hamish's, or Guthrie's? Her bra was black, the kind with wired undercups and lace that Rita Hayworth might have worn – but not shown. 'Why?' she repeated. It was too glamorous for out here among the clover. But Dorcas, instinct ever true, returned gracefully to nature by unhooking the sophisticated contraption and tweaking it off. She cast it aside. Her full breasts swung. She lay back, her top half softly pink and utterly voluptuous, on the sappy bed of the tennis-court slope. Her hair, so silky fine, seemed spun of the same stuff as belonged there, thistle silk and the tassels of the grass. 'You do this too. Come on, Beatie.' She toed her sandals off heel by heel. 'Now's your chance. No one's about.'

I clutched my coffee mug.

'Why?' She was asking that again. Her nipples were pale, like marshmallows. 'Why do you want to see him now?'

'Are you sure no cars mean no people?'

'Usually.'

'Sure?'

'I can't see any.'

'Your eyes are shut!'

'Warm. It's warm! Feel it. Feel it, Beat. Come on.' She patted the grass invitingly beside her. She was now unzipping her skirt and, still blind, pushing it down over her hips, casting it aside. 'Whole hog. Come on. Feel the warmth. The sun on you.' Her panties were skimpy. Her thumbs nudged the side seams to an essential brevity. 'Go on, Beatie. Let the sun get to you.'

'But we've to *work*!'

'I've *been* working.' A sweet smile lay on her closed face. 'Now I'm tanning my tits.'

'For Hamish?'

She answered with a wider smile.

'You're sure then?'

'Sure.'

I pulled my short-sleeved jumper above my head.

'Bra too.' Dorcas opened one eye.

That too.

She was smiling a lopsided smile. 'You've certainly grown a lot since last we did anything like this.' There was a pleasing wonder in her tone. 'You're all lovely . . . all golden.' Slowly, she closed her eye. I lay back. I had never felt so bare. Bare to the blue above. More bare, though still with a skirt, than I had been when naked for John Rose. But the sun's warmth began to bake away the strangeness. 'Now. Tell me.' Dorcas was waiting.

My tale moved into a key appropriate to our garb, or lack of it.

'I changed my mind. I didn't want any more what-ifs and if-onlys. People waste their lives doing that, you know – people who spend their time in libraries and who work in libraries . . . like Agnes. I could have done that. They asked me was I interested in a career in a library. A career? A sentence to fiction for life.'

Dorcas gave an appreciative shudder. Her eyes stayed shut. She was waiting. The next bit of my story was not so easy.

'Remember . . . I told you we had a doctor staying and you said "Watch out"? Well, I did. I . . .' There was something so relaxed about her mouth and her neck that I demanded suddenly: 'Are you listening to me? Have you fallen asl—'

Her lips curved to a bow. 'Spit it out, Beat. Give. Come on.'

How had she described Hamish – a boyfriend, a man-friend? John Rose was not really any kind of friend.

'He and I had an affair,' I said; it sounded cold and over.

'I knew something was different.' Her voice was deep and soft. 'You can't hide things from me, not things like that.' Dreamily, she said, 'That sun's really hot. You should put cream on your nipples.'

'Should I?'

'I read in a magazine: they burn.'

'You read a lot of magazines, don't you?'

'You can pick up useful tips, here and there, you know, among the rubbish.'

'My . . . nipples . . . look different from yours.'

'Tawny. It must be your Italian blood.'

'Have you got cream on?'

'It isn't my first time. Which reminds me – what's his name? What's he like, this man of yours?'

I plucked at the grass stems, considering how best to describe John Rose. 'He's not tall but he's . . . neat. He has fine hands with long fingers . . .'

There was a new sound, a sound above the drone of insects and the odd sheep bleat, an approaching sound. I sat up, arm over breast, and immediately lay down.

'What is it?' from drowsy Dorcas.

'There's a car coming.'

'Rats,' she said. She stretched for her clothes. With her legs and arching back she propelled herself to the foot of the slope. I copied her but my skirt was still on and as I slid I got into my jumper. I stuffed my bra into a pocket.

'They can't see us,' Dorcas said. 'Quick. I haven't a pocket. Put mine in – where's mine?' We turned. It was the black squiggle at the top of the bank. 'Oh heck! Well, I'll fetch it later. What timing! It could be the butcher. Is it a van, this car?'

'No, it's a black taxi.'

'What?' She did her zip and got to her feet. 'But we're miles from town. Who the . . .?' She watched its approach, its official shiny black, purring along under the wellingtonias. 'Who would do a thing like that – come twenty miles by taxi?' Her eyes narrowed. 'Unless it's . . . I know!' She turned to me: 'An American. I bet it's an American.'

My heart stopped. I wailed: 'Tomorrow! But Guthrie said tomorrow!'

'Come on.' She tugged me by the hand. I stumbled after her across the lush deeps of the old lawn court. She tried to run but her breasts bobbed. Over her shoulder, she gasped, 'God! I need a bra, don't you?' She slowed: 'Hamish gave me that one. Glam, isn't it?'

'Yes. Ouch!' There were nettles in the shady end. We scrambled up the far bank but came to the top with caution. The taxi swept round to the front. A man got out.

'People don't do this to Mr Ingram,' Dorcas muttered, 'usually.' The man was now standing with his bag and looking about. I stepped back. 'Wait here. I'll see to it.' I crossed my arms. She strolled over.

'Hi,' I heard him say.

Dorcas put out her hand.

'This Dewar House? Is Mr Jimmy Ingram here?'

I saw Dorcas shake her head, then nod and make a gesture towards the steps.

Like a film on rewind, I let myself slide back down the bank below their line of vision.

I lay spread-eagled and pressed my hands and heels into the slope till I felt the cold soil under. I heard the taxi tyres score the drive, then the sound of their voices again – my friend's light and high, and his voice. 'Bornati . . .' then 'London' and 'hassle', hissily.

But I had not needed that proof. I knew him from the way he stood there, tall – not towering as I had thought – but familiar in the inclination of the head, tilt of the mouth, the wide swing of his arm reaching for the grip. There was something odd about his hair. It was flat against his head where it should have been springy. One long finger held the loop of a tweed jacket not needed this hot noon and slung over a big shoulder. His clothes were a monotone, grey open-necked shirt and trousers. An outdoor strength bulged in the muscles of his tanned forearm, the kind of strength you saw in a labourer. I thought: iron man.

When they were inside, I slunk away. In the back courtyard the sheets stretched across and made a sun-starched maze to confound me, so blinding-white that the kitchen was dark after.

I saw stars. My case was there where Guthrie left it. But I stood in limbo. I did not know where to go with it or what to do. At the sound of a footstep I got behind the door. It was Dorcas.

'Beatie, Beatie. It is him! Wow! Quick!' Her cheeks were flushed. 'Switch the kettle on. He wants a coffee. Look. I must get a bra. This feels . . . I *know* he noticed. X-ray eyes, that man! Sorry but . . . you know! Your bag. Yes. Follow me. I'll show you where we are.'

We went out the back way. She stroked the sheets. 'They're dry already. Everything's happening so fast today! Be an angel. Bring them in later. I haven't time.'

'Why?'

'I told you: Hamish.'

'When d'you go?' We were across the yard.

'This bit of the house has the billiard room in it. We're above that. The maids' dormitory, I call it. We've our own entrance.' She opened a green door. 'Easy access for the grooms.'

'When?' I repeated.

'What?'

'When do you go to see Hamish?'

'Now. Soon as we've done the pies.'

'You can't!' My sandals slapped after her up the wooden stair.

'I can't not! Now, be quick!'

It was a very long attic room with a low-eaved ceiling. She couldn't go! How could she go? How could she leave me on my own so soon? I dumped my bag on my bed, which was the one at the far end. There was such a big gap between us, Dorc was making a play of waving at me to emphasise the distance. Then she rummaged in her chest of drawers. I was just afraid. I did want to be alone with him. It was what I had always wanted. But I was afraid.

'Where can I hang my dresses, Dorc?'

'There's a row of wee hooks, see? Between the chests. I'll get you hangers.' But she was still chugging drawers open and shut.

Immediately above my bed was a small skylight. Perhaps I could watch the stars through that at night. The neat pile on the mattress must be my bedlinen.

'Damn! You haven't any glam bras, have you, Beat?'

I shook my head. I had one nice set of black but the bra was nothing like the one she'd taken off. Besides, I knew Dorc's way with clothes.

She sighed loudly and clipped on some old thing. Someone was just going to have to lump it she said. I pulled my own bra from my pocket and slowly put it on.

Back in our kitchen quarters she was businesslike. She took Bornati coffee. I peeled and cored the apples.

'You'll have to face him sometime,' she said, rolling out her pastry brusquely. 'He's bossy. He paws the ground a bit. Said he wanted to climb hills. I told him some of the walks.'

'So he's going out?'

'Perhaps.'

'Which walks?'

'The Rings. The Big Farm.'

'Do you *have* to see Hamish? Do stay with me. Please, Dorc. Since he's come.'

'I can't. You don't know Hamish. He'll *kill* me if I don't. Are the apples ready? He's handsome, your dad.'

' "Dad"? My "dad"? Please. Don't call him that!'

'Did you see his hair? Did you see it was a wee ponytail?' She wrinkled her nose. 'I didn't. Not at first.' She looked at me. 'What's wrong? You're so touchy.' She shrugged. 'Funny, for a man, though, isn't it? You get off with anything if you're an artist.'

It *was* funny for a man but it annoyed me to hear her say it. I cut leaf shapes out of pastry scraps. Dorcas said they were good, I could be a sculptor – which was not so funny – and I was going to be fine, she could tell, as a cook. Just as the pies went in the oven, a bell buzzed. She spun and glared up at a box on the wall. On its black glass face were rows of dials, a red needle still dancing in one. 'The drawing room. It's him.' She washed her hands and went to see.

When she came back she said, 'He wanted to use the phone. Now if he does that again and I'm still out you'll have to go. The drawing room's to the right diagonally across the hall. His bedroom is at the top of the stairs, first left.'

'I won't need his bedroom.'

'Room service "is expected", as Mr Ingram puts it. ' "Is expected",' she repeated. Her green eyes met mine. 'You're free, of course, too – when the jobs are done. It's thirty minutes more for the pies.'

We wheeled her bicycle out past the pegged sheets. Mounting, she balanced there, leg cocked, toe on the top pedal, ready for off. I saw her bite her lip. Then she squared her shoulders and wiggled her hips. On the handlebars her little chrome bell winked. Did they 'do it' in the afternoon? To me, sunlight was the wrong light for sex. The cottage was dark inside, of course. I could not see a man resist an armful of Dorcas after a day on the hill and a can of McEwan's Export. How had Hamish come by that black lace bra? His truculent Highland ways in a lingerie shop defied imagination. Mail order. It must have been. That said something else . . . What did he have her do in it: pose? Or what? With a thrumming ping she coasted off down the track and turned to meet the tarmac drive. The cheeks of her bottom were rounder than before. Dorcas was putting on weight. Since John Rose I had lost it.

I was alone in the house with my father.

The walls were feet thick but, afraid he heard me, I put the utensils back with care. Still the sounds I made wiping up and washing the chopping boards seemed loud. I kept imagining . . . my head kept turning to the bell box on the wall. But the red needles did not twitch. Outside I folded the sheets into a laundry basket. The linen was warm, smelled of the open and of pine resin. With the courtyard empty, I had a clear view of the far end and a path which appeared to lead through the trees and up the hill. Was that one of the walks? Bornati could have gone there already, silently; I remembered thick soft-soled shoes.

The smell of baking apple pies met me at the kitchen door. I put the basket down inside. What if he was hungry? He might come . . . But he would buzz first. This anxiety was silly. He might well be out. It was so beautiful out. The sun slanted across the floor. His first time back in Scotland, weary of 'hassle', of cities . . . he must have gone out. He would be halfway up to the top already. That was where I wanted to be. I wanted out too. But I still had duties.

One glimpse I had had. And he of me, hiding behind Dorcas. My glimpse had been seeing, though, because I knew what I was looking at. His had been ignorant.

I checked the coast was clear, went by the back, kept to the shadow of the house, dashed out across the tennis court and recovered Dorc's black bra. I stuffed it into the top corner of one of the chests, hers, I thought. I made up my bed. Dorc had forgotten the hangers after all. I rearranged her clothes and took two for myself to hang up my yellow mini dress and black Moygashel. I hoped the creases would come out. I sat on my bed to change to gym shoes – my sandals were slippery for exploring. I hesitated: staying in the kitchen would be safer. Or in here even.

Then I heard the noise, the knocking. It came from somewhere underneath. It was not a real knock. I remembered what Dorcas said and recognised the sound of billiards. It must be him, my father, playing, in the room below. He was the only other person here. I pictured him angled over the baize table, the cue, javelin-like, pointing. So he had not gone out at all. There was the smack of a sudden shot and then between pauses, some long, some short, the clip and knock and knock again. The sound was lazy yet had a reserve of compacted violence about it. Its very desultoriness, however, persuaded me he would be involved down there for hours. In American movies didn't they spend whole nights in pool halls? It was a relief. It was as if the game had captured him and left me free. I could go quickly up the hill and not be afraid of an encounter. I left quietly as I could.

I took the uphill path. Round me were tall plants whose sparse leaves hid fruits like raspberries: they were soft, ripe to the touch – yet oddly pale, albino with orange globules. Dorcas would have eaten them. I did not risk it. The valley lay below already. When I emerged above the trees it was clear this track was the one I had hoped for, the one which lead to the hilltop called The Rings. I looked down on the roofs of the Big House. No car had arrived nor was there a sign of anyone about.

The slope ahead was twitching with rabbits. Though I approached in peace and alone, their heads went up. Sun shone through their transparent ears. They ran off, white scuts bobbing. I remembered Dorcas's tale of a wild night, of Jilly-Willy and company, Hamish too, with shotguns, driving their Land Rovers the length of the valley field with the headlamps on, firing at them. They had killed hundreds, she said. *Hundreds*. She relished it as she relished the rat killing.

On the last shoulder I stopped for breath. The final climb was steep. I changed my approach from head-on to zigzag and reached a glimpse of the next valley. It was shallow compared to ours. Beasts grazed.

The ground opened out on top. Sky was all about me. Birds complained, piping a bleak falling note. The sun shone still but a wind blew, chilling my bare arms. I reached the first of the concentric circles, a double ditch and bank, three feet high at most, fifty yards across. There were gaps which could be entrance ways. Man had come here for safety in ancient times. I was surprised to see cowpats: there must be an easier way up. Perhaps it was from the east or from the other valley. It was not so remote, then, as it felt. I stood looking south towards the Borders. Guthrie said there were other hill forts on other summits, that beacons had been lit to warn of trouble.

The wind was tiresome. I went back into the circle. I dropped to my knees and already the wind was less. I lay flat on my back. Everything went quiet. Faint clouds moved high across the blue. Beside my face were the stems of grasses, bleached, bending, magnifying themselves as I looked at them. With such infinity of sky I lost perspective. Strapped to the back of the world I felt it turn.

★ ★ ★

138

A man was standing by my head. Wind steered against his limbs, which were stout as pillars. His grey clothes filled behind him like a sail. He was a colossus staring out over hills. But I felt cold in his shadow. His shadow froze me. Froze me stiff as iron. I wanted to struggle up, to run. I was afraid in case he moved and turned, in case he looked down and his eyes met mine.

I was reaching for the lid of the kettle when the bell buzzed. I jumped. It went on buzzing. Which was normal, I told myself. It was normal for a bell to ring for the maid in the kitchen. Quite normal. More than I was at that moment. I slapped my hand to my forehead: hot as a furnace . . . even after the splashings of water. Was I still beetroot? I peered into the chrome kettle. No comfort in that distortion. But I had been imagining things. The bell box told me he was in Bedroom 3. Bedroom 3: not scouring hilltops. He was here in the house, had been all the time. Playing billiards. Another buzz. The red needle jiggled: Bedroom 3. My hand shook, clattering the lid on the kettle. I clipped it home. Calm down. What a stupid thing, that rush downhill, that sliding descent! Just. Calm. Down. This had to be. It's what I wanted: feared but wanted. 'At the top of the staircase, first left' – I had not forgotten.

On the landing I knocked.

'Come in.'

The room had a blue carpet.

'Good girl,' he said. His back was to me. He lay propped on one elbow on the far side of a wide bed. He was on the telephone. Without looking round he said, 'Get me a Scotch, would you? Scotch on the rocks. A glass. The bottle. Ice.' It was like a film. I was there, but I was not really there. It was such a moment of truth that I was hardly conscious I was part of it. I realised he was waving at me. His hand . . . it was dismissal. Yes . . . Good girl. Get me . . .

I backed out of the room.

Downstairs I managed to find the glass and the ice cubes and eventually discovered the whisky was kept in a black cabinet in the drawing room. It was all modern in there, oil paintings, abstracts in wild colours on white walls, black floors. Bedroom 3: blue and mahogany. Blue the colour of infinity. A white corner, the pillow behind his head. He must have dragged the cover down when he settled to phone. His face was indented, craggy as a mountain, more maleness there than I had been prepared to meet, lips rather full. He had hardly looked round. He had not seen me. Such arrogance . . . Me with my too big beating heart. He had confused me, yet denied me. I put the drink things together on a tray.

I knocked.

'Come in.'

'Good – Hey! Hi! Who are you?'

I said, 'The maid.' And, since I had no black dress and white cap, I half shrugged. Almost, anyway, I meant.

He saw me this time. 'Where's the other girl, the blonde?' His hair had grey in it. Drawn so tight back, it made him like a thirties slicker. His attention was particular. His head, neck, eyes held quite still.

I had lost my voice. I stared.

His body was long under the covers; the big hands lay easily on the cuffed sheet. He pressed his head back into the pillow. His eyelids shuttered.

He was seeing 'not the blonde'. Fright made my voice sound much too shrill.

'She . . . she sees her boyfriend in the afternoons.' I put the tray down smartly on a stool.

He was still watching me.

'And what's . . .?' he said.

I was rooted to the spot.

'And what's . . .?' The hand was beckoning to me now, wanting me to come closer. It reached back to plump the pillow.

I turned and rushed from the room. 'And what's . . .?' His words went churning in my head. 'And what's . . .?'

What's your name?

Your game?

He would have to get out of bed to fetch the drink himself.

CHAPTER THIRTEEN

'That Dorcas is a rare girl, don't you think?'

'Dorcas is great.' I looked at the clock above the bell box. She was also late.

'My! But aren't they bonnie apple pies!' Mrs Caird had arrived that afternoon wheezy from her exertions on the bicycle. 'You'll be the friend then – Beatie, is it?' Her hair was grey wool and her fat cheeks were veined like dunking apples. She dumped a bag by the sink. I was to start with them, they were Epicures, just lifted, the skins slipped off a treat.

When Dorcas did arrive she looked flushed. She was strangely quiet and avoided my look. I kept glancing across expecting to exchange a smile but got no response. I asked how Hamish was.

'Don't speak to me about Hamish,' she hissed, then, loudly, as if to a deaf person: 'I'll set for dinner, shall I, Mrs C?'

'Do, dear. That's the ticket.' She fetched steaks from the fridge, slapped them on a plate and ground pepper over them. Mrs Caird was businesslike with bloody meat.

Mr Ingram and the American Gentleman, as the cook called him, ate alone that evening with Dorcas doing the serving, then they drove off in the car. Mrs Caird left the moment the steaks were on the plates. I had to stay in the kitchen the whole time and ended doing the washing-up. Dorcas took the tea towel.

'I climbed up to The Rings,' I told her.

'Energetic.'

'And when I got down here again he buzzed.'

'So?' She carried the dry plates to the end of the counter. 'Did you tell him?'

'What?'

'Who you are, of course!'

'I can't tell him. You know that. What's wrong with you?'

141

'I'd tell him – what's wrong with *you*?'

'It could jigger the whole thing. He might run off before the opening . . . And Guthrie—'

'To hell with Guthrie! Whose father is he? I'd have faced him as soon as I clapped eyes—'

'He's *my* father – *yes*!' I confronted her. 'And I'd appreciate it if you'd let me do this *my* way.'

'But you're such a scaredy cat! Out with it! Why don't you? Go to his room. Tell him. Go tonight.'

I tipped the basin up.

Dorcas banged a cupboard door. 'It's not *so wonderful*! So you're his daughter – so what? What d'you think he'll do? Buy you a cashmere twinset and a string of pearls!' She stood there bristling. 'Well?'

I wiped the sink. 'I might even settle for that, you know, Dorcas – now you mention it.' I propped the mop behind the taps. 'But I don't know he's the type, do you? Where do these glasses go?'

She stomped out.

She was not in our attic room when I went up later. Perhaps she had gone back to Hamish's or down to see Guthrie. I did not sense either of these moves would help. She had been rather odd and very mean. Hamish must have done something.

Through the skylight the fir trees drew closer. The sun was almost down. I heard a pheasant shriek its clackity alarm. Had Dorcas frightened it? For a moment I thought I heard the billiard balls. I was not such a scaredy cat as she thought, though. Go to his room, she said. Go. Hadn't I done just that, as bidden? And, yes, I had taken fright. But I had not been frightened to go to John Rose. Look how I had gone and done just that . . . and everything else.

I stretched an arm between my thighs and tensed. But it was better to be here alone in the iron bed below the eaves away from Edinburgh and the looming images: his small jockey features that I now disliked, his curls my fingers itched to knot and tug and hurt. I knew sex now. The bare bones at least. It was over. They say you feel a woman, but I felt a fool. I shut my part in it away. But now I saw sex everywhere, like a new coinage minted, even in this man who was my father. My own mother seemed of a generation quite beyond it: he, on the contrary, had passion in him still. Despite my instinct – which had been to run, condemn, suppress – a feeling was stirring in me now that could not help admiring that.

Another pheasant squawked. Dorcas whipped them up, these men. I watched how she did it. Hamish would be alone in his cottage brooding by the small black grate. The flick of his crow's wing of a forelock, the look in his cold Celtic eye – they flashed like the blade of a knife. In Edinburgh I had pushed my days along like a woman shuffling behind a pram. Out here in the valley, life darted at you from all sides. There was an urgency about it. What had Hamish done to Dorcas? Go. Just go, she said, so impatient with me suddenly. But I would wait. The exhibition opened in two days. So – not tonight, or the next, but the next . . .

I turned on my side. It was not a time for prayers. I knew what my father looked like now, had him here at last, familiar but a stranger, huskier than I thought, not the aesthete, the artist with the long white hands whose fingers sensed the grain, but a harder man, a man of the fiery furnace, a welder, cindery. The eyes were not brown animal eyes as I had made them in my dreams: they were set in deep, hidden almost, they were so guarded. He was returning from another country, after all.

I woke suddenly from a dream of billiard balls and sap-filled Durex, grey giants and woods with trees from whose branches hung glossy aubergines that were deadly poison to the touch. I was locked in a wooden turret being besieged by hordes, half-animal half-man, which clawed and battered at the boards.

Something was scratching somewhere. I got out of bed. Pulling on my sweater, I hurried past a sleeping Dorcas, went down the stairs and opened the door at the foot. In the middle of the courtyard was a Border collie standing with her ears pricked watching me. Beyond, a man was disappearing round the corner of the kitchen wing. The dog's flagged tail waved from side to side. It looked like Midge or Madge. At a low whistle the dog sprang away. I recognised the figure now: it was Hamish.

Back upstairs I checked my watch. Perhaps it was not too early. 'Dorcas?' I shook her gently. 'Dorc?' She lay humped up under the faded cotton cover. Only one forearm and her pale hair showed. This struck me that morning – it was so different from the spread abandon of her body when I shared her bed. She was fast asleep. I roused her.

'Whasse time?'

'Six.'

'Sleep,' she moaned. 'Seven. Wake me . . . seven.'

'Mr Bruno Bornati, sculptor extraordinary, has not come down this morning, Mr Bornati having been last observed lurking in Rose Street after the pubs shut. Apparently he and Mr Ingram came home separately in the wee small hours. Mr Ingram will see you now, Miss Brown.' Dorcas served me this once she had served breakfast.

I took my apron off.

'They won't be around today, James says, but we've to get food ready for tomorrow night.'

Mr Ingram sat at table, but stood up to shake me by the hand. He had pale smoothed hair, a freshly laundered look. His boyish jaw was rounded. He wore a pink shirt, navy tie with white spots and a handkerchief to match tucked at the breast of a navy blazer.

He asked if I had cooked the scrambled eggs and congratulated me, saying I had passed the test. His voice was Scottish, just. He had nice teeth when he smiled. And strange golden eyes. He called me by my whole name, Miss Beatie Brown, like they do in Victorian novels, and it sounded quaint. He said they were very glad to have me to help, that great things were expected of us the night after next when some VIPs were coming to dinner. He paused and looked at me for a moment. Then he said I looked a bit exotic for a name like Brown. I assured him quickly I was Scottish. He went on to give details about the following night and said he had told Dorcas that if we had everything prepared ahead for the late buffet supper he had put in Mrs Caird's capable hands, and she was happy, we two could go in with the Drummonds in their car to the opening of Bornati's show – 'if you want to, of course. Are you interested in that kind of thing?'

I assured him I was very interested.

'Are you going to art school like Dorcas?' he asked.

'No. Yes. Well . . . university, actually.'

He looked puzzled. No wonder. What *was* this I was saying? I knew I could be good at art but I had not chosen that. I was to read for a Master of Arts degree at the University of Edinburgh. I should do well enough for Honours then I would become a teacher in a good grammar school and be safe, wear a black gown over my tailored costume, maybe run a Mini Minor, have my holidays in Skye and a pension at the end of it.

'Well, Beatie. I hope when the work's done you'll join in the celebrations. The more the merrier. Glad rags too.' He gave a nod. 'You've got some, I suppose?'

'How glad?' I asked him.

'Glad as you like. If you're stuck, ask Deirdre. She's a dresser-upper. She'll help.'

'I don't think she's around at the moment.'

'Ah, no. But she's coming. You'll see. Deirdre doesn't miss a party.'

There was no sunbathing on the tennis court for us that day. Mrs Caird went wheezing round the kitchen, opening cupboard doors and shutting them again, lifting out pots, bowls, baking sheets and setting them round the worktops. She said in her experience if you cooked you had to be well organised. It was pheasants for that night and salmon for the party. Her husband had plucked the game and was bringing them up with the vegetables. 'Thank goodness I've got you both, my dears,' she added, beaming round at us. 'The American Gentleman enjoyed your apple pie, Dorcas.'

'A man of lusty appetite,' said Dorcas with a glinty look in my direction.

Pudding that evening was to be another pie and meringues with raspberries. Dorcas was to prepare her fancy French dish with the purple things, unconventional, but tasty with the birds.

Mr Caird arrived and lowered his load of produce to the kitchen floor. Removing his tweed bunnet, he stroked his walnut cheeks with a rather comical mixture of pride and regret. The box overflowed with an earthy oniony abundance: waxy potatoes, carrots, mounds of pea pods, tomatoes, cucumber, lettuce, plums. New leeks and frills of parsley were tucked down between the blue flesh of the plucked birds, tawny tails included.

I was set to podding the peas. Dorcas took a broad-bladed kitchen knife and attacked her exotic vegetables. Once cut, the purple aubergines revealed their pale dry flesh.

'Gosh!' I said.

'What?'

'I thought they would be dark inside, or horrible. They looked too beautiful – they had to be sinister.'

'See! You're frightened of your own shadow.'

I detached myself from this prickly friend. There was a patch of sunlight in the yard. I made a newspaper parcel of peas, took a bowl, a low stool and went outside.

I had hardly sat down when suddenly Bornati was there, standing looking over at me from the pine wood. I pushed open the bundle on my lap. He and Mr Ingram should have been on the Edinburgh road. I started shelling the peas but I knew the soft-soled shoes approached.

He stretched his arm out: it was brown, coated with dark hairs. 'May I?' His voice came twanging like a double bass. He took a pod. I nudged a waiting line and sent peas jumping into the bowl. 'Mm.' Eating his, he stretched for another. 'I haven't seen that done for years.' When he said 'years' he sounded Scottish.

'I haven't done it since I was a wee girl either,' I looked up at him then away quickly, 'in fact.'

I felt his eyes on my bowed head. A wee girl. Either. Since. In fact. My primness simpered in reverberation round the yard.

He spoke again: 'I haven't heard it said like that for years.'

I pursed my lips. His hand was in my lap again making the pea pods squeak as he groped for a fat one.

'You'd better watch, eating them raw. You'll get a pain.'

' "A pain?" ' He mocked my flat rising Edinburgh note. Again I pursed my lips. He stooped, tilted his head, to see my face.

I shut up as best I could. 'Smooth as a madonna,' Guthrie had said once. But a muscle twitched beside my mouth and I knew, despite my efforts, there was transparence there. You can only completely cover up when you are old and wiser and your skin is thick and pouched and pocked like leather.

Making the peas dart into the bowl, my fingers spidered in agitation while my hand expanded wide as a cinema screen with the awareness of him close. His corduroys were creased across in ridges at the crotch. His shirt was soft, velour, grey, touchable. His belt looked new, so shiny black, its silver buckle at my eye level. Italians liked good leather. I had always wanted a real leather belt or a leather bag. His hand came for another pea pod. My hand. His hand again. He had no inkling that this arm of mine had come from him, this thumb at the green seam, this index finger making spurt this sudden row of baby peas. Kin skin. Mine olive too but city-pale compared to his, so weathered. We touched once. I felt brushed by silky hairs.

Guthrie, another wearer of the crepe-soled shoe, came suddenly upon this domestic moment.

'Bruno Bornati!' I ducked under his outstretched hand and tried to buck away but the stool jammed on the cobbles and I was stuck there under his greeting. 'Drummond's the name. Guthrie Drummond.'

Bornati drew back to see better. The groove from nose to fleshy lips lengthened. He hesitated. Then his hand went out.

'Drummond. Do I . . . Perhaps I . . .?'

'It was a long while ago. Back in student days in Edinburgh.'

Under a black brow Bornati struggled to remember.

'My lady wife might be the more familiar. I think you knew her . . . Deirdre. Deirdre Drummond. Of theatrical bent . . .'

Now Bornati's eyes went crinkling up. 'Huh! Yes. Sure. I do. I do – Deirdre!' He looked to the ground for a moment. Not seeing Guthrie's Viking-blue gaze made it easier to recall the wife. 'I do remember Deirdre. Deirdre was smallish, darkish—'

'Correct.'

'Say! And you're . . .?'

'Still married,' Guthrie nodded, one quizzical eyebrow hitched.

Bornati's teeth were very white. I did not like the way his lips turned down at the corners. There was a sneer there. 'Am I to meet the lady?'

'She's up staying in our Edinburgh flat at the moment. She's in a play next week. Rehearsals are keeping her in town. But she knows you're coming. She'll get down here for the big shindig after the opening of the show tomorrow evening.'

There was a pause.

Guthrie asked if he was pleased with how his pieces looked in The Fruitmarket.

'I haven't been in to see them yet. That's where Jimmy and I are going now.'

'The new gallery has caused a stir.'

'And my work?'

Guthrie said of course it was not what Edinburgh folk were

used to. He confessed he was curious himself. He had seen the occasional piece featured and reviewed but photographs were not the same as being there, sharing the same space.

'You know something about sculpture then?'

'Oh – but I am an artist.'

I was piggy-in-the-middle underneath. I felt sorry for Guthrie. 'A *good* artist,' I said with emphasis, indignant that he had not been remembered when he had remembered Bornati.

But Guthrie dismissed my interjection with a small explosive sound. He looked over towards the kitchen door. 'Here's my daughter,' he said. As he spoke he placed his hand on my head, which misled the sculptor whose eyes fell on me expectantly.

Guthrie explained that his daughter was the fair one emerging from the kitchen.

I twisted under the gentle pressure of his hand which I had taken as some kind of compensatory blessing but now read as a warning. 'This dark young lady is her friend – but I thought you two had met. When I arrived you seemed in cahoots over the pea pods.'

I tossed my head to indicate we had not been in cahoots.

'Don't you know each other yet?' To me he said, 'Haven't you introduced yourself?' Guthrie's eyes did not match his easy smile: lighthouse glints stretched across deep water.

'The young lady works here: I know that.' Bornati's hands were in his pockets. I had been more interesting to him the afternoon before when we two were alone and he had woken from a nap. Guthrie said, 'Meet Beatie, Beatie Brown.'

There was hardly a clue in my name now, with the Catholic Mary gone and the Bornati too. So I gave him one bold, clear look. 'I . . .' That was Dorcas's footstep behind me. 'I *half* introduced myself,' I said, making sure Dorcas heard it. 'Yes. I'm Beatie. Dorcas and I are here to help, aren't we? But you know Dorcas.'

'Sure. Dorcas showed me round. Hi, Dorcas. Hi there, Beatie.' Bornati nodded drily.

Mr Ingram appeared from the billiard-room wing. The men strolled off.

'You've taken it. Where is it?' Dorcas demanded.

They had disappeared through the doorway.

'Where is it?'

My father's brief dismissive look was in my mind. They had

all three simply walked away from us with their grey-trousered unsmiling self-importance.

'Where's that bloody bra?' She pinched my arm.

'Ouch!' I slapped her off. She still confronted me. 'Didn't you fetch it from the tennis court?'

She shook her head. 'There's no sign of it.'

'A dog? A fox? A prowler?'

'I thought *you'd* fetched it! I was *sure* you'd fetch it.'

I stared her back.

She rounded on me, her eyes flashing. 'Why didn't you? A good friend would have thought of that – when I had to see Hamish. A good friend would have remembered!'

' "Had to see Hamish"! Really? I'm not your nursemaid, Dorcas. Anyway, it's too silly.'

'I have to find it.'

'For Hamish?'

'Or he'll *kill* me.'

' "Kill" you?' I said in scorn. 'He loves you, doesn't he?'

'He'll kill me.'

'Can't it be in the wash? Can't you say I borrowed it?'

'You don't understand.'

I wrapped the empty pea pods in the newspaper. Then I said: 'Perhaps he found it himself. He was round here with one of the dogs this morning.'

'You didn't tell me.'

'It was very early. You wouldn't wake.'

'Why didn't you tell me?'

I stood up. 'Last night you said not to breathe his name again. You confuse me. You really do. You're—' But I did not know what she was, she was so awful suddenly. I was not going to tell her I had fetched the thing after all – not now! The newspaper parcel split then and all the pods fell out. I got down and scrabbled for the shells. I missed so many I felt blind and the knobs of the cobbles dug into my knees. And it was then I heard the sound of car tyres sweeping the gravel at the front and going away down the drive. You could not win, somehow.

In Bornati's room the sheet was flung wide back over the bundled covers. When I came close it was all written with wrinkles. 'Be quick,' we had been told by Mrs Caird. 'Just make the beds and flick the duster. I need you back down here.' I placed my cleaning things beside the telephone.

I was not going to be afraid.

My father had slept here. That was where his head had pressed the pillow. I put my hand to it and imagined the place warm. His knees, his legs, his toes had left these rumples on the sheet. All night long. Had he given one thought to the girl who had dumped his whisky tray and fled? Had he given a thought to the blonde? But he was mine. This was my right. This act. This bedmaking. Stretching both arms wide I pulled the linen tight as a drum, ran my hands over the expanse where he had lain, and sweeping, sweeping, the arc getting wider, stretched far across and deep, my body bending closer, feeling the flat of my palms were in need, in need of the flat of my cheek to help. I touched it with my face and caught his scent. I smelled his smell, the sweat of his pores, oil of his hair. I lay like that, face down, arms reaching for the pillows, pulling them close, embracing them like warm creatures, and in their yielding caught him close.

'Get up!' A flex slapped. 'Up! Get up!' Dorcas jammed a plug into a socket by the door.

I did not move. Then, but only slowly, I backed my body off the bed and, mute, with heavy arms, obeyed . . . but, reluctant to leave the place I had stolen I stopped even then with my back to her, kneeling, and smoothed over my own traces. I was not a very guilty thief. I took a deep breath. Dorcas was holding hers.

She came at me suddenly, wrenching a surge of bedclothes. 'Get up! You haven't even started here. I've done the other room. Get up! Finish the bed, can't you! Dust!' Back at the door again, she kicked the switch and the Hoover roared into life.

CHAPTER FOURTEEN

With Bornati in the house I felt joined to him as if I were on the other end of a taut string. The moment the car vanished down the drive I was at a loss. Dorcas always saw her father's absence as freedom. But this absence tangled me in thought.

Later in the morning, Guthrie stuck his head round the kitchen door, and, with a sidelong look at Dorcas, said had I seen the studio yet, what about us going up there later, he'd give us a lesson in something new.

'What could be new?' said Dorcas. I could have pushed her bored expression into the soup pot.

'Will you, Beatrice?'

Dorcas disappeared anyway after lunch. I did not search for her and would not have begged, this time, for her to stay with me. I was to see the studio. I was to be instructed. I went because I thought it would bring me closer to Bornati. I went alone, up the grand staircase and round to the left down the uncarpeted passage and through double doors.

The three windows, tall and many-paned, admitted an all-seeing but indifferent light. The room had once been an elegant one: its size and height, the plaster moulding on the ceiling and the cornice were signs of that. But the floorboards were stripped bare now and the furniture was a random hotchpotch of uprights: plinths, easels, a chaise longue shrouded in a brown cloth, a screen, a bench. Bald sky looked in on the objects on a table – brushes sprouting from pots, jars jammed with rulers, pencils, palette knives and tools – and found its own reflection, clouded, in the mirror above the marble fireplace. I crossed the room. Leaning my knees against a sill I looked down on a new view of the tennis court. In contrast to the green outside, the studio was grey. I felt a vague unease. Or was it disappointment? There was no sign the

151

room had been in use for ages. I blew fluff off the brushes, described a face on the slope of a drawing board then wiped it out. Perhaps I had expected an assault upon my senses: a ravishment by colour, some knock-out blow by the bizarre.

What lesson had Guthrie planned? There were the familiar still-life props: fabric remnants (gingham, ticking, plush), a stone jug with dried umbellifers, a pewter plate. I scoured round for other signs and found black wax driblets, a patch of fine white dust, a chisel with a flared head, plaster gone solid in a pouring pan, a mallet hairy as a coconut. With a jolt I saw the vice. It was fixed on a corner bench with its jaws clenched tight. I had last seen one like that when I was five, seen the knobbed handle from underneath, knew its cold smoothness. I had the feeling suddenly, a feeling that rose up and exploded high in my chest – enough to make me catch my breath – of having made a real arrival at last.

Guthrie entered with a gnomic smile. 'Been waiting long?' he asked.

'Dorc wouldn't come.'

'No? Well . . .' he shrugged, 'I hardly expected it.'

'She has got something on her mind, you know.'

'Oh, I know. I know . . . ever since she ploughed Hamish up out of the turnip field she's had something on her mind.'

'Something more, I mean. Something about—'

He presented his face, a mask, so close to mine that I recoiled. His hair was as fine and fair as Dorcas's. He put a forefinger to my lips. 'Don't!' he said. 'Do not tell me any more. I came here to teach you something, something exciting – and that's what we are going to do. Banish reality, the humdrum, lost causes. Escape – to Art! I may have a promising pupil in you. I am looking forward to the next few hours. I do not want to be reminded of . . . that. This is between you and me and this stuff.' He strode across and pulled the lid off a plastic bucket.

Inside was a drab mass.

'Clay. We are going to model heads.'

He delved and touched it with the full palm of his hand. 'Perfect. I think perfect. But we'll see.'

From a cupboard he brought out a wooden stand with wire loops bulb-shaped at the top. He told me it was an armature.

'I know. I've read about how to sculpt.'

'Because you wanted to try?'

'Because I wanted to understand Bornati.'

He gave me one of his quizzical sad looks. I thought he had another question for me but he changed his mind. He told me this was a special armature called a head peg. He produced one with a head already modelled on it, wrapped in a wet cloth.

'Who's that?'

'Guess.'

I had an awful suspicion.

'A girl like you . . . I made it up. The hair's still to be done. It's for demonstration purposes. I'll work on it for half an hour using the real you as my model – which should improve things. After that you can do a head by yourself.'

We were standing side by side with these things in front of us on a table. He put his arm round my shoulders and gave me a hug. 'You and I, my Beatrice, shall get on well.'

You get warmth and strength from such a hug. I let myself lean on him just a little. 'I thought we did already.'

'We do, we do. But this is new territory, isn't it?'

'I've been in an art room before.'

'At McGillivray's High? Dear girl! Rows of desks ranged round a rubber plant. Sugar paper that dissolves to mud. Miss Whist with her Arts and Crafty half-drop repeats, her ogees and her "or whatevers".'

But that lady had been unlike any other Edinburgh teacher.

'You must put that institution behind you, Beatrice. You're grown now. Free. You'll not find a studio like this again till you get inside an art school.'

'But I'm not going to art school, Guthrie. I'm going to university, don't you remember?'

'I've seen sketches by you. You could draw as well as Dorcas when you were twelve. What's happened? I don't accept that. You can change.'

'It's not so easy. My mother—'

'It's never easy. But there's always a way if you're deter-mined. Don't you draw now? Ever?'

'For fun, only – Oh, Guthrie, I would have turned out quite differently if *you*'d been *my* dad!'

He looked at me, a light burning in his eye. Then he said, 'Work can be fun. Even work you do for a living. I know this is anathema to one of your Calvinistic upbringing but life need not be one long, teeth-gritting, self-denying penance. Here!' He flung some kind of cloth at me. 'Well, don't just stare at it.

It's your artist's smock, Beatrice. An old shirt of mine.'

I put it on happily and rolled the sleeves up.

Guthrie arranged plinths for us so that our head pegs were at a comfortable working height. My armature needed a better base board. He had me screw it on. 'Clay is very heavy. You know how heavy your head feels sometimes. A clay head is twice as heavy.' He corrected me sharply when I let the screwdriver go squint and spoiled the notch on the head of the screw. His hand squeezed mine. He demonstrated the exact angle and pressure that must be used. 'Screw and driver make the one line, the one driving shaft,' he said. 'A tool is not a wooden spoon. Hasn't anyone told you that? It's a precision instrument. Sculptors have to learn techniques. How are you going to control an arc welder?'

I rubbed my hand. 'What's that?'

'An electric welder.'

'I never said I wanted to use an arc welder. Will Bornati use that?'

'Yes, yes.' He was impatient now. 'Bornati'll use one.' Guthrie now had the lump of clay out of its tub and on a tray where he cut it in half with a wire and put one lump back and closed the lid. 'That's yours. Always seal it away to keep it moist and workable. In the air it dries out.' He lifted the tray and put it on the upturned tea chest between our plinths. 'Help me now. Feel it. Put your hands on it.

'Clammy.'

'Experiment. Be bold.'

I pushed into it, nudged, pummelled, pulled it away. The nearest thing was kneading pastry. Clay wanted to be handled. It mellowed. Kept the imprint of my thumb, thumb nail, knuckle, poking pinky. I could cut it, smooth, tease . . . no; then a bit dropped off.

I took both hands to it and went heeling in and at the same time clenched out great lumps which I moved against, squeezed, drew forth and then slapped back to stick on the main mass. I cupped out egg shapes, stippled them, nipped them, with my nails striated them like hair. If I urged both hands up I made a climbing lily form, or was it a trunk, or could I make it grow . . .? Something made me look at Guthrie. Crinkles had come to the corners of his eyes. 'Guthrie, it's wonderful. You do some too.'

He needed me to be his model. He engineered a dais and sat

me on a chair on top. He lifted my hair from underneath and let it fall down my back then he said it would have to go up. Since I did not have a ribbon I twisted my hair on top and tied it with itself. It stayed like that if I kept still.

'Find a fixed point now and keep your eye on it.'

'Am I not to talk?'

'As little as possible. I have something nice for you at the end . . . if you're good.'

'I'm always good.'

'Are you?'

John Rose betrayed me with a blush. Guthrie showed his teeth in an odd smile.

'You make it look easy. And you're a painter.'

'I like heads. There's one I did of Deirdre up on our wardrobe in disgrace . . . And of you-know-who as a child. Sometimes I give a lesson to a class. Now. Would you undo the top button and push your blouse open? I need your collar-bones. At the back too . . . push it down. More. That's it. I need the nape of your sweet young neck.'

'Sweet young neck' – that was just Guthrie being Guthrie. Generously, I granted him artistic licence.

Besides one's hands, he told me, you could use modelling tools – wooden spatulas and looped wires. He wanted me to use only hands to get the feel of it.

'This stuff's primordial mud,' he said, 'eroded volcanic rock that's been washed down into riverbeds and absorbed organic matter and minerals and oxides. It looks dead, doesn't it? But it's living. If I keep it moist the organisms in here go on decaying and the clay gets more and more plastic – malleable, that is. See how big the cranium is.' His hand curved with each finger extended to show what he meant. 'And at the back. I began with a smaller mass than I now have. Always start that way. I make these pellets of clay and stick them on. You can leave them rough, impressionistic – you know Rodin, you've seen an Epstein – or you can smooth them. It's up to you. You can even let the clay get "leather hard" and then carve it. It's a matter of preference, of style. But your hair . . .' he breathed, slurring the sibilants '. . . so lovely like that, threatening to fall – a luscious weighty mass!' He lost himself applying the clay, moulding, tooling it. I seemed not to exist for him. 'Ah!' He stood back. 'It's coming now. But—' he checked himself. 'Do you know you have the same forehead as your father? Exactly.

And that notch – see how my thumb can hollow it – that notch in the inside corner of the eye that defines the bridge of the nose and then swoops out, under, out along the line of the eyebrow. It's strange he doesn't see the likeness.' He shot me a shocked glance.

'Is it? Oh, I can't tell either. Perhaps . . . if my eyes were dark like real Italian girls he might . . .'

'He must be blind. And look – now! When you frown!'

'I can't look! Do I frown? Does he?'

'You're doing it now. And he does – the wrath of all the gods is there!'

'Guthrie, you do exaggerate!'

'What?'

'You're ridiculous.'

'Impassioned, maybe: not ridiculous.' His thumbs drew together down the line of my throat. 'Passioned. Passionate. *Patior* . . .'

'What? That's Latin, isn't it?'

'*Passus sum*: I suffer . . . Steady! Hey, eyes front.' He impressed the clay, dismissing me again in his preoccupation. But what had he said? How could a sculptor be blind? 'That frown of yours – it's there again. Look! This is no good. I need a week, a month of afternoons of you sitting for me. I should never have begun without you. But its purpose was to show you how, quickly. So . . . Down you get! I'll wash my hands. Have a look, if you like.'

He went over to the sink in the corner.

The lavish hair had improved the head but it was not impressive as a likeness. The eye sockets were too deep. The lips protruded, ugly in their exaggeration. They made me think suddenly of a moment in that very first weekend. Unlike the balmy September Saturday the Sunday had begun wet. I remember standing by the window watching rain teeming down, glossing the rhododendrons and blackening the earth. Suddenly I had turned, sensing Guthrie's eyes on me. I caught the furtive movement of his hand and knew that I – and not the park outside – had been the subject of his sketch. 'Beatrice, smooth-browed as a madonna,' he had said. He saw my anger. 'But what a delicious curve under your mouth – as if you had just popped in a cherry – a dark and juicy cherry.' Under the fair hairs of his moustache his own lip had glistened.

'It's not good. I know that,' he said now. 'It's a demonstration model only . . . but do go round the back: the back is as important. Girls get so obsessed with faces.'

We arranged the things for me then. I stood with my clay, armature and my model, Guthrie, suddenly solemn sitting on the raised chair where I had been. I walked about and eyed and measured the volume of his head. Then I set to, quickly, with pawfuls of clay to build up the mass.

Guthrie's brow was high with the fine hair springing back in wings. Under this fairness the skin of his scalp was tanned smooth, thin over the bone. The physical identification I made through the tips of my fingers with the structure of his skull was an exciting intimacy. I worked hard. We had breaks. Guthrie offered advice. From talk of mass we turned to talk of rhythm. I worked on the different planes, cut angles, exaggerated the ear, the overhang of the brow, the way his beard made a short, downward jut, a line which I followed again in the back of the neck. There were echoes too from cheek bones to moustache. It did not seem like work. Guthrie was generous, uncomplaining. Hours passed. His lips at rest were sensuous. I had always noticed that. Why did he not shave the beard off? Was there a weakness? He was not fat. There was no receding jaw. 'He thinks he's an artist,' Dorcas always said, to explain, but she did not like how it felt she said. When he tried to kiss her, she wriggled away because it was scratchy. But Deirdre kissed him, beard and all. She would kiss anything, of course: she was a kissing kind of person, Dorcas said.

'Dorc should be here doing this with me, Guthrie. Has she ever worked in clay?'

'Coil pots p'raps.'

'I wonder what she'll do with her art.'

Guthrie went pointedly mute. The silence that fell on the studio made a great deal more that I had meant to of my remark. Into my mind came Dorc and Hamish romping on the sheepskins.

'What do you make of Bornati?' I asked suddenly.

'He hasn't changed. He's a ruthless bugger.'

My hands went up. 'What?' They were like claws clarted with the clay. 'That's a bit strong, isn't it?' Guthrie sat sphinx-like. 'Self-absorbed,' I conceded. 'OK.'

'And lecherous.'

My mouth opened to protest again but I shut it silently. I had seen Bornati watching Dorcas too. And I had felt the lingering

look fall upon my own body. 'Has a roving eye . . . perhaps?' I
put in.

'Arrogant.'

'*Amour propre*?'

'He's a pseud, a laid-back bumptious American.'

'He's British!'

'What do you mean? He hates this country. His return
flight's booked first thing the day after tomorrow. He can't get
away quick enough. That's the difference, isn't it, dear Beatrice? That's the difficulty you have viewing the world through
those rose-tinted, would-be-daughterly spectacles of yours.'

I brushed my hand across.

'You've smudged your cheek.'

'I'm stopping.'

'What!'

The clay was sticking to my fingers.

'See!' he roared. He stood up on the dais shaking his fist at
me. Veins rivered up his forehead. 'See! Don't you see,
Beatrice, he's just done it again? He's stopping you. All the
time he's stopping you doing things: being yourself. What are
you up to?'

The shirt buttons were very small and difficult.

'Don't take that off!'

I tore at them.

'Beatrice!' It was a roar.

'Have your shirt! And your primordial mud!' I ripped the
garment off, and flung it. It landed on the head and hung
there.

He stared at it. His colour was high, his hands made fists.
Then he leaped to the floor and stormed across. He circled the
box. A sleeve of the shirt hung from the thing like a limp
proboscis. He reached out. Gently he removed the offending
cloth. And it was just a clay head, the first one I had ever tried
and it looked now as if someone had given it a slap in the face.
'Why did you do that? Why?' His face was red and angry close
to mine.

'I don't know, do I? I don't *know*! I *don't*! I *don't*!'

'Because I criticised your father: that was why, wasn't it?
Wasn't it?'

'I DON'T KNOW!' I screamed.

'You don't know. You don't know. You don't know . . .'

I hated him the way he stood there.

He gripped my upper arm and pulled me round and made me look.

'This head is good. Best I've seen done by a student for the first time.' He walked me round the tea chest. 'You are good. It's good. Already, it is a fine head. Vigorous.' I shrank from this praise. He was trying to make me look at him. 'There's more than meets the eye in you . . . and quite a lot does meet my eye, believe me. He makes me so mad, your father—' Here Guthrie broke off. I tugged to get away. He mastered his emotion, ignored my tugging, still kept a hold of my wrist. He scrutinised the surface of the clay. 'The damage is superficial, thank goodness. You'll go on with it now, won't you?'

Only slowly did I lift my eyes.

He let me go but brought his arm around, 'Come,' and on my shoulder, that weight, that warmth. 'Come. Come over here.' He took me over to the sink. Even turned on the tap. Handed me the soap. Helped me. 'Wash yourself. I'll wet the cloths and cover what we've done.'

'Guthrie, wait!' And in a small voice: 'I will go on with it.'

'I want to talk to you first,' he said.

We sat at the same window, side-on upon the big low sill but our backs against the folded shutters. Our eyes did not meet at first. His glance was on the wrapped clay heads. Mine turned on the tennis court below. I held a glass. A suspicion had begun to creep around my mind. 'Did you come up and plant that bottle earlier?'

'No. There is usually wine in that cupboard. It's known.'

'By whom?'

'By those on whom Jimmy Ingram is pleased to place his patronage.'

'You?'

He smiled. 'I am one. He owes me a favour or two. I can use the studio for instance. So could Dorcas – if . . . And, yes, of course house guests like your famous fa—'

'What does he owe you?'

'That's not any of your business.'

I guessed it was something to do with Deirdre.

We sat there in silence for a little. I could not trust myself to speak. Things came out wrong this afternoon. I resented Guthrie's criticism of Bornati. And he had built me up and knocked me down almost simultaneously. For some minutes I could not look him in the eye. Anyone seeing us from below would read this as a heart to heart. But I was not sure what it was. I was not comfortable.

Guthrie, maestro, could control the trickiest orchestration. Words came from his lips, so low, so deliberate, they were like the commiseration of doves: 'What will you do? What will you do? What will you do now, Beatrice? When will you tell him who you really are?'

The wine was red. It would have been so good this: having wine together after such a revelatory session in the studio if I had not had such a difficult task ahead. But the wine gave me strength. I kept my eyes on the glass. 'Tomorrow night. When we get back here.'

'You'll do it then?'

'I'll tell him, yes. Then it doesn't matter if he runs away, does it? Everyone else will have got their money's worth: the dealers, agents or whatever, Ingram.'

'Beatrice . . . why do you bother about everybody else? You're more important.'

'But *you* said, didn't you . . .' I thumbed the glass. 'It was you who said months back get him over for the opening and *then* tell him. It was you who set this up for me.'

'I have, haven't I? I've brought you to this point. You are still what's most important.' He chinked his glass against mine. I had to look. His eyes were that greenish-blue, water frozen over snow. I turned away again at once.

'You!' Out it came, this accusation, from nowhere. 'You want something out of this too, don't you? You—'

'Me?' His hand smote his shirt front, his eyes sparked with incredulous appeal. 'What do you think I want?' I looked away. I could not say. But I did not retract. 'Beatrice? What will I get out of it?'

Leaning back against the shutter I felt my twined hair uncoil. 'You tell me,' I said.

'I want what you want – your father to recognise you.'

'Recognise! I want him to love me, Guthrie!'

A low sunbeam shot straight into his fair-lashed eye. ' "But to see her, was to love her",' he added softly, 'to quote the words of our Immortal Bard . . . Och, lassie, I wish my own daughter needed me or wanted my advice as much as you need and want your father. But listen, how can you honestly say you don't care if he runs away afterwards?'

'Did I?'

'You did.'

Pushing myself to the brink of this game of consequences I confessed it was not what I longed for at all. I did not dream it could end like that. When he did at last meet me, he would never, never just go off. After. Never. Surely. I leaned away, my forehead up against the window pane. 'Why don't they play tennis? Fix that stupid post and play? Look. There's Dorc.'

'Keep her out of it.'

'I can't help it if she walks right across my line of vision. She's looking for something.'

'Beatrice, look at me. *We* were talking about *you*.' He touched my wrist to make the point.

'Oh, Guthrie. I wish you were my father. I do. I really do. I'm sorry Dorcas is so mean, so offhand with you – but it's because she's got you; you've always been there, to flop back on like an old armchair.'

'Is that all?'

'It's a huge thing, to be there. Her mother never is . . . if you'll forgive me saying that. And you offer much more too. You open up opportunities – look at this afternoon for me. You teach. You warn. You care!'

He patted my arm. He was looking past me out to where Dorcas, searching, mooned disconsolately up and down the tennis-court slope. The expression in his eyes was distant.

'Thank you for this afternoon.' The clay heads when I jerked my glance in their direction looked like props in some absurd play. I turned. I wanted to bring his thoughts back to me. 'Thank you for the wine too. Thank you for making me face all this. For making me grow up.'

The blue Viking look came round at last.

'You took that on yourself, Beatrice. And you'll be brave. I know.'

CHAPTER FIFTEEN

Dorcas had a heavy step when she was sulking. A heavy jowl too. She crashed on her bed and lay staring at the ceiling, her hands rigid by her sides.

'Listen . . .' I was going to say that I had found the bra. She did not even turn in my direction. 'Listen . . .' Her eyes were cold as jade glass marbles. Her lower lip stuck out.

Could Hamish have another woman: could that be it? To me Dorcas was Venus, an irresistible milky, soft, exciting perfection of young womanhood, peerless. It was inconceivable that any man could leave her once he had won her. It must, therefore, be something else . . . more difficult, bigger. Frustration was swelling in her like a gross bubble. My knowledge of the sins of man was limited. Lechery, adultery and fornication were what Mr Sturrock had hurled at us from the pulpit. I knew the consequences all right: they came hopping with frogs and swarming with locusts. But there were darker things that still remained obscure to me.

Why would she not confide? She had come upon me that morning, lying like a self-sacrifice prone upon my father's bed. She had stood apart then lashed me with her tongue. She knew my pain, my secret.

I had to leave her to her mood. I went outside.

The air held the stillness of summer in suspended animation. Soon I should report to the kitchen. I was by the tennis court, standing where I had seen Dorcas stand. From here she could easily have looked up. Those last three windows were the studio. She could not be jealous of me and Guthrie, could she? As I was jealous of her and Guthrie? No, that was impossible. She had been invited too; she could have had a lesson with the clay. I had not been down at the lodge since I arrived this time. My memories of the miniature house with its crow-stepped gables were fond. I could have gone there now to visit Guthrie, to tell him Dorcas was upset . . . but something bigger filled my mind. And he had said I must be brave. So there could be no running back to him now, no hiding, no snuggling into his Icelandic jumper and adopting all its borrowed warmth – not yet.

I wanted Bornati to be back. Soon he must be back. We were preparing a feast for him tonight. The sun was warm. It pressed me. Stay, it said. Wait. Its warmth pushed me forward to meet him. I went down the drive to the last curve before the gates and I stood and watched the cows in the valley field, the rotary mastication of the square, pink-nosed faces, the shudder under the flank, the whisked tail; I heard the run of cow pee, the slurry of a cowpat: I envied their complacence. The stillness, held in the warmth of the days, held in the green arms of the trees, stretched and stretched. There was this buzzing like a bluebottle in my head: I wanted Bornati to be back.

I turned towards the Big House but still listened for the car. I had to get closer to him. I might be serving tonight. Dorcas could not do everything herself. The way she was . . . perhaps she would cry off: my spirits leaped at that thought. Beyond the verge reached the arms of brambles. The nuts were ripening over them. This was near the season of my first weekend, the one I had called Sex and Slaughter.

The table, like the sideboard, was of a rich red wood and long as a loch. The walls were damson-dark, hung with the heavy gilded frames of paintings, peaty oils, each with a glowing core of pigment showing huntsmen, grouse, cut pomegranate, quince. It was so different from sitting in our dining room where the tables were a motley lot. Instead of dingy Scottish bridges, I laid out mats of holly-green tooled leather. The cutlery was gleaming silver from a baize-lined box which Mrs Caird unlocked. With each addition to the table, each crystal goblet, knife, fork, spoon, each candlestick and flower, my heart beat faster. I returned to the kitchen and to my job behind the scenes.

Dorcas was there. She was backing through the kitchen doorway, her hair flax-straight against her curving body which was zipped into a black dress. I heard male voices in the hall. She was laughing at something they said. She had emerged from her sulk for the men but she still refused to meet my eye.

Despite the soft hair there was something hard in her face, something of a carapace about her linen dress. Raising a silver tray she announced she needed ice and went over to the fridge.

Mrs Caird suggested I change too.

'There's no need,' snapped Dorcas. 'She'll just be in the kitchen.' She sailed out with her ice-bucket.

But Mrs Caird said she wasn't having a Cinderella. I was to run over quickly and put on a frock.

I wriggled into my yellow dress, the one Ninian had wanted to seduce me in, gave my hair a quick brush and twisted it on top. I looked older with it up. Lipstick, quickly, yes: there was to be nothing schoolgirlish about my image, briefly glimpsed though it might be – if Dorcas had her way. I was Beatrice Maria Bornati not Beatie Brown tonight.

I slipped back across the yard, in this yellow more butterfly than moth and too brilliant for the gloaming. Above my head I saw the sky was overcast with blue-black clouds.

The soup tureen, borne by Dorcas like a trophy, heralded the start of the dinner. I watched the door close on her, engineered by some patented pneumatic arm. I saw nothing of her serving and heard only a snatch of conversation when the empty plates came back. Next Mrs Caird took in her pheasants, roasted gold, plumed, garnished, arranged on the biggest ashet I had ever seen. Dorcas followed with the vegetables. I heard appreciative noises, glimpsed the handing round of the big blue and russet plates and saw the door close once again. Mrs Caird gave a sigh of satisfaction when she came back and said that dish always went down well.

She was over by the window suddenly, squinting out. 'What's the dog doing here?'

A tail bobbed beneath the sill.

'Looks like one of Hamish's, the shepherd up the valley.'

'Aye, but why's he here at this time o' night?' Mrs Caird's voice dropped an ominous octave. It rose again. 'Mind! That's Crown Derby, dearie, and it's priceless!'

When Dorcas reappeared at last, her face above the debris of the game was flushed.

'Did one of the old men pinch your bum then?'

'Mrs Caird! You mind your tongue! I've never heard you speak like that.'

'Well it's Beatie's turn now. Let her serve the puddings.

You're the one that knows how to make the coffee and I'm going off. My man's waiting for his sandwich. I always cut him one at nine o'clock. You know that. Come on now. Give your friend a chance of the limelight. Did you ever see such a lovely colour as that frock?'

'Nice for the Riviera.' She looped a fair tress behind an ear. 'Not so sure about the Scottish Borders. They're getting Bruno's life story in there . . .'

'What's that?' Mrs Caird was tying a headscarf over her ears. 'Gossip. Gossip.'

'I like gossip. Tell me.'

'The American Gentleman. He's telling them about himself.' I had untied my apron, had my hand on the pudding trolley.

'Hey!' Dorcas lunged forward. 'That's mine.'

'You let her do it, Miss Dorcas.'

'No.'

Staring into her defiant eyes, I said, 'You know who's out there, don't you? It's your Shamus. With his dog.'

She turned away from us for a moment. Her sulky lip was back. She said she had to go. Reaching something from a shelf she went quickly out the back.

'Then I'd best stay. I don't like her knowing that man.' But Mrs Caird hesitated, her hand-knitted woolly buttoned over her nylon housecoat. I told her I could manage. I insisted. I could see she was relieved. 'If you're sure then . . . Dorcas is a bit daft. It's youth, I suppose. Mind now, Beatie, be careful with that china.'

I pushed my trolley to Bornati's place. He helped himself to raspberries and two of my meringues and kept talking. His speech was a low-key account with pauses.

'My father ran a café, like many Italian immigrants. You know the kind – marble counter, black bentwood chairs. They sold their own ice-cream, fish and chips, cigarettes, confectionery too . . .' He paused.

'We're all waiting, Miss Brown,' said Mr Ingram. 'Those puddings you've got there look delicious.'

I served the next gentleman quickly. The men were all in dark suits, indistinguishable one from the next.

'My father . . .' Bornati spoke in an elusive dark voice, a mixture of mellifluous American and soft Scots. He cleared his throat. 'In 1940, when Italy entered the war, my father, who had been here since the twenties, was suddenly interned. He was one of the thousands of Italians taken away to camps. I was too young, still fifteen. We heard nothing, my mother and I, not for weeks – not until the news got out of the hundreds of Italians drowned when the *Arandora Star* went down and his body was recovered.'

I stood there, staring. Mr Ingram's prompt broke the awesome silence. 'Serve the next man his pudding then, young lady.'

A bald gentleman with a yellow tartan tie asked, 'Was he a Fascist?'

'He had applied for British citizenship two months before the war began, as it happens. He was a socialist.'

'Weren't we deporting Nazis and fifth columnists?'

'No one knew what was going on in the panic. Many foreign nationals were interned. They said they graded them according to security risk but it was muddled. A few weeks after the news about my father they interned me too because I had reached my sixteenth birthday. Grade 18B we were, British-born Italians, all there together on the top floor of Barlinnie Prison. They were security mad.'

'We thought we were about to be invaded like Holland and Belgium. We had to be suspicious. That's what Alec's driving at,' put in Mr Ingram. 'They must have had some reason to take your father.'

'Oh they did. He had some raffle tickets on him sold in aid of the Fascist Party. He'd brought them from some schoolboys, quite innocently, just as if he had been asked to support the Boy's Brigade.'

'Come off it! A Fascist youth group!' Alec was scornful.

'Remember you speak with hindsight. To young people in Italy it was popular – like the Boy Scouts.'

'It was an awkward time for foreigners . . .' Mr Ingram paused to let me serve him.

'The press whipped the whole thing up. I had a foreign name but I spoke like a Scot. My parents didn't and they were more suspect. The enforcement of the Internment of Aliens Act was blimpish bungling at its worst. What was really happening was exposed too late for my father. When that ship was sunk by that German torpedo some would-be traitors but many innocent men went down. Then my time came.'

'What was it like in prison?'

'I can still remember a sour face saying, "What have we got here? Another of the little buggers!" An enormous wall – that was my first impression of the prison – an enormous wall. But we could mix with each other – unlike the Italian-born internees who were locked up with the convicts. We were moved from there to a camp at Douglas on the Isle of Man. I was drawing again there. Got out eventually on condition that I undertook work "of national importance". I became a lumberjack in Ayrshire. An open-air job I thoroughly enjoyed! Got two pounds, one-and-eight a week and a half-day Saturday.'

Someone tapped my elbow. 'Sorry!' I gasped, caught out again. This one wanted pie. I had no knife.

'Take this.' It was Guthrie, one guest down the line, who now said, 'And after the war you got into art school, which was where we met, of course.' Leaning back in his chair he exposed me, included my presence in this unfolding of his past. I cut the crust.

'Then taught a bit. Then went to the States.'

'I seem to recall – for I saw quite a bit of you around the place in those days – that you had a wife. A Scottish girl, wasn't she?'

The face closed up, darkened. My hand holding the knife was shaking. We were all waiting. We all wanted to hear about this Scottish wife. In the awkward pause Guthrie whispered, 'I'll have a meringue and a slice of that delicious apple pie, Beatie.'

He had not called me Beatrice as he sometimes did. I cut the pie and conveyed the wedge shakily to his plate. But I need not have worried. Bornati was too involved with his own story to make any connection with me. There was no reason why he should. I manoeuvred the trolley. Guthrie said, 'And my meringue?' I had forgotten his meringue. I served it and moved on again. 'And cream, my dear . . .'

'Double cream? All over? Yes? Or – what?' It was going to be Guthrie who got me into trouble at this rate.

'All over. I don't get this often, you know, Beatie. Smothered is how I like it. Thank you.' His eyes were shining their support. I turned my back, feeling safer not seeing these signals however well-intentioned. Guthrie waxed expansive for the company. 'My Scottish wife, my Deirdre, does not serve me up dainties like this. But some of our native lassies do do it very well. Very well indeed. Does . . . er . . . did yours,

Bruno?' Surely this was Guthrie going too far. Had he drunk too much? Was this still for my benefit? I slid behind the chair backs.

The next guest was already welcoming my arrival and had his podgy index out. In serving him I dropped the dish, which spewed its contents on the carpet. 'Sorry!'

'Come on, lassie!' Mr Ingram said. 'All fingers and thumbs. Shall we summon your other half?'

'I'll manage.' What humiliation! But I had saved Bornati from having to answer.

'Were you making sculpture then?' Briskly, from Ingram. 'What medium did you favour: clay, plaster, wood?'

'Moore and Hepworth revere wood, don't they? I understand they talk about discovering the truth within the block?'

Bornati pushed his plate to one side, leaned his forearms on the table, opened his hands. 'Yes. Wood was my material then. I was given a set of tools by a craftsman friend of my father's. I'd whittled away in my lumberjacking days. Carving wood is an adventure. A frustration. A revelation. You never know exactly how the grain will come up.'

'I haven't seen any piece in wood by you.'

'I only used that years ago, Jimmy.'

'Is there no one in Edinburgh who would have kept . . .?' Guthrie on the probe again.

'I expect she put them on the fire.'

'You mean . . . Did your wife not—'

'Life was difficult. Most of us had our troubles, didn't we, Drummond?' He frowned at him. 'I don't recall much about that time. I remember the postwar despair in many artists' work . . .'

'You always come back to the subject of work.'

What else was there? Bornati's gesture said. Then, 'I remember the distortion and contortion, the brutalism of that time and how I was drawn to that. In 1950 my mother died. It brought home the treachery of my father's end. Everything changed. I had to get out. I had to work with new elements. The perfection of form that I strove for when I carved in wood, the cursive, elegant finishes were suddenly irrelevant. Edinburgh had just about strangled me. Tell me,' he leaned back suddenly, 'does it still do that?' It made me curl inside to see his sneer.

The men in their dark suits shook their heads. One said, 'We have an international festival for the arts, Mr Bornati. We attract international stars. Visitors flock.'

'Good. And does Edinburgh know that sculpture has come off its plinth?'

'Well, well, Mr Bornati,' Alec smirked, 'some think it's gone off its rocker. Indeed they do. Your own work takes a lot of getting used to.'

'You speak, of course, as one of the more traditional members of our purchasing committee, Alec.'

'Indeed, Jimmy. Well, I am not ashamed of that. And I am eager to see how Mr Bornati's much-praised but by all accounts strange sculptures – are we to call them "constructs"? – appeal to me tomorrow.' Alec was the one with the unsettling tartan tie.

The host turned to his guest of honour. 'Bruno, I assure you I am not ignorant of modern trends. And I have read your C. Greenberg and appreciate his thesis that we must try to view the new sculpture in a new way, without the preconceptions we usually bring to bear, loaded as we are with the whole history of Fine Art. As you say we are traditional here, have been, perhaps, too traditional for too long. Our job is now to inform a conservative public and to look to the future by investing in a major work.' Mr Ingram smiled. 'This is why you and your sculptures are in town.'

The artist put both hands against the table and pushed his chair back. 'The Americans have already invested. Generously. I am glad to say.'

'Does it mean anything to you to sell a major work to the country of your birth?'

'I am not a sentimental man.'

'Come on, Bruno, it must mean something!' Guthrie coaxed. 'You lived here. Married here.'

'I explained my problems about that. As for my wife – I left her when I left the country. She had no interest in art. Her own family were Edinburgh . . . all that.'

'You had a daughter, didn't you?'

He gave a tight shrug, almost imperceptible.

Guthrie dared me to look. His eyes were two lit points. Tell him, they said.

'Beatie.' Mr Ingram, diplomat, beckoned. 'My dear, if you would . . . the cheese.' He got up to pour more wine. 'Have an oatcake, anyway, Bruno, for old time's sake.'

I rearranged plates, presented the cheese board and set the biscuit basket by Bornati's place. Then I wheeled the trolley from the room.

Minutes later I returned to do my last round of the guests by handing out the little cups of coffee while Mr Ingram offered brandy and liqueurs. I got a particular look from my Bornati this time, a moment's warmth from the brown eyes. When I looked at him again he was drinking, sucking down the corners of his mouth. I must have been frowning too for Guthrie intercepted me, lunging back in his chair, and mimicked the expression, pulling his blond brows down between his eyes, looking like the American Eagle.

Dirty dishes were stacked by the sink. The window was black. There was an infinity of space out there but it could have been the coal hole. 'Her own family were Edinburgh . . .' Another camp. Another kin. In the black glass I saw that shrug, the tension that at last, at least acknowledged me. My hands were submerged in the hot suds. I found a moment of comfort. So my father was injured also. I mopped and sloshed. That made it easier. I could not believe what I had heard. His father, my grandfather, had been imprisoned, deported and then drowned. Why had Mother never breathed a word of this? My father's letter said she was 'embarrassed' by him. You would be if your father-in-law was a Fascist or a fifth columnist – but not if he happened to buy the wrong book of raffle tickets, not if he was about to be made a British citizen! I put the plates one by one steaming in the rack. And he thought Edinburgh suffocating – didn't I too? I let a handful of cutlery crash on the drainer.

A torch – that was what Dorcas snatched when she rushed out!

CHAPTER SIXTEEN

Imperfect by a sliver, the moon now up above the knuckles of the clouds, cast a wan light on the cobbles. A furtive wind was out. To my right the track dipped black as a pit then grey again meeting the drive. Dorcas had swerved there in the sun yesterday, bell trilling, bottom shifting . . . and she had gone that way tonight.

Lights snapped on in the billiard room.

Inside a red wood lip, the table was a green pool.

'Hello.'

He was rubbing something on to the tip of the cue. His head was bowed. He must have heard me. He must have seen my yellow dress. 'Hi,' he said without looking up.

'Will you play?'

Now he straightened. His mouth seemed long-closed like a mollusc. His hand stroked up and down the shaft. It was as if he was coming round to something. He replaced the stick in a rack and came towards me. 'Why are you doing that?'

My two hands were up against my chest. It felt as if an iron bar was there. I took a deep breath then let my arms go.

'You are a jittery young lady.'

He was wearing the fine black belt. The light was behind him, a low band above the green table. When I looked up the skin of his face was dark as an Indian's. 'I'm fine,' I said.

'Where's your friend?'

'You asked me that before, do you remember?'

'With her boyfriend?'

This time – the way his eyes were bent on me – I could not feel the same anger.

'Where did you come from just now?'

'Outside. There's a moon.'

'I'd like some air. That's what I need. Let's go.' His hand, arm, massed pressure of his whole body propelled me. 'To see the moon, the Scottish moon. OK?'

We went outside swiftly, down to the side drive. I was so buoyed with his coming that I let myself go blindly. His footsteps mixed with mine on the gravel. It was like the films . . . the blackness, the breath-stopping excitement.

'Your dress – it's luminous.'

'I can't see you.'

'It shines like the woman's dress in a painting I know. Munch, I think. Do you know Munch?'

'*The Scream*. I know *The Scream* . . .' I was pleased to show I knew this.

'It's not that one. So you know something about art, do you?'

'Something about history of art. I can draw . . . Guthrie Drummond started me sculpting a head in clay today up in the studio here.'

'Good results?'

'He didn't do much of me. The point was for me to do *his* head.' Then I added, 'He did say it was good. Actually.'

' "Actually",' he mimicked, as he had done before, making my voice sound light and prim – except that this time the darkness exaggerated every sound. 'What does a young lady like you do with herself?' he asked.

'I was at the same school as Dorcas.' I hurried on. 'Working in clay is wonderful. You feel you can do anything. You don't want to stop.' I felt him searching my face. 'Why do you ask me things, though? I don't think you're really listening. What did I just say?'

'H'm. That you like work? That something was wonderful?'

'It's only play: that work. For me.' I knew he had hardly listened.

'Show me this head then so that I can see what you've made of Mr Drummond.' His footsteps slowed. I was walking just in front of him now. 'Tell me,' his voice was different, thicker, softer, 'are Edinburgh girls as prim as they used to be?' His hand reached out. Large, dry, it closed – not on my arm, my shoulder, but on the nape of my neck.

I froze.

I tried to protest. Leaned back. Felt his fingers in my hair.

'Is it a full moon then?'

I was dumb.

'Let's go up.'

'But I must watch for Dorcas!'

'But she's canoodling with her boyfriend!' He laughed a soft laugh that seemed to roll out of him and spill away across the black void that was the tennis court. 'I want to see this studio; Jimmy told me there was one. I want to see what you and Drummond have been up to.' I ducked. I tried to walk more quickly to get free. I thought I had succeeded but his hand dropped to my waist and, square on, he was pushing me again. I seemed not to be escaping so much as conniving with him – skipping on ahead to do his bidding. His advance embarrassed me but I could not have run away from it, not now, not for the world.

He went round the front. He pulled me back from the big doorway. My dress was bright yellow slipping past the lit porch. But in the rhododendron darkness of the south wall beneath the hill we were in that Munch blue-black again, with that same melancholy weirdness and the sounds of clashing leaves, trodden pebbles, his breath at my back. Would he touch me again?

He must like me, though. I wanted him to like me.

Neon strips hummed on in the studio. They were waiting for us, the swathed heads on spikes, the attent ghosts of me and Guthrie.

We unwrapped them.

'It's my first head.'

He faced the faces.

I faced his silence.

Unspoken words went racing. Remember. It's my first head my very first and it's damaged it had an accident but I have drawings perhaps they're better I wish you could see stay on and I can show you all my everything about my . . .

He went close to the head of the girl (I could not call it me, it was such a parody). He made as if to touch the brow. I noticed suddenly how his two thumbs bent right back, sickle curved. Of course they had! How could I have forgotten? I watched them ease along the contours yet not quite touch the clay. I cried out inside. I did not trust myself. But I was standing too close. I backed against the corner of the plinth – backed, tripped, clutched, brought some object toppling with a crash.

A pottery jug. In bits on the floorboards.

'Uh-huh . . .' he said, sing-song.

My fingers scrabbled round.

I heard him sigh. He said nothing, though. He was still intent on the heads.

'Drummond's of you is an awful piece of work,' he announced. 'Yours of him . . . is interesting. It's all over the place in a way, of course, but—'

'Yes?'

'It has life, Beatie. Also some peculiarities. You exaggerate. Is that characteristic of you – that you exaggerate? It's bold, though. See that line.' I watched those remarkable thumbs again at Guthrie's cheekbones. 'It's a pity I'm going.' He eyed me. 'I'd like a session with you.'

'I'd like a lesson from *you*, Mr Bornati.'

With his head tilted, he still eyed me. He made me feel naïve.

He went moseying round the room then, picking up things, peering. He glanced behind the screen – it was the kind you see in French farces draped with lingerie. He flicked a rush of silky bronze stuff from the shrouded chaise longue. He looked over at me. I drew away behind the easel, round the table with the paint brushes on it and backed up against the bench. 'What are you doing so far away? I thought you wanted advice. Hey-ey!' Swinging round the obstacles, he was coming for me. I could not manage this. I felt along, knocked the handle of the vice. It dropped with a clang. Running scared . . . running scared, I was, and he would think me silly – a silly little chit – and he would not bother, he would go, he would be flying off the day after tomorrow.

'You're doing that again? Why do you keep doing that?'

My hands were up tight against my chest. The iron bar was there.

I breathed in, closed my eyes and willed myself some magic, willed till my fingers, like little elvers wriggling, took their way, probing in at the curve of each breast, sinuously down to feel the point of each hip, the wild quickening possibility . . . and opened my eyes and saw he had stepped forward and was watching everything with concern on his face – wonderfully – concern on his face, for a moment, and then I gave him, quickly, rushing forward holding his head – such a fine dark head between my hands – one kiss, the most soft, deep kiss I ever gave to any man, so full of meaning yet so contradictory it was like a poem packed with beauty, mystery and hurt and I gave it darkly, pressing to his dry, astonished lips.

And pulled away.

Left him puzzled. A smile beginning—

Hand over hand, bench, table, door, banisters, I fled.

You wear short little skirts and you make sheep's eyes and you're sexy and you go around seizing men old enough to be your . . . You go kissing them full on the lips and then you ask – but you didn't, you ran away – but with that kiss you asked . . . No, with that kiss you said, you said something. That kiss was an imperative. That kiss said Like me Want me Love me. Oh God. But what kind of a kiss was that to get out of the blue from a girl? What kind of a kiss was that – for Chrissake? He must be saying that. 'What now, for Chrissake?' That's what he must be asking. Surely.

With this I went into the dark.

The darkest dark I had known before was when we killed the rats and the torch failed.

'Nae moon the nicht.'

'George!' Dorcas had climbed the bars of Jilly-n-Willy's dodgy gate and was stretching her hand back. 'Give me the string. You hold the torch so I can tie them. There!' The faint but fading beam made limeade of the leaves, red-veined worms of the bunch of tails. We three stared.

'Nae clypin' noo,' the boy warned. Dorcas gave one nod accompanied by a solemn throat-cutting gesture. George parted from us then. We heard the hollow sound of his wellingtons getting fainter on the road. Then the torch finally went out.

'Oo-oo-oo!'

'Don't, Dorcas!'

'It's fun.'

'It's dark.'

'It's this way home.' She pulled me.

I felt gravel underfoot.

'Keep talking,' I begged.

I stumbled on a verge.

'Hear the water.'

We skliffed along.

'After the bridge there's the church.'

'Doesn't your house have a light?'

'But there's a bend.'

I looked up. Not a single star.

'Scary, this.'

'Smell the church trees.'

Where the cypresses curtained the road it was even darker, if it were possible to blacken pitch.

We began a dragging run, veering from side to side. When we brushed the bearded seeds of flowers, got caught by a reaching bramble, stumbled into hedges stinking of ripe growth, kicked a turf or grazed a knuckle on a wall, we gasped, and clutched, and pushed away from it.

A plaintive sound woke me, beached me from sleep out of a horrid tumbling dark. I thought at first it was the cry of seals. Oblivion had been hard won after that moment with my father. I was annoyed. Was it those dogs again, whimpering?

Then I knew it was the sound of sobbing.

It was Dorcas.

I turned towards her bed. At least she was back. I had heard her squeal and hoot – but I had never heard her cry. It was no small miserable snivel and it was amplified by the long vault of our room.

I begged silently from my pillow. Fall asleep. Just fall asleep. We'll talk about it in the morning. Please. It's not so bad. It can't be . . . Off to sleep now. Tomorrow is my big day, my biggest day – Dorc! Go to sleep! Come on! There was a pause. But then she gave a dreadful howl and the sobbing went on, in spasms, dry and slow then light and quick. I could not escape, not by burying under the blankets, not by anything.

'Has he hurt you?' I sat beside her on the bed. She faced away from me. I held her shoulders, 'What is it?' my cheek against her hair. 'What is it? What's all this? Ssh. Ssh.' I stroked her back. Underneath the bedclothes she was crouched up, still dressed. 'Where's your nightie? You'll be more comfy in your nightie. Can I put the light on then I can see?'

'No light.'

Under the pillow I found a soft garment. I tried to get at the fastening of her dress. She raised herself on one arm and bowed her head. I pulled the zip making a V of white open down her neck. I felt her shudder and clutch the sheet up. I did not know what to do next. She seemed to be naked under her dress. But she was becoming calmer.

She sat up, sniffling. 'I'll do it.' She peeled the dress off and groped for her nightie. Then she lay down again on her back with a great sigh. I could see her face for the first time now, eerily lit by my skylight. Her features were swollen, the eyelids puffed up.

'What happened to you? It was Hamish, wasn't it? I shan't tell Guthrie. Honestly. What's he done?'

'Just lovers' tiffs,' she sniffed. She sucked her breath in suddenly. 'That hurt. Ow! That hurt. When I lie that way it hurts.'

'How did you get back?'

'I walked.'

'Alone?'

'Yes.'

'In the dark? All the way from the shieling?'

'I'd the torch. I always do that. Mind you, not with,' she sucked her breath in sharply, 'this.'

'What is it?'

'Cracked rib . . . feels like.'

'Let me get something? Water? Cocoa? Aspirin?'

'Water.'

I brought her water in a toothbrush mug.

'He's a devil when he's drunk, that's all. I thought he was exciting. You know what I mean, Beat? Well, after George he was exciting. George would always rather be down in the pub with his mates, or gawp at television. I had to coax him even for a kiss.'

George who had beat the drum for us.

'But not Hamish?'

This night was like a ship on the high seas where there were calms and storms and I found myself unexpectedly on the bridge with the steering wheel in my own hands. I had sailed into the wind when I kissed my father. Now, with my friend, it was gently does it, bring her round.

'Hamish always wants me all to himself.'

'You don't like that?'

'He's jealous if I'm even *with* another male!'

And Dorc loved the company of men, rose to it, glowed in it.

'You should be proud of that.'

'I was!'

'But not any more?'

Her head shook vehemently like a doll's pinging on a spring. Her speech was punctuated by short whistling breaths when the pain in her ribs caught her. 'He wants me all to himself. He makes sex exciting too. P'raps you're too – well, *nice* – to know all this, but he makes sex fun, or did. That's why he was mad about that lacy bra. It's the one he makes me wear. He says it's important to know what turns him on. He makes me do it slowly. Undress. Slowly. He's trained me. It's like those magazines I showed you. I get marks! Well! And now he's got it into his head that the men in this place are after me! He's angry. He's trained me, as he puts it, and he thinks I'm going off with someone else.'

She turned on me.

'Don't laugh! When Hamish drinks he's lethal. Now he doesn't trust me. He's been coming spying on me.'

'Can't you handle him?'

'Does it look like it? I went over there tonight to try to smooth him down. Prepared to do the whole lot, take my time, be really good for him . . . *prove* to him. He sat there drinking whisky and watching and then he went over to the corner where the crooks are, those stick things they use to pull the lambs out of gulleys, they get them by the leg . . . I was doing my stuff . . .'

My eyebrows must have been up.

'Wiggling and wriggling, you know, in my bra and knicks . . .'

'Not the right bra?'

'No.'

I felt awful. 'Sorry—'

She paid no heed. 'I was trying to make up for that. I was watching him. I felt nervous, yes, but wasn't really worried: I had it in the back of my stupid head that he might have some special surprise for me because I was trying extra hard, really hard, if you see what I mean, though it wasn't fun. He must have seen through that. My heart wasn't in it. Och, it's so stupid! So humiliating when I spell it out like this. Sex is all right in the films, isn't it? It's great when you're carried away by the passion and all that – but there's nothing more grotesque than trying to pretend when it's gone wrong.'

'Oh, Dorcas!'

'Well, I am more experienced than you, I suppose.' Her eyes had a bleared gleam. 'Just look where that's got me. It's not natural, that's the trouble. It felt like fun, then suddenly it felt like – prostitution!' She leaned suddenly away from me and howled.

She had said it.

'He started to whack me with the stick. Not in a fun way, you understand, ticklings on my botty – God, no! I'm black and blue. That's why you've not to put the light on. I'm black and blue. I got away at last, after a struggle. Not after sex. There's no sex when he's drunk. Only beatings. Gentle shepherd!' Her voice and her body shrank again. 'I'm scared now. I'll have to get away.'

'It's happened before then?'

'Yes. But he said he'd never . . .'

'Just don't go near his place.'

'But he's started coming here. He didn't do that before. He's got a thing about it. Mad. Jealous. I told him there was no one else. He doesn't trust me. Says he sees all these men here and us dancing round all dressed up! I don't want him now. Hate him. I'm really scared, Beat. How did I get into this?'

'You can tell Guthrie. You can go up and stay in town. Stay close to us. Don't wander off.'

'Don't leave me, please.'

'I won't.'

'Thanks, Beat. You don't think I'm too awful?'

'That's what I count on you for. You go where angels fear to tread.'

181

CHAPTER SEVENTEEN

We were in a public place at a public function, the Private View. I was supposed be seeing his work, the Bornati abstracts, which were ranged around, large and difficult, on the floor of the new Fruitmarket Gallery. But it was Bruno Bornati I saw – their maker, my own master builder. When I came in he was surrounded. This was a relief. I had not seen him since the night before. That morning he and Mr Ingram had disappeared very early up to town. I presumed these people were dignitaries, dealers and the art-daft. Then I saw he had spotted me. Above their heads, he held me, claimed me by the way he looked across.

He was ugly like that. Disguised. It made me angry. He was not my father with his hair drawn so tightly back. I wanted to snap that small elastic band. Otherwise I liked his looks, the high temples, cheek bones, the long nose. The tweed jacket, the charcoal one, sent me that irresistible message of comfort (I had fallen for Guthrie's too), the serviceable cloth was fatherly, huggable. His shirt was terracotta, his tie Tiepolo blue. He almost smiled.

I sipped my wine.

Where had Deirdre got to? Why wasn't she rushing forward making herself known? She had been silent coming in with us in the Morris and I had put it down to pre-first-night nerves. She wore an actressy outfit today, scarlet, dress, pillbox hat and signature scarf for flourish. I felt superior in my black which was very plain, sleeveless, a boat neck and well above my knees. It had taken hours sewing in the long back zip by hand. Italian women should wear black. I eased my toes. The shoes were new from Dolcis and said 'Made in Italy' underneath the soles.

I thought of the kiss I had taken. I sipped more wine and raised a charged look up.

He was watching. He beckoned to me with one brief finger. But Dorcas stopped me.

'Deirdre's got lipstick on her teeth,' she hissed. Dorcas had sat silent too, slumped in the car. Our relationship was fragile. The drama of the night before had made a whiteout of the cracks but there were crevasses underneath. The ice plates were still shifting. 'She's had lipstick on her teeth ever since we left the house.' Dorcas herself was ugly today. I raised an eyebrow at my friend whose bruises I had helped disguise. Her eyes were bleared and puffy yet she cared only how her mother looked. 'Her make-up's as thick as a pancake. Th-thick.'

Guthrie came close. 'It's an allowance we make for actresses. Did you know that, Beatrice?'

I kept my eyes on Deirdre.

'They always do their faces up for the spotlights. Mere daylight is a naïve scrutiny with which they are unfamiliar.'

'*She* says she *has* to go over the top or her public wouldn't look at her. *She* says: "All art needs exaggeration." ' Dorcas sounded breathless.

'Which is why,' Guthrie explained to me, 'when we played our game of clay heads I made your eyes such deep-set orbs, Beatrice, why I made so much of the ovoid, the perfect madonna shape, the key to the planes of your face.' His voice changed to a softer tone. 'You're looking very comely tonight. Very comely . . . You'd make any father proud.' But when I turned to look at him, he began his teasing again. 'Is this exaggeration of your Mediterranean beauty – this dramatic application of the khol pencil round they dear grey e'en – what they call "The Cleopatra Look"?'

'Oh shut up, Dad!'

So rude, his real daughter.

'Tut, Guthrie,' was all I said.

He kept his sympathetic gaze on me and then, to my relief, withdrew it and strolled off. I felt easier being alone with my troubles.

We were left to contemplate *Balance*, two curved sheets of aluminium, crabwise, back to back.

'Your father's in a funny mood,' I said.

'Is that what you call it? I call it flirting.'

'It's not flirting. You've a one-track mind, Dorcas. You make me so angry sometimes.'

She retaliated. 'This stuff, this so-called "sculpture" of *your* fa—!'

'Ssh! Don't you *dare*!'

'What?'

'Say it.'

'What?'

I glared.

'Dinna fash yersel'!' In a childish playground voice. 'Well, this stuff makes *me* angry, OK?'

'I told you. I said that. I sneaked a preview last week. I think it's horrid too. But ssh!'

'You don't trust me?'

'You're in such a queer mood. I—' I did not.

Dorcas hooted. Somebody looked round. Poor damaged Dorcas! I saw all the soft blossoms of her girlhood gone. We stood awkwardly together.

'Look at her,' Dorcas said. 'Over there. My mother. She's trying to fathom what it's all about. Look. She's given in. She's reading the label.'

Deirdre, poised, was indeed mouthing the name of the piece, as if she needed to rehearse it. She appeared to absorb the concept and stow it away, then she turned and looked about her. She went very still all of a sudden. Then I watched her face clear, her body assume its graceful purpose as if it were an empty vessel standing to receive its fill. She brimmed. It was Bornati she had seen.

'Where are you off to, Beat?'

Mine. He was mine. Come to me: he had beckoned.

But Deirdre also moved out across the room.

She slipped between us. I felt her buttock, small and soft, push against my hand. I itched to punish it. There was a viperish flick in the corner of her thin red mouth. She took up a place in the group which had formed, standing behind a gentleman in a suit.

The man was saying: 'In this series, Mr Bornati, you work exclusively with the sheet steel. The piece *Stack* uses horizontals set across uprights: a lintel. This is not so new, surely. It's an old device. Its sculptural antecedent was the henge.'

'Actually, it's in-between the parallels that the power lies. Stacked on top they do not *appear* to touch. If you want sources – the idea came from an electric generator . . . high voltage, high fence, danger! The levitation *yet* the massed weight of the

185

material – that's what it's about for *me*.'

The man's hand went unsatisfied from jowl to chin.

'Also, in the work you call *Support*, you bend one of the steel sheets and set the other on top, tablewise – derivative of the dolmen, surely?'

'In that and in *Back to Back* I was playing with repulsion, the flat, the convex – and containment, the invert curve.'

The man trapped his hand in his armpit.

'Permit me to suggest that you are using a literal, historical approach which is quite out of date in this context. Relax, man. Forget antecedents. Let the sculpture speak.'

Some listeners smiled at this. Others were doubtful. Deirdre stood out now in her red outfit for all that she stayed in the back. It made me wonder. Perhaps she needed him to come to her. She needed him to come to her as if, in some way, it was her due.

'So you do not want us to find human reference in these works, Mr Bornati, am I right?'

'Find what you like. I – I do not *intend* human reference: that's all. Look at them. Be moved, changed, made afraid. Be struck by the fact of it standing there the way it does – but not in reference to something else like human form or myth or . . . feeling, even.'

'This is very far from Henry Moore.'

'Henry Moore is not so far from Michelangelo as I am from Henry Moore.' This, the condescending, curt dismissal.

Deirdre was on her toes.

Bornati must have seen her, her snaking lips working under the pert hat, wiring for him. But he turned his back. In coming round his eyes rolled like an animal's, like I had seen the bull, Big Daddy's, do. He knew her: I knew that. But I saw he knew her enough to care not to meet her now.

He pushed away. Deirdre and, more discreetly, I followed. The noise of people talking hummed. She was catching up. She came behind him standing with his hands in his pockets, his chin on his chest, in a far corner of the gallery.

The work he appeared to contemplate so morosely was an ugly thing. It was a large black box – which was all it was as far as I could see. It rose from the pale floor like a piece of debris from a salvage operation. It had none of the burnished glow of the other pieces. Instead the surface was a tarry black with crusted patches where rust had etched its way.

Deirdre's red arm went climbing up his spine, her fingers took his tailed hair. 'Bruno, big black bear, my big black bear . . .' Her voice was deep with the attack of a well-rosined bow. 'Remember how I used to call you that?'

His shoulder stiffened. Slowly he turned round. 'Deirdre . . . Hi, there.' He barred his teeth in uttering her name.

A dramatic pause from Deirdre, with lowered lids.

'Let me look at you. You have changed. You're a husky bear now. Hoary.' She played this hoarsely. 'Ulysees back from his voyages.'

So this was how you did it if you were skilled: you invoked the myths. The Greeks would be on her mind, of course, with that play. But it did not work, that trick . . . the tuck beside his mouth told me.

Her hands were on his arms. I admired her nerve. I should take a lesson. From where I stood I could hear the actressy tones carrying the emotion, delivering it at him, charged and live.

Now she was touching his tight hair.

He looked down at her and I heard him say, 'Not so old – yet.'

'No. Oh no, Bruno, you can still string the great bow. I can see that.' Her hands moved up his arms. 'You are stronger, aren't you? More vigorous. What a lot you've done! What a long way you have come!'

She leaned in to him so that her red body was framed against his dark one.

Only then I saw it. Only then – like a dart quivering in the target – I saw that these two, this man and this woman, had been lovers once.

They stood matched limb for limb.

I should have been glad to see the way with one hand and then the other he peeled away her grasp.

The way one high heel stepped back.

'Is there a Penelope?' she asked.

I should have been glad.

But he said: 'I don't go in for wives.'

'I remember,' which came deep from Deirdre, echoing like a bucket down a well, 'nor did you in the old days.'

I should have been glad . . . but she meant my mother. *She* meant *my mother*!

He was pushing her away. He was looking over. Pushing her. Wanting me.

But already people in twos and threes were crowding us again.

Deirdre was at her best with a crowd. If she had not been convincing enough in the love scene she had to try her success with the crowd.

Her sudden gesture sent a length of scarlet unfurling like a banner. Against the black sculpture she was a slash of red. All of us were watching, those standing near and those who came gliding from far corners of the gallery. Deirdre delivered her upstage centre smile. 'Talk to me about all this, Bruno. This is wonderfully modern stuff. I've not seen anything like it before. Not ever. It's surely *terribly* new. I need instruction. I've never *seen* a BOX on the *floor* called *art* before. What on earth made you *think* of something so . . . so basic? Is it an *objet trouvé*?' She had aggressive French.

His face was dark.

'You *made* it?' She was incredulous. 'It's no beauty, is it?' Deirdre was no fool. 'It isn't even smooth. It is *strong* – is that what it's meant to be? What's it called? *Void*. So negative! Strong. Negative. And ugly.' She hooked him by the arm. 'Let's go on to the next one. See if I like that better.'

'So.' Her grizzly had a growl on his face. 'You don't like it.'

'So?' she said. 'But I shall persevere.'

People pressed close, people whom Bornati's frown would have had stand off but who were drawn towards the actress because her voice projected such intimacies. They did not stare, of course, they looked away, but stood there all the same. There was plenty to distract the eye but it did not draw their fascination quite like the sculptor himself and the woman.

'Isn't the floor a beautiful wood? I like *that* finish. I like the *floor*,' said Deirdre.

Bornati's forehead had that knot in it.

At the drinks table by the door the woman in charge was polishing glasses, holding them up to test for sparkle. My heart felt twice its normal size.

'Red or white?' the woman offered.

'White.' It was too big, too big a thing for me, this. 'When will it finish, do you know?'

'I've to stop pouring soon. It'll tail off after that.'

Two red-haired children in jeans and rainbow stripes lolled against a wall. They made circles with their arms. Whey-faced, they were familiar in a strange way. Perhaps they were the progeny of that Mr V-neck, a man with orange hair and a Fair Isle jumper who had let me in to the unfinished gallery for a glimpse the week before. Their windmilling was slow and rhythmic, co-ordinated like a dance.

I could not drink. My head was swimming. What had that meant, that last look?

'So sculpture has come off its plinth.' It was Guthrie. 'Beatrice.'

'I am not.'

'What are you not?'

'Beatrice. Because he might hear. Just call me Beatie . . . like you did at the dinner.'

'Beatie sounds like a biscuit.'

'And like "beaten",' under my breath.

We exchanged a sharp look.

'It offends my sense of the beautiful. If you were my daughter, I wouldn't allow—'

'Guthrie,' I interrupted him, then hesitated. Something in my tone made his pupils shrink to points.

'What?'

'What did your wife do?'

'What do you mean? She's always doing something. When? Where? With whom?'

'Exactly.' My mouth went bitter. 'When you knew my father in the old days . . . she was one, wasn't she? One of Bornati's women.'

His eyes dulled and slid from me. I pushed home the hurt at his averted face. 'She was one of the women who took my father from me. She was one of *them*! She took him from me – and from my mother! Wasn't she? Wasn't she, Guthrie?'

He would not look at me.

I flung away.

But I was stopped by Dorcas.

She was red in the face, tight-lipped. 'Get my mother out of there! She's making an idiot of herself. Can't you see Bornati's livid?'

'What's eating you, Dorcas?' Her father's voice came low and slow. His eyes slewed round, his mouth was slack. 'What is eating you?' He was looking at her as if he had not had a good look at her for a long time. 'You've had a rough night of it, haven't you?'

'I'm all right.'

'Was it Lover Boy?'

'It was a tree.'

Guthrie stared.

'I banged into a tree! It's so fucking dark in the—' She cringed.

Guthrie had stepped forward, about to hit her for the swearing, the fibbing – and everything else too, I supposed – but he stopped himself.

'Perhaps it'll teach you a lesson,' he said.

'Get my mother out of there,' she begged.

He turned into the room. 'Don't take your own troubles out on your mother.' He found Bornati. 'No,' he said, his eyes narrowing as he watched, 'he's not livid. No man could complain about being so stylishly seduced. He's loving it, this adulation. It may irk him that she can't tell the sculpture from the architectural fittings but he's lapping it up. She strokes his fur quite nicely.'

'She's ridiculous. Come on. Get her out. Dad! Don't just let her. Don't – please don't just stand there!'

'Didn't you see the whispering? When she hid behind her scarf? That's Deirdre's style . . . solicitous,' he hissed.

He would not look at me. He put his hands in his pockets and went on standing there.

'Dad,' Dorcas tugged at him, 'come on!'

It was too horrible to watch.

I was out on the street. The air was cold on my bare skin.

Up in the studio after the lesson with the clay, I had suspected there was something Guthrie wanted out of all this. And I suddenly remembered he had been the one who had talked at our fireside tea in the lodge that snowy day about how to 'catch him in the end'. He wanted his own revenge on Bornati. I was furious he had not told me. I had told him so much. This affair between my father and Deirdre had divided my first family. Now it divided Guthrie and me. We were not so different though. Revenge was what I wanted too, in my peculiar way. But I wanted him first: I wanted my father.

Why should I, his daughter, be out here in the cold when he was proudly pacing round inside?

But I was shivering. I had to calm myself. I began to walk to and fro in front of the entrance.

It was one of those Edinburgh nights when you could smell the beer brewing, a sickening unpleasant smell.

Even without the Drummonds I might still have got here. Between the buildings the Bornati banner hung across. There was the name. Had my mother seen it yet? It grew white under the slate sky. She might even have come. She might have made enquiries – you needed an invitation, of course – but she might have wangled it and come here tonight, down Fleshmarket Close, round the cobbled turn of Cockburn Street . . . I peered into the doorway opposite. Blank shuttering, clean threshold stones. There was no one about. There was no one here but me. She had settled her score. So, Deirdre Drummond was one of *them*. I rubbed my goosepimples, remembering what she had said. Down the steep vennels poured the dusk. Not *the* one – one of *them*. That made Deirdre a little less wicked, and a little more ludicrous. And Guthrie, a little pathetic. If she had been *the* one, it would have been worse: it would have put my mother in the wrong. One of *them* was different. And one of *them* made him lecherous: him, Bornati, artist obsessed and womaniser. It fitted. It even added to his stature.

People were emerging from the gallery behind me.

'I need a wee dram after all that ironmongery.'

An eerie roar and clapping surged across.

'The Tattoo aye draws the crowds.'

'It's the Pakistani Pipes and Drums.'

'Now that's a show that never misses. But . . . och, I suppose the new gallery's nice enough. Now what pub do you fancy, Jean? Is it to be Deacon Brodie's or Greyfriars Bobby?'

Their voices faded. Their shapes merged with the railings and shadows rising towards The Mound.

I went in to see the work again.

Beauty was not a word he wanted to come near. If the surfaces were smooth the shapes were confrontational. If the shape was familiar the surface repelled. There was a deliberate brutality about it. The hammered, riveted and welded plates, the cuts and angles were hard for me to understand. I could not accept. I could not see. I kept remembering how he had worked when I was small, the chug of the mallet, squeak of the chisel, patter of the woodchippings as they fell, the way his large hand came and lingered on the surface, as if he trusted, knew some prize hid there.

191

I stood before the box called *Void*. I thought I had it to myself. It was the worst, I thought, the bleakest. A black cry. A gaping maw. Then I saw that it was occupied. The two children had found a place to be, a place that suited them better than hanging against the wall. They sat cross-legged face to face, drawing invisible pictures above each other's head. I watched their pink fingers, soft as the bellies of little mice, exploring the black surface.

'So this is where you got to?'

Blood flooded my cheeks: 'You escaped then?'

'I can always get away,' he said. 'Like Houdini.'

I pointed, expecting fury.

'H'm. I see my *Void* is occupied.'

'They seem a kind of double act.'

'I have in mind,' he looked round to see if anyone was near, 'another double act.'

'What kind?'

His forefinger curled from me to him. His eyes were warm.

'We can't just go! We've got this party laid on for you after.'

'I want you to come.'

My feet were making for the door. I was going. His big frame shunted me along. 'What about . . .?' His eyebrows went up as if he listened, but all the time he pressed forwards. '. . . the provost? Photographs? Aren't there important people?' I fussed with my coat.

'I'm important, aren't I?'

I met his eye: he meant it.

'Ever eaten oysters?'

It was a dark dusk now. Splats of rain struck the pavement. My knees went whisk, whisk under my white mac. Obediently I hurried down the street. Then I said, 'The woman serving wine will tell.'

'So?'

'Perhaps they'll follow?'

'So?'

Clip. Clip. The smartness of my shoes.

His tweeded warmth bulked behind me. 'So? I'll tell them to skedaddle. I showed up, didn't I? That's all they wanted. Anyway. Openings. I hate the things.'

CHAPTER EIGHTEEN

'One.'
'*Coràggio.*'
'Which means?'
'Be bold.'
'Just one.'
'It takes two to tango.'

I looked up from the solitary oyster on the big indented plate and saw Bornati frown. We were on this row of high stools at the Café Royal Oyster Bar. My face was a pale oval in the fancy mirror.

The waiter flicked a white napkin, 'French bread, madam. You, sir?'

Bornati, eyes low, fleshy lips pushed out to slurp, seemed suddenly a pig at the trough.

I had wanted a table *à deux*. I expected a private seduction.

Was this how he might have me too? Would he cast my remains upon the heap when already he was reaching out, roving the dish, for the next more succulent succubi?

That hand now patted my knee.

'Delicious. Delicious.'

High on my thigh, I crossed one stockinged leg. 'Do you really need to eat so many?'

'Ha! But I like oysters.'

'It's my first time.'

'Try.'

I broke some bread and eyed my plate.

'It's *the* place to have them in this town. I came here as a boy only the once – my cousin brought me. The occasion of my eighteenth birthday. We dressed up in suits, I remember.' He turned to look around, wiping his mouth on the large white damask square. 'It was just the same, the bar, Art-Nouveau swirls, dark wood, brass, stained glass, people . . .'

'Old school ties.'

'You think? That doesn't figure with me, though. I went to school but we weren't . . . we were always different, being immigrants. We were grateful enough to make a living. Our café was on the Promenade down there in Portobello. We were the Italian Scots – gli Italo-Scozzesi.' He was looking at me. 'You're smiling,' he said, leaning his elbow on the counter near my plate.

'The way you said that. Ital—'

'Ee. Eetalo-Scozzesi.'

'I *love* that.'

'You *love* that?' He was staring at me. 'You don't like oysters, but you love that?' He made dog eyes. His hand was warm on my thigh. 'Would you like more of my Italian words?' His face was close; he had big pores on his nose. 'I once knew someone with eyes as grey as yours . . .' at this there was a pause in his caress, 'eyes as grey as the Firth of Forth.'

'Mine should be brown.'

'Why?'

I looked deep into his.

'This woman was cold. You're not cold.' His shoulder pressed me. 'Are you?' A solemn scrutiny.

I sipped champagne.

He drank too.

Did he suspect? I watched his profile. Then he turned back to look at me again – this time a lidded look.

So I reached for the cragged shell waiting on the plate, squeezed lemon on, put it to my now moist, now pouting lips and, exactly as I saw him do, with one slurp, I sucked the oyster down. I found it cool, tender, a delicate fruit of the sea. There in the mirror, a white blur, I saw myself with my throat stretched back. I held the pose, the screen test for my life, half-blind, refined . . . then I let my body melt and my unfurling look come deep and daring into his.

One big arm covered me. 'That's all I need to know,' he said.

'Is madam finished? . . .Sir?'

I snatched a crust before the plates were whisked away.

'You nervous?' Bornati asked.

'Hungry.'

He inclined his head. 'That was just a start – we'll have more. But you are nervous. Aren't you? Your friend's the one who's easy in men's company. You're . . .'

I did not trust speech.

All ears, the barman scanned the room.

'. . . more complicated.' I could feel his hand creep up. 'I don't want to go all the way out there again tonight, do you?' he murmured.

'There's food.'

'So?'

'It'd be a waste.'

'You're so Scottish.'

I hated the way he said that. 'They'll be waiting. Now. With the cars.'

'So?'

'You can't *do* things like that!'

'My dear child, I do exactly as I like. They've had their pound of flesh.'

'Now you're after mine, aren't you?'

It was as if we had drawn swords.

'You don't put it very graciously.'

'And don't call me your "dear child".'

'I don't like this "Beatie". What is this "Beatie"? You should have a lovely name like Carla or Leonora, Julietta . . .'

What else could I be but silent? At last I said, 'I don't mean to put you off.'

'Good. That's good.' His speech was softer. 'Wait here then; I'll be right back.'

Every long second he was gone I felt the barman watching.

When he returned he was annoyed. 'They've no rooms free. It's the goddamned Festival,' he said. Brusquely he propelled me through the lobby.

We had crossed Princes Street when the floodlit castle high to our right went dark. Rain still flustered about. The audience at the Tattoo had needed their tartan rugs tonight. Then we heard the music, the final moment, the wail of a pibroch being played by the lone piper from the battlements. It came threading out across the night like an ancestral cry. A lump was in my throat. I felt suddenly moved as if my heart would break.

He had turned to wait for me. He must have seen something in my face. 'Makes you proud to be a Scot, h'm?' I did not even nod. He watched me. After a pause he came back and put his arm round me. 'Come,' he said.

I could not.

He tugged.

'Mr Bornati,' I began, 'Mr—' I struggled with the name. I could not call him that. 'Father' was what I wanted to say. 'Father.' 'Dad.' That was the moment. I wanted to tell him then: it's me, Beatrice, your daughter. You called me Mary. Really. It's me. I'm fine. See. Grown-up. I just wanted you to know that: that's all. I want nothing else of you. Nothing . . . But the words would not come out.

He was smiling lopsidedly. 'Hey,' he said. 'Bruno. You can call me Bruno, surely. We're good enough friends for that.'

Just then a car drew up. 'Bruno! You two! There you are. Get in! Before the crowds come milling out from the Tattoo and jam the High Street. Quick!' Mr Ingram was leaning from the window of his Jaguar.

I was alone in the rear seat, vaguely regretful. In front was Mr Ingram's neck and to the left Bornati's profile. They talked about the show. The wines had made me sleepy. I drifted in and out. The car wound over the black land, purring down the green tunnel of its own headlamps. Nodding awake, I felt taken care of – not like a child, though. More like a captive.

'Don't drink any more, Beatie. I'm warning you.'

I laughed in Guthrie's face. We were all, all his women, out of his control.

A saxophone wailed. We had trooped through with loaded plates to the drawing room and were now gorged with food. Shaded lamps cast pools of light. The paintings above glanced crimson and purple. Dorcas sat like a dumpling on the floor spooning up a creamy pudding from a bowl. The record playing was a blues. Deirdre was swaying to its slow rhythm, threading her red scarf through her fingers like a conjurer then letting it float and fall. Jimmy Ingram stood at the side, apparently amused. She sidled up to him, took the glass from his hand and, head right back, swallowed wine from it. Then she approached Bornati. 'Dance with me. Dance with me.'

'Hey, lady. It's been one helluva night.' He pointed at her stomach. 'I haven't seen you eat yet.'

Deirdre jumped back. She laughed, deep, short laughs. 'Well, how funny! I don't need food, Bruno. Don't you remember? Don't you – how I don't need food? I ate. I ate already. What I need's a man. Dance with me.' Her hips insinuated. 'Dance.' She closed her eyes and began to move as if he had complied.

'Where can we get peace?' he asked me.

We found a sofa, leaned back in the darkness and watched Deirdre circling by herself. Guthrie sat on an armchair opposite. Mr Ingram plied more drink. At my turn he hesitated. I did not want more anyway. Bornati reclined by my side, close, proprietorial, one leg crossed on one knee, one hand making his brandy swill round and round the glass. Mr Ingram surveyed the pair of us for a moment? 'Happy?' he asked.

Bornati raised his glass.

Guthrie was watching too but when I glanced over he looked away.

Dorcas started the fireworks. She flung her bowl spinning across the floor and sprang to her feet. 'Stop staring. Do something, Guthrie. She's drunk. My mother's drunk. Do something!'

'Daughter, spare the crockery. What will Uncle Jimmy say? It's not as if it's the first time.'

'Do something!'

'Jimmy here can take her up to bed. Can't you, James? You're handier.'

'If you think that's best. Certainly.'

'Och, so pompous, Jimmy! It's the bed she's used to, man, isn't it?' Mr Ingram's face had a schoolboy smoothness. 'Well, isn't it?' challenged Guthrie.

The other gave nothing away.

Deirdre stood stock-still.

Dorc tugged her father's arm. 'She's got a performance tomorrow.'

'She's always performing, for God's sake!'

Deirdre approached, mouth and eyes widening in readiness. 'You will come, won't you? You will all come and see me in my play. I'm a bird in it – a burdie, a bonnie burdie in a lovely ruff and yellow feathers.'

'She's so ridiculous. My mother is ridiculous! Take her away! Take her to bed! Anyone. Someone—'

'To bed?' On cue, Deirdre again. 'Where's your Hamish Shamus tonight, darling?'

'Shame on us,' echoed Guthrie.

'I am giving him a rest.'

'Out of the mouths of babes,' said Guthrie.

'Didn't you have a wee baby too, Bruno?' We were back in the shadows. Deirdre was swivelling in search him. 'A baby. A wee baby. Same as Dorcas was.'

He kept his mouth shut.

'What became of that baby?'

I felt his weight beside me on the cushions, not a dead weight any more but tense.

'Go to bed, Deirdre.' Bornati's words: the stutter of a gun.

But she came on towards him. She teetered on her high heels, then she hitched her crotch on to his crossed knee. 'Dancey, dancey. Jig, jig.'

He tried to shift her. 'Jimmy!' He was urgent. 'Will you get this woman – OFF!'

Dorcas was there first. She was bigger than her mother but she was weak in her distress. She pulled at the red figure with its angling arms and legs. She wailed for help. 'Guthrie! Dad! Dad-dy-y!' she cried. But it was not he who rescued Deirdre from her own indignity. Lisping and leaning, laughing a little, but without fuss her mother left the room on Mr Ingram's arm.

The father had gone to the daughter. Dorcas crouched as if over some pain, her shoulders heaving. I was near too, ready. Guthrie appealed to me. I bent and tried to comfort her. She did not respond. 'You'll have to take her down to your place,' I said. 'It's not just this, you know. It's . . . it's everything! She's exhausted. She'd better not be alone in case Hamish . . . you know.'

'What?'

'They had a fight last night. She didn't sleep.'

'Some "tree"! Och, I saw she wasn't well. All that make-up on her face. But why didn't *you* tell me?' He challenged me with such a fierce look that it made my tight heart jump. Then he shot a glance at Bornati who was sitting quiet as a shadow. Very curt, he said, 'Where's her jacket thing, her anorak? It's wet out.'

I fetched it from the hall for them. At the door I draped it round her shoulders. 'She needs a good sleep in her old bed.' Dorcas gave a loud sniff. 'I wish . . .' I was going to say I wished I was going with them.

'Her own bed is not all she's needing,' said her father grimly.

I waited. Guthrie was fumbling with the anorak, trying to keep the slippy thing snugly in place. In the end he put one of his big arms round his wayward daughter. The other came clamping across her chest pinning the blonde hair flat. Her drooping face was half-curtained and she was enfolded like a baby. He had something more to say to me. His eyes were dark.

'Be careful, Beatie.'

I nodded.

Slowly they turned and shuffled out together.

In the room behind Bornati was watching from his black corner on the sofa.

We were alone.

At the open threshold was the smell of rain. I reached for the torch. He was behind me in the dark. He unhitched some garment from the kitchen door and, hooding me, draped it round my shoulders. The torch flung a thin beam which swooped then darted round the yard, lighting up cobbles, pines, bent bracken glistening. Bornati grunted, covered my faltering grip and pointed straight to the green door.

'A candle? Jesus. That's quaint.'

'It's for reading in bed.'

He had followed me the length of the low attic room. It was stuffy. Already he was tugging at his tie, shrugging off his jacket. I needed air. I kneeled on my bed to get at the ratchet of the skylight and pushed it up into its last hole. As I straightened he clutched me from behind, my hips narrow as a rabbit's in his large hands. I writhed away and perched at the end of the bed.

He leaned facing me.

I heard myself declare, 'I know someone who knows you very well.'

'Dramatic Deirdre, you mean?'

I did not mean Deirdre.

'There's no need to be jealous of Deirdre. Deirdre was the easiest lay in Lothian Road, as long as you appealed to her sense of theatre. Come here.' He stretched out his hand.

'You have a great conceit of yourself,' I said.

'Oh?'

I met his look. Then I began: 'Dorcas always calls her mother Deirdre, and her father Guthrie sometimes, sometimes Dad. That's funny, don't you think? Do they do that in America?'

'Sure. It's usual. I guess it's less confusing. So many second, third, fourth marriages even.'

'I call my mother Mum or Mummy. Mother when I'm cross with her. What did you call your mother?'

'Mamma.'

'Mamma.' I tried it out. 'Mamma mia.' I had heard that.

'Ma-am-ma mee-a,' he improved the accent. I could tell he was wanting to touch me again. 'Ma-am-ma mee-a,' he repeated, with his warm brown look.

'Your father?' brusquely, my question.

'Pap-pa.'

'Papa.' I repeated.

'I liked him, my father. I liked him and I loved him.' He looked up. 'Pa-pa, I called him. Pa-pa. You say it.'

I said it like that.

He approved.

There was this painful lump high in my throat. I think I shook my head. 'And I don't even understand your work,' I said, looking at the wall.

'No. You don't like it. I can tell. Come here.'

'I hate it.'

'Come. I can take it. Tell me. Come.' He removed my shoes and dropped them on the floor. 'No human reference. Right?' His hand closed round my ankle.

'It is a dead end.'

'What you need are some lessons in Pure Form.'

'I do need lessons. I need lessons in loving.'

His face was a crossroads for an instant. 'Are you a virgin?'

'That's sex not love.'

'Have you had sex then, Miss Pernickety?'

'Yes.'

His relief was obvious. The quirky smile made something go hard inside me. He came lowering up. The bed creaked. His face pressed against my stomach. My hands came together to push him away. But when they closed on his hair and felt the heat of his head, the throb of blood, the hard skull under – they held on instead. He began fondling me, handling my bottom, feeling my thighs. All the time his head was in my hands. I bent over and bit at the elastic holding his hair.

'Hey! What's that you're doing?'

I was roughing it up. He was a Technicolor Jesus with the long waves flowing. 'Wait.' I bunched it loosely behind. 'That's better. Yes.' For a long moment I stared at him.

He looked back at me in some confusion. Then the moment

passed and he looked at me with lust. I could not go on gazing at him any more because he looked at me with such lust. I slipped from him, lunged across the room, to hide myself from him pressed against the wall opposite, arms up, hands flat to get away from seeing the way he looked. But he was behind me, feeling for me again, always this feeling . . . It was not to be like this. No. It was not to be . . . but his hands were moving round, taking hold. Iron man, his hands like iron bands. But when I strained away I found they let me writhe inside. They let me move. Urged me. In their own way they instructed, coaxed me. Wine had made my head swim and now it made my body melt. It would not take much . . . to let . . . I leaned back into him. His fingers were cunning. I moved against him.

Felt his mouth.

'You're a strange young lady.'

On my neck.

'Beautiful . . .'

On my cheek.

'You like this?'

The corner of my lips.

'Because this. Is fine. By me. If I touch you . . . touch . . .' My knees were somehow against the bed. He had the zipper of my dress and tugged it down in jerks. 'What goddamned knicky-knicky things you women wear.'

On the skylight the rain was stars. A runnel stealing down was falling in, wet on my bare shoulder.

I was standing in the black bra, and pants, stockings and suspenders: accoutrements I had first been introduced to in those sexy magazines. Bornati drew back for a better view. It made me think of the Labrador suddenly and of the thump, thump, thump of the black tail on the lavatory seat. I gasped and caught my breath: this bra of Dorc's was tight. With parted lips I watched Bornati smoulder. For that one instant I was glad I had stolen the black lace things. Then I, too, felt treacherous stirrings.

'The breasts of a very young woman offer themselves . . . did you know that?' His voice was very low. He sounded as reverent as a tourist in a church. His hands moved over my skin with an explorative seriousness. 'They tempt.' He waited for me to look at him.

'Aren't you often tempted?'

His lopsided smile. 'I am a lover of women. Aren't all Italians, all artists, lovers of women?'

I met his eyes. I saw a flicker. He had noticed I was trembling. 'How old are you again?'

'I told you.'

'*Carina*.' He put his hands on my two arms. '*Carina*, tell me.' No.

He shrugged a slow Italian shrug.

Above was the spangled reflection of us both: my pale blur inside the ring of his incestuous arms.

When he stroked my skin he barely touched me, as if he were afraid to bruise, or held the petals of flowers. Pursed to kiss, his lips were soft. His tenderness was the most terrible thing. He eased off the straps, unhooked the lace. His eyelids drooped. All other senses now came into play.

I stood feeling I was falling. It was as if he worshipped at the temple of woman. He was so serious suddenly. As serious for me as for his art. I was dissolving into sin. Come down, ye floods, ye cataracts, ye plagues. I do deserve you all.

He loosened his belt.

I would not touch it. I would not do that.

He was a strong man but he was vulnerable: he was a man with an erection he needed a home for.

I would not let it touch me.

Small shivers ran along my limbs. He calmed them with his big warm hand. I lay back on the bed. I had not imagined this, the physical step by step. This, though, was how we had to move towards the moment: it was the only way. But as he took my stockings off, one by one, tugged, plucked and pulled, my fear grew. In a slow silence he was stripping me. I was afraid he would be too strong to stop. I could not breathe. He was looking at my nakedness without a change in his expression as if I was one of his pieces of work and the surface quality was under scrutinous review. It was too late. I lay quiet, weak as the baby he had known.

He prepared himself. And me.

'Pa-pa!'

He was not stopping.

'No!' I gasped.

He had not heard. I dug my nails in, bunched all my muscles up against him. 'Didn't you hear? "Father," I said "Father!" Get off, YOU ARE MY FATHER!'

He was staring.

'Is this . . .'

Shrinking from me. Horror in his eyes.

'. . . the only way you want me?'

Lower teeth barred, narrow as a dog's.

'. . . the only way you'll have your daughter?'

A face that sagged like rags.

'I'm Beatrice. Beatrice Mary. Your Mary. I do have a nice name, you see.'

'What? Wha-a-at? WHAT IS THIS YOU'RE TELLING ME?'

'Please. In Italian. Call . . . call me by my name. Bay-ah-tree-chay – isn't that the way it should be said? Don't—'

'Beatrice?' Hissed like 'cockatrice'.

'Don't you like it? You chose it! Say it! I want to hear you say it . . .'

Now he was cupping his hands over his groin. Something dangerous was mounting in his face but I could not stop myself.

'Have you lost the power of speech . . . too? I gave you a chance before this. I told you. I—'

His hand sent me reeling. ' "Nice"! "A nice name"! Where is she? Where is she?'

I was on the bed, one side of my face ringing with pain.

'Where is she?'

The fork of his legs.

'Where is she?'

His sawing breath.

'You bitch! You little b—'

'Don't!' I reared up. 'Don't you call me that!' Jockey John Rose had called me that: I was not that! I was a Fury. From spiked fingers I flung curses. 'I gave you a chance,' I blazed at him. 'I wrote. You know I did. Twice! *Twice* I wrote. You said no, though. You said no. Go away. Go away, you said. Just like that. GO AWAY. *Forget* it. *Forget* me. Oh! . . . And you said look at my sculpture. You gave me that. Thanks! But what sculpture, Fa-a-th-er? What sculpture? What can I get from that – that . . . *stuff*?' His stupid question came again. Full of scorn I said: 'That sculpture leaves me cold. That sculpture denies the artistic development of the whole human race! And you can leave her out of it: my mother knows nothing about this.'

He stood down slowly from the bed and turned his back. I heard the zip. I watched the black belt tighten round.

The shuddering took over then.
He was standing looking at me.
'You'd better get dressed.'
'You wanted me undressed.'
'Get dressed.'
'Undressed – that was the way you wanted me.'
'Dress!'
I could not stop the shuddering.
He came at me then, hauling the bedcovers up. I pushed them off.

I sat naked under the noise of rain. Heavier now, it was drumming on the skylight. A drop on the inside of my knee . . . sliding round underneath . . . another joining it. The shivering made it go faster. I could not look higher than the buckle of his belt. He stood between me and the door. His hands hung by his sides. Another splat of rain. Come down, ye floods! The sound of my own juddery moan.

He reached suddenly for the bar above my head and yanked the window shut. The noise was like a shot. I crouched in fright. There was a squeaking wrench then the shards of glass pitched down. I screamed without sound. I was that skull face in the blue dark. Help me! Why did he not help me? Why did he look at me like that? He was not seeing me. With those staring eyes he was not seeing me. What good was all that agony, those circling whites, that beseeching now? My blood began to seep.

CHAPTER NINETEEN

It was like a beach, the way my steps made that bleak sound. Water was still dripping from the trees into the long puddles on the drive. I shifted my case to the other hand. The pain was raw. I did not want the bleeding to begin again.

The curtains in the lodge were still drawn, not neatly but bunched over the objects on the shelves: I pictured Guthrie doing it, in agitation, to screen his troubled daughter from the dangers of the night and the intrusion of the day: the father protecting his own, despite her waywardness. A bitterness came to my throat. I tried to swallow this away but it etched itself in, burned upwards, made my head feel as if it would burst again.

The big gates were closed against me too. If they were locked I would have to scale their pointed heights. I knew I had to be on the other side of this, of all that had gone on here. I dropped my bag, ready to rattle, curse, ready to climb – I grasped both handles: they opened at a touch, swung apart on oiled hinges without a sound.

Would Mrs Caird still think Dorcas such a rare girl when she saw the mess this morning? Or would they put the blame on me? I felt guilty enough. I was sneaking away like a thief. All I wanted was to get out – in person: it could never be in peace.

The hills were sending water running ringing into the field drains. Clouds had rolled off. I was miserable that the landscape could with such indifference brighten round me. I had wanted the gate shut. I wanted the weather to be foul.

When I was standing at the bus stop the sun came out. I kept my eyes on the tarmac road. Warmth stirred the smells of sap and earth. The brown suitcase beside me on the grit made me conspicuous. How much lighter my escape if I had been empty-handed. When the bus came I hauled myself aboard and thrust the offending object behind the driver's seat.

'You're up with the birds. Running away, eh, lassie?' the man winked. I told him I was going home. With a mock apologetic face he released the brake. I lurched the length of the aisle. Ugly red swirls writhed on the upholstery. From the rear seat I looked out in time to see the pointed roof of Dewar's deserted railway station disappearing round the bend – but no one, no car anywhere in sight.

We bowled along, barely even slowing where we should because nobody was waiting. To my relief we stopped for a while in Dalkeith. The people who got on settled composedly into the seats as they must have done every morning. We pulled out again. Too soon we reached the outskirts of the capital. Too soon I was able to identify the sandstone walls, the trim villas and the tidy tenements. Milk bottles still stood by doormats. The odd newspaper protruded from a letterbox. I envied the rest of the world this morning, everyone who could rise after a sound sleep to the old routine, easy and familiar.

That was the fish shop. We had passed the end of our crescent now and were accelerating up towards the park. I would get off there, instead. I would cut through to Salisbury and phone my mother, pretend it was from Dewar, make it sound as if everything was fine. I could waste an hour or two somewhere and arrive later, appropriately.

'Why haven't you been in touch? I didn't like to phone you there . . . Coming home? But – you can't come home so soon. I thought it was a job. A summer job. I've let your room. Isn't it nice there? Can't you stay on a bit? Is it not nice then? What's not nice? What's Dorcas doing?'

'What's Dorcas got to do with it? Mother, what's that about my room?'

'I've let it.'

I thought I knew my mother.

'Just for the week. Remember how you said I could. It was you gave me the idea, Beatie, I'd never have dreamed of such a thing at all if you hadn't said. I've got the rates bill and the electricity. This family's very decent, a widower with four children. What could I do? It's just for the week.'

'Mother, I'm on my way.'

'You are coming then . . . There's the sofa, I suppose. But when . . .?'

'When the bus gets there. I can let myself in. I don't know exactly. OK?'

I put the receiver back. The callbox stank of pee. A hostile stench. Presentiments of things to come. Was I to be out upon the streets already? How dare she rent my room! I saw red, the red rectangles of the booth, through that the front of Brattisani's café. I shouldered my way out. One of its portholed doors stood open.

Everything was painted that orange-red you call vermilion: be warm, be happy, welcome back to the womb. The partitions dividing the place into cubicles had portholes in them too. I pushed my case under the seat at the window. A cleaner with a floor mop came. 'There's no waitress service here,' she told me, then called over her shoulder, 'Counter, Mario!'

Mario was waiting behind the chrome machines, his head tilted expectantly. I asked for a coffee.

'Anything else?' He said it in a sing-song voice. 'Toasta, bacon rollsa, eggsa?'

'How much is a bacon roll?'

'One and six.'

'And toast?'

'Fourpensa. Toasta? OK. Toasta comin' uppa. One and one penny.'

Back to my corner. 'My' – possessive already. Was this what a tramp felt about his doorway? The coffee was cappuccino, hot and frothy. I reached for the sugar, a glass ball with a chrome spout and I poured it in, needing sweetness, needing strength. I put it back beside its companion piece, a red plastic tomato. I sat staring at this ugly object. Last night I had sat before oysters and champagne.

'Toasta!' It was Mario's sing-song from the counter. I got up. He handed me the plate, his brown eyes eloquent above the melting butter on the golden toast, 'For you, younga lady.' His interest made me look away.

I knew what my mother had seen in my father. His was black wavy hair just like this boy's but he had height and those demanding eyes, a daring look that made you melt, prim though she had been. With her good bearing, her clear look, her straightforwardness, of course she had been a challenge when they first met at that dance. I could imagine that meeting now. For some reason, I had it taking place in the obscure corner of a crowded panelled hall.

I nibbled. I sipped. I had very little money. I could not wait here for ever. They would throw me out. Even Mario. I heard him welcome the delivery of a batch of morning rolls, then resume the clatter and shoosh of the morning's preparations.

I knuckled the knot that was in my stomach. I had to rub that knot away. But *he* was doing it. All night his face had been there, then at dawn, looming, even as I went down the wet drive, as I sat in the bus and now above the red Formica table – his face, dark with engorged anger, hanging there twisting me up. Anger I had not expected. I had missed that out from all my calculations. Calculations I had worked out my way. I was the one with the rights. So when the skylight broke over my head it brought a welcome pain. A real wound. Relief of a blood-letting. I cupped my hand over the place. The small Elasto-plasts rummaged from Dorc's spongebag were still in place. His efforts with the bandaging, his pressing my chest, the tremor in his fingers told me what his mouth, his eyes could not. For he could not even look at me – looked all the time at the hurt, the sliced flesh above my breast – said not one word. When he left me, he walked out with a slow tread, carrying his shoulders stiffly in a way that shortened his neck as if he had taken one great deep breath and could not then or ever let it go. He left me mute, refusing. About as loveable as the plastic tomato. I squeezed it. Air came out. Squeezed again. A splurt of ketchup.

Get lost. That was what they said. Get lost. That was what men said to me.

My bare legs were sticking to the plastic bench. The mini dress – black because it was the first thing I grabbed, black for mourning, black for morning – was all creased across the lap. I reached down, undid the locks of my case and put my hand into the corner where I knew they were: my sunglasses. Further in I felt my new high heels. But keep to sandals. You never knew what running you might have to do. I stuffed the brown anorak I had worn for the journey inside the case. Ran a comb through my hair.

I sat for as long as I could. Tried to banish the bad pictures and focused on the tomato. Pinched it. Poked. Poured some sugar. The cleaner came in to remove my plate and cup, to wipe the table, to wipe me away, if she could. 'You have to order at the counter, miss.' Her cloth flicked the rim where I was leaning. I smelled bacon. Did I want a bacon roll? Could I afford one? No. Anyhow, I felt separate from my body. I seemed to have stepped to one side of it, though my brain still darted about. One shilling, I had. One sixpence. Some pennies.

Round the chrome columns ducked Mario's gleaming head. I told him I had to use the phone outside and would be back.

'Ah! I lika the glasses.' Mario smiled. 'Lika Natalie Wood.'

You looked blind in black glasses. And they let you behave as if you were dumb.

'Where are you phoning from?'

'Edinburgh. A box. Guthrie, don't phone my mother. I've done just that. I've told her I'm on my way. Don't you – I'm fine.'

'Bornati just roared off in a car minutes ago.'

'Where was it going?'

'Beatie, how— Didn't he have a plane to catch?'

'Was he going to catch it?'

'He's gone. That's all I know.'

'Let me speak to Dorc.'

'She's still asleep.'

'Please.'

'She needs to sleep. After last night.'

'What about me, Guthrie? Why do you think I ran away? What do you think last night was like for me?'

'You told him then?'

My silence.

'What did he say?'

My silence.

'Beatie?'

'Get Dorc for me.'

'She's dead to the world, Beatie.' No more 'My Beatrice'. 'She's no use to anybody. You know what she's like even on normal mornings. And I am concerned about her now. She's had too much rope. I am actually glad, Beatie, that it has come to some kind of crisis. Knew in my guts that that lover boy from outer Celtic darkness would be trouble . . .'

On and on about His Own . . . The black receiver was growing larger in my hand. I heard only my breath in, out, in, out, sucking from the stale mouthpiece the past breath of a million urgent messages. Then the pips. 'What did Bruno look like, Guthrie? What kind of expression did he have on his face?

Tell me . . . Try—' I had no more coins. I thumped the box. Pushed the buttons A and B. Thumped again. Traffic sound surged in. I tugged the door. Mine. This smelly booth was mine. Mine. This single square yard. I could not leave it yet because I still had Guthrie's voice gravelly in my ear. My father had left. I made this fact multiply along and up on all the little panes. To look for me? Someone was knocking on the glass. According to Guthrie he had gone to catch the plane. Someone pulled the door again. But had he? One shilling and six pence. No pennies left.

'Hello.'

I butted out into the street. A hand was on my arm. A male hand.

'Hey! Hello, Beatie.'

It was Ninian. His skin was tanned, his teeth white. 'I thought it was you in the box.'

'The sunglasses . . . I thought no one would—'

'No. Legs, arms . . . just the same.' A shy but smiling glance slid down my body. Ninian was radiant with clean health. 'I thought you were away,' he said. His Adam's apple moved above the crisp V of his open shirt. I felt dirty suddenly. I wanted a bath. I put my hands out to say, as he could see, that I was back.

'Can I see you?'

I repeated the gesture.

He repeated his question, brusquely, not to let exasperation show.

I felt so dirty.

He kept up that steady stare of his but his smile was not quite a smile any more. We were blocking the pavement. I stepped back to let pedestrians go by. That dark forelock had fallen on a frown when he pushed his way to me again.

'What are you doing today for instance?'

What indeed!

He had grown, was more thick-set. Yet when he stuffed his big hands into his trouser pockets there was the old hurt Ninian again, waiting, watching me.

'Swimming,' I said. 'I'm going swimming.'

'Along at Warrender?'

'In the sea,' I said.

He looked happier. 'I've passed my driving test, you know. I can nip back for my mother's car. Get my things . . . Where shall we go? Gullane? North Berwick?'

'Portobello. I thought Portobello.'

'Is it nice there?'

'It's the nearest sea.'

'Will you come back with me?'

'I've . . . messages to do.'

'Shall I collect you from your house?'

'No. No. Meet me here. Outside this café.'

'I'll hurry but it'll take me fifteen minutes. You will wait? Have you got a towel and things?'

I nodded slowly, thinking. 'Things,' I said.

'Right.'

'Right,' I said.

You got a bus from George IV Bridge that took you all the way. I knew the number. When I was working for the library I had been transferred once. The Portobello Branch was treacly Victorian, a gloomy maze of precipitous dark stacks. At a bakery on the main street having lunch I remember getting hiccups drinking hot tomato soup – but I never saw the sea. The journey was easy: you just sat on to the terminus, the very end.

It was when Ninian said did I have my 'things' that I knew I did not want him. I did not need 'things'. But he had helped me to see what to do. Mario was going to look after the case. The sunshine would not last, he said, so I got out the old brown anorak again. It would always do for a quilt or a mattress. Right now, it was bunched beside me on the front seat of the top deck of the bus to stop anyone sitting there.

This was the traffic lights at Jock's Lodge. A clutch of children's windmills like a bunch of flowers was strung beside some fishing nets on canes outside a corner shop. Top deck, front seat, both seats – all to myself, the best place to be where you were king of the castle and captain at the bridge, the big road, the high sea all yours, waiting. The engine throbbed up from underneath promising we would soon be off coasting along above the metal tops of cars, with the pavements like the wash from ships spreading wide below. People were dotted like flotsam then – foreshortened, woolly-headed, bowed, breasts and knees bobbing – and I did not have to bear them staring at me, at my pale face, my skimpy dress. What a weight of stone lay upon a city smothering weed and seed and growth for the sake of being neat and decent, grey and trim. Even these corporation buses were turned out in a uniform, washed and polished, striped white and maroon, like the pupils of the town's best schools, the ones you paid for if you had parents who could and did the right thing, which parents did in Edinburgh, nicely, all the time.

Which did not mean behave like I did. Black elastics stretching down my thigh, the impending ping of the release, silkyslack of the stocking on the slide, access to my wicked olive flesh, the horrid moment when the shivering began, the awful shivering that was as bad as hiccups, as acute, as embarrassing, until he stopped it with his big warm hand.

The small wound was tight now. Like a new stitch.

No! Those footsteps skliffing up the boards, I did not want them to come and sit . . . I put my arm, my hand out over my anorak. But across the aisle a pair of feet extended. Those sandals were Le Touquet made by Clarks. My mother had had me wear them too – till Dorc said something and I had slip-ons which slipped off and made my feet ache. A good girl this to sit, pink hands cupped in the lap of crisp cotton frock. I knew what it felt like to be inside that laundered cloth, your bare arms touched by the lined sleeves of your school blazer, the tightness of clean ankle socks, the lightness of sandals, a new morning. Could school be back already? Not for me. I'd left for good. Or ill. My arm rested on the cushion of my anorak.

The chimney of Portobello Power Station stood out against the sky. Which was a misty blue. Which was where his aeroplane would fly, soaring off up, roaring. Like him. Yet he said nothing to me. In the end not even angry words. No words. Looks only. Looks that had wide spaces behind them. I had seen him look at me and shut his eyes. Look and shut his eyes, then turn away. The shut mouth. The turning . . .

Room to dissolve the pains away I wanted. Somewhere not beautiful. But real. And not a place they would connect with me. People made jokes about having holidays at Portobello now. In those years before the war when the Bornati father ran his café, it had been a place to go. I knew there was still an esplanade with those wide iron railings; you saw photos in the *Scotsman* of the waves crashing when there was a storm. I wanted the sea. For whatever changes to the waterfront, beyond must stretch the sea, grey, infinite, strong, salt. I wanted to feel cold sand beneath my feet and the cold sea welling, circling my ankles with its clean grip.

'Terminus! Everybody off!'

I gathered my anorak like a warm creature to my hip and joined the world below.

A short passage between some grey houses and I could see the watery horizon. The air was very still with no sun: all had begun too brightly. There was sand beyond the rails and the sea was far out.

In ones and twos some old people sat on benches gazing at the view. Behind them stretched the drab stonework of town tenements. Mothers pushed their prams past and dragged children wanting things, potato crisps and ice-creams, pink sticks of rock. There was a dingy row of shops: dung brown, the wee tobacconist's with Tam O'Shanter Flake and Player's Please, green, the barber's under the fat spiralled pole, and black, the ladies' hairdresser's with New Look glamour photos faded pastel pink and blue and the card announcing Marcel Waves. I detected relics of better days in the chipped plaster of acanthus leaves beneath a lintel and a marble threshold the colour of raw mince with 'Café' spelled in bits like jet. This could be it – the Eytie ice-cream parlour from my father's past where customers bought 'Pokey hats' or sat inside on the black bentwood chairs.

I was on the edge of a small fairground, stepping over oily puddles and the vinegared newsprint from last night's fish and chips. The rides and roundabouts and mobile homes were sleeping late. In sleep-stale boxes a thin wall away the hard women were still in curlers, bedded in old eiderdowns with dark-jowled men snoring hoarse from shouting out their wares, their wall of death, their waltzer, helterskelter roll a penny shoot a duck och awfie luck see candy floss and take your chance and spend and spend. All spent the morning after. Like me. All spent. But they would pick up again. Together they would mend and paint, crank up and generate more honky-tonk and rum-te-tum.

I got deeper in instead of getting out. The gaps between the vans were alleys in sideshow land and rides and roundabouts in gaudy livery. I met their officer on watch, an old teddy boy with sideburns, who told me they were 'No open noo till five', and watched me till I went away, picked my feet up and over the last bucket and bar of the stockade.

213

On the edge of the ground was a stand of yellow swingboats. In one a man and a child sat face to face.

'Push, Daddy. Make it go.'

The teddy boy had seen them too and went over shaking his head.

'You there! Can you unlock the bar, please? Is it you we pay? She loves the swingboats.'

Still he shook his head.

'Can't you open just for us?'

'No way, mister.'

The girl looked cross. The father climbed out. 'There's the swings. We'll go to the swings.' But the girl hung on where she was and gripped the edge of the boat. The man had to prize her fingers off and lift her clear. She slithered down and flattened herself on the ground. He pulled her up but had to hold her at arm's length because her feet were kicking like little hammers. He raised his voice, which stopped her, then he whispered something. She allowed herself to be hoisted on to his shoulders. 'Buy me a strawberry ice-cream, Daddy, with a big milk Flake,' she sang.

I could smell the sea. I was halfway down the sand. It refreshed my face and clapped its hands over my ears with its long roar. Where the breakwater tailed like an eel, I stuffed my brown bundle in an iron ring and put my sandals on the top.

The sudden coldness of the water made me gasp.

I went wading forward. Long shallows. So cold. So strong. Clean me. Cut through. The water circled my shins, my knees. Deeper in, made me catch at my black dress. Two rings were brimming round my thighs. I picked clear patches, my toes big and pale upon the bottom. Away out the water weight was vast, like lead, and with a wind whipping the surface. Close to me though, it played a waiting game, limpidly, the cool rim quietly, quietly . . . The rings at the top of my legs made a figure of eight. I twisted my dress up higher. A finger of wet sneaked into my knickers. The bottom shelved abruptly. I felt water cinch my waist. Away down under I saw my legs distort, whitish, bloodless, cramp-cold already. Breast high I was taken now by this edge of the northern sea. I wrung my dress tight up. Had the small Elastoplasts come off? The cut felt raw again. It stung. My feet were lifting. I lunged. Was that me? That splashing? Something was after me, coming from behind . . . I glimpsed in that instant my wound opening, the edges of flesh fraying white threads. 'No!' I dragged forward. No fish, no fins. Strong brown limbs closed round me like a gate. 'No! Leave—' Pinced my head in a trap and hauled me backwards.

I bit at that shoulder. Clawed at those arms. The legs kept kicking, propelling me along till I grazed the bottom and was brought up beached on the sand.

Then the blows came. Blows between my shoulder blades that made me cough and retch. 'Stop!' I moaned, to the long thighs holding me so tight. 'Stop it! Who . . .?' Jackknifed legs trailed with hairs. I jerked round. That black streak dripping down his nose, that long lip, that shirt transparent to his skin made up one Ninian. 'You! How did you—'

He was staring at me. 'What did you think you were doing?' His hooded doubtful eyes.

'You should have left me!'

The blue hanging lip. 'You were in too deep.'

'I had to be in deep!'

All his bones knuckled me then, rubbing the punishment in with the towel while the water dripped down his hair, his nose, his long blue lip.

'Dry your*self*,' I begged.

'Where's your stuff?' he sniffed.

I pointed to the wall.

'Towel?'

'No.'

He kept sniffing. 'That all? That jacket?'

'My money's in it!'

'What's that blood?'

'Och, you get cuts on a beach.' I got up. My teeth were chattering. My hand came away with a pink stain, scarlet in the cracks from covering the place. 'I have enough to buy myself a chittering bite.' A chittering bite was the snack my mother gave me when, as a child, I had been taken bathing in the sea.

'Haven't you anything to say to me?'

'I have enough money. I'm going to buy a strawberry ice-cream cone and a big milk Flake.'

He wiped his hand across his nose. And sniffed. His lips hung darkly miserable like blue grapes.

'How much – exactly – is a strawberry ice wi—'

'What if I hadn't come?'

215

'I didn't want you to come. I said I was going swimming and here I am.'

'We arranged to meet.'

'I changed my mind.'

He was shivering with anger. Trembling like a vaulting pole. 'You're impossible! Look at me! Say you're sorry – at least!'

I felt calm when I faced him. 'Why are you bothering with me, Ninian? I'm too much trouble. You do find me difficult, I know that. Look how you signed yourself on that postcard you sent from France! You botched it! You don't know what to think or feel about me. It is nice of you to keep trying, of course . . . I know I don't help.'

'You speak as if you're some kind of problem. Some kind of difficult maths problem.'

'I am.'

'You're a girl . . . a lovely girl.'

I was shaking my head.

'I went to your house this morning when you didn't come. Your mother was waiting for you.'

'I had phoned.'

'She couldn't understand why you hadn't come straight home. We kept expecting you to turn up. Then I thought of driving down here.'

'Did anyone ring the bell when you were there?'

'Guests went out, I think.'

'Did you see a man . . . tall, a dark Italian-looking individual?'

'We were looking out the window: no.'

'My father,' I said, to explain. 'I thought he might have come to see if I was . . . But he didn't. I don't know why I keep . . .'

'Was he expected home?'

'Don't call Parklea my father's "home", Ninian. I don't know why I call him "father" . . . now.'

'When you spoke of him before you sounded proud of him.'

'Dreams, fantasies, notions I had . . .'

'And don't have any more?'

'And do not have any more.'

A silence followed.

Gently, Ninian asked, 'Shall I take you back?'

'No. I'll go back by myself.'

'Your dress is wringing.'

'My jacket's dry. I'll wait a bit.' I felt him hovering, wanting to help but still awkward. I leaned away shaking my head. 'Please.'

'Why won't you?'

'I have to do this myself. Make the return journey. I've paid for it.'

A selection of quality fiction from Headline